PRAISE FOR TH

"[*Those Who Make Us*], an all-Canadian anthology of fantastical stories, featuring emerging writers alongside award-winning novelists, poets, and playwrights, is original, elegant, often poetic, sometimes funny, always thought-provoking, and a must for lovers of short fiction." —*Publishers Weekly*, starred review

"In his introduction to *Clockwork Canada*, editor Dominik Parisien calls this country 'the perfect setting for steampunk.' The fifteen stories in this anthology...back up Parisien's assertion by actively questioning the subgenre and bringing it to some interesting new places." —*AE-SciFi Canada*

"[*New Canadian Noir*] is largely successful in its goals. The quality of prose is universally high...and as a whole works well as a progressive, more Canadian take on the broad umbrella of noir, as what one contributor calls 'a tone, an overlay, a mood.' It's worth purchasing for several stories alone..." —*Publishers Weekly*

"[*Playground of Lost Toys*] is a gathering of diverse writers, many of them fresh out of fairy tale, that may have surprised the editors with its imaginative intensity... The acquisition of language, spells and nursery rhymes that vanquish fear and bad fairies can save them; and toys are amulets that protect children from loneliness, abuse, and acts of God. This is what these writers found when they dug in the sand. Perhaps they even surprised themselves." —*Pacific Rim Review of Books*

"The term apocalypse means revelation, the revealing of things and ultimately [*Fractured*] reveals the nuanced experience of endings and focuses on people coping with the notion of the end, the thought about the idea of endings itself. It is a volume of change, memory, isolation, and desire." —*Speculating Canada*

"In [*Dead North*] we see deadheads, shamblers, jiang shi, and Shark Throats invading such home and native settings as the Bay of Fundy's Hopewell Rocks, Alberta's tar sands, Toronto's Mount Pleasant Cemetery, and a Vancouver Island grow-op. Throw in the last poutine truck on Earth driving across Saskatchewan and some "mutant demon zombie cows devouring Montreal" (honest!) and what you've got is a fun and eclectic mix of zombie fiction..." —*Toronto Star*

THE EXILE BOOK OF ANTHOLOGY SERIES

DEAD NORTH
The Exile Book of Anthology Series, Number Eight
CANADIAN ZOMBIE FICTION
Edited by Silvia Moreno-Garcia

FRACTURED
TALES OF THE CANADIAN POST-APOCALYPSE
Edited by SILVIA MORENO-GARCIA

THE EXILE BOOK of ANTHOLOGY SERIES Number Eleven
playground of LOST toys
Edited by Colleen Anderson and Ursula Pflug

THE EXILE BOOK OF NEW CANADIAN NOIR
Edited by Claude Lalumière and David Nickle
The Exile Book of Anthology Series, Number Ten

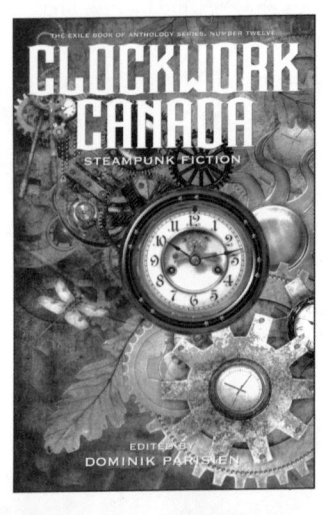

THE EXILE BOOK OF ANTHOLOGY SERIES, NUMBER TWELVE
CLOCKWORK CANADA
STEAMPUNK FICTION
EDITED BY DOMINIK PARISIEN

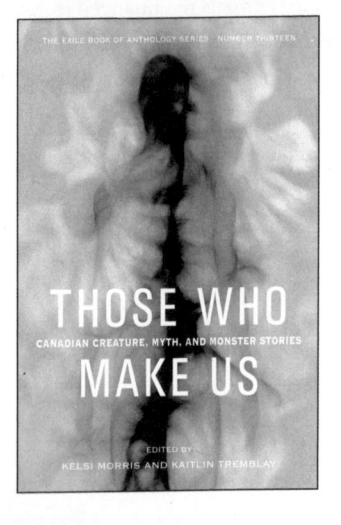

THE EXILE BOOK OF ANTHOLOGY SERIES NUMBER THIRTEEN
THOSE WHO MAKE US
CANADIAN CREATURE, MYTH, AND MONSTER STORIES
EDITED BY KELSI MORRIS AND KAITLIN TREMBLAY

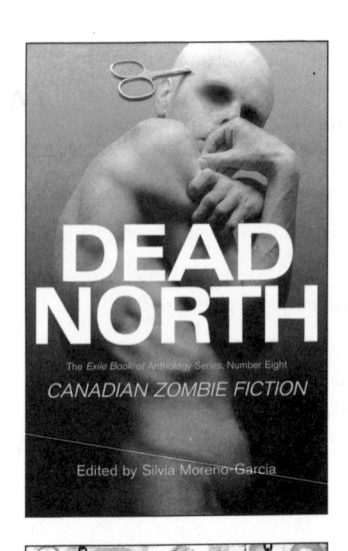

CLI FI

CANADIAN TALES OF CLIMATE CHANGE

THE EXILE BOOK OF ANTHOLOGY SERIES NUMBER FOURTEEN

Edited by
BRUCE MEYER

Afterword by
DAN BLOOM

EXILE
editions

Publishers of Singular
Fiction, Poetry, Nonfiction, Translations and Drama

Library and Archives Canada Cataloguing in Publication

Cli-fi : Canadian tales of climate change /
edited by Bruce Meyer ; afterword by Dan Bloom.

(The Exile book of anthology series ; number fourteen)
Issued in print and electronic formats.
ISBN 978-1-55096-670-1 (softcover).--ISBN 978-1-55096-671-8 (EPUB).--
ISBN 978-1-55096-672-5 (Kindle).--ISBN 978-1-55096-673-2 (PDF)

1. Climatic changes--Fiction. 2. Short stories, Canadian (English).
3. Canadian fiction (English)--21st century. I. Meyer, Bruce, 1957-, editor
II. Series: Exile book of anthology series ; no. 14

PS8323.C6C55 2017   C813'.010836   C2017-901178-2
                                                 C2017-901179-0

Copyrights © to the stories rest with the authors, 2017
Text design and composition, and cover by Mishi Uroboros
Typeset in Fairfield, Copperplate and Akzidenz Grotesk fonts
at Moons of Jupiter Studios.

Published by Exile Editions Ltd ~ www.ExileEditions.com
144483 Southgate Road 14 – GD, Holstein, Ontario, N0G 2A0
Printed and Bound in Canada by Marquis

We gratefully acknowledge the Canada Council for the Arts,
the Government of Canada, the Ontario Arts Council,
and the Ontario Media Development Corporation
for their support toward our publishing activities.

The use of any part of this publication, reproduced, transmitted in any form
or by any means, electronic, mechanical, photocopying, recording, or otherwise
stored in a retrieval system, without the expressed written consent of the publisher
(info@ exileeditions.com) is an infringement of the copyright law.
For photocopy and/or other reproductive copying, a license from
Access Copyright must be obtained.

Canadian sales representation:
The Canadian Manda Group, 664 Annette Street,
Toronto ON M6S 2C8   www.mandagroup.com   416 516 0911

North American and international distribution, and U.S. sales:
Independent Publishers Group, 814 North Franklin Street,
Chicago IL 60610   www.ipgbook.com   toll free: 1 800 888 4741

*In memory of Claire Joyce Weissman Wilks,
a passionate gardener, and artist extraordinaire,
who knew how to make the best of the weather...
and for all those who feel the climate of the times
and choose action as a way to sustain Mother Earth.*

CONTENTS

THE CLIMATE OF THE TIMES
AN INTRODUCTION TO CANADIAN CLI-FI · xi
Bruce Meyer

MY ATLANTIS · 1
Seán Virgo

CHILDREN OF THE SEA · 22
Rati Mehrotra

YOU NEED ME AT THE RIVER · 34
Linda Rogers

THE FARMER'S ALMANAC · 48
Halli Villegas

THE HEAT WAS UNBEARABLE · 61
Frank Westcott

ANIMATE · 77
Kate Story

DEGAS' BALLERINAS · 90
Leslie Goodreid

INVASION · 107
Phil O'Dwyer

THE WAY OF WATER · 117
Nina Munteanu

ABDUL 131
Wendy Bone

NIGHT DIVERS 153
Lynn Huchinson Lee

CAPTURED CARBON 170
Geoffrey W. Cole

REPORT ON THE OUTBREAKS 189
Peter Timmerman

AFTER 199
John Oughton

WEIGHT OF THE WORLD 213
Holly Schofield

LYING IN BED TOGETHER 231
Richard Van Camp

REEF 243
George McWhirter

AFTERWORD 256
Dan Bloom

ABOUT THE AUTHORS 258

ABOUT THE EDITOR 263

The Climate of the Times
An Introduction to Canadian Cli-Fi

BRUCE MEYER

There are those who deny that climate change is a problem. They believe that there is nothing wrong with the planet and that humanity should continue on its current path in order to preserve jobs and foster the economy. They claim that there is nothing wrong with our carbon-based technologies where tons of exhaust are pumped into the air each hour and billions of gallons of waste are released into our lakes and oceans. They see this as the necessary process for progress and profit.

The Earth's climate is not infinite. The air we breathe, the water we need to sustain life, even the temperature of the day, are all necessary ingredients for the survival of human beings. That said, what we remove from beneath the ground – the coal, oil, gas and metals – do not simply disappear because we release them into the air or the water. The more we make, the more we need to unmake, and that creation of new things, that use of non-renewable resources for energy is an enormous expression of our self-deception: we merely rearrange what already exists in the world, and those rearranged things do not simply disappear because we want them to. The world's capacity to absorb and tolerate misplaced carbon, among other things, has reached the point where the balance of nature has been permanently altered by human activities. What is one day's resource will become another day's waste, and another day's waste will become another day's poison. The result of this process is already evident. The polar ice caps are melting at an alarming rate. Greenhouse gases remain trapped in the Earth's atmosphere and the atmosphere, denser and less receptive to cooling, heats up the air we breathe and melts the ice caps. The melting of the ice caps raises ocean levels at a dangerous rate. And each year because of this ouroboros of demand, production, and waste, the world IS growing warmer. The air in major cities such as Paris, London, Beijing and Mumbai is unbreathable because there is nowhere for pollutants to go except the atmosphere. If we think of climate as a series of balances, what goes out of balance in one place becomes an imbalance somewhere else. Climate is the ultimate cause-and-effect relationship, and we are living not merely with technological and industrial success but the negative effects of our own success at being technological and industrial.

Imagining the results of climate change is nothing new, though it has not been a topic of necessity for most writers in Canada. We learn to ignore those things that do not celebrate our potential for failure. We write about our successes because success reinforces that status quo and comforts us. The uncomfortable topic, the unsettling reality, is a hard sell to readers and an even harder sell to writers as subject matter.

Canadian author, Helen Humphreys, penned a fascinating book of vignettes, *The Frozen Thames*, about the impact on Londoners when the Thames River has frozen at various times. One of the freeze-overs, in the winter of 1683-1684, is recounted by Virginia Woolf in her novel *Orlando*. Woolf describes seeing a corpse looking up through the ice of the frozen river. When these frozen Thames weather events happened during the Medieval and Renaissance periods, they were celebrated with "frost fairs" while the life of London ground to a halt, its main artery for transport and commerce solid ice. The freezings of the Thames, however, were not merely causes for winter jovialities and sporting activities. They were indicators that there was something wrong with the climate.

Many climatologists argue that these freezings are part of eleven-year cycles that are predictable; yet the worst period of climate imbalance experienced in England and in Europe brought European civilization to the brink of extinction. That period was the Great Famine of 1315 to 1317. The weather was not merely unusual: it was awful. During that two-year period, increasingly warm and wet weather destroyed crops across Europe from Spain to Russia. Ireland, for example, stopped producing wheat as a major crop and turned to husbandry to feed its population. The result of Europe not being able to produce enough food during that two-year period was that nations were forced to expand trade at an exponential rate, especially trade with the Middle East and North Africa. The expansion of trade signalled not only the end of the Crusade philosophy which had dominated European beliefs for centuries, but also ended European isolation. Those developments would have been viewed as good things if it had not been for the rats. The rats that came in on the grain ships from Africa and the East brought with them fleas that spread the bubonic plague. In 1348, almost two-thirds of Europe's population was wiped out by the Black Death. Those who survived the Black Death bore a unique gene that innoculated them against the disease; that same gene today has been identified as one of the root causes of Alzheimer's disease. The sad poetic irony in that realization is that we could live but would eventually leave ourselves vulnerable to losing our memories. The maxim of this litany of events is that everything in nature carries a consequence.

When it comes to climate change, it is difficult to imagine what the consequences look like, let alone to put those imaginings into a work of fiction; yet authors have been writing about our relationship with the climate for centuries. Some of Shakespeare's most memorable plays – *Twelfth Night, The Tempest,* and *Hamlet* – open with bad weather both as a narrative device for scattering characters and as a metaphor for chaos and political upheaval.

Climate change fiction is not new. It is now, in the face of real climate change and its consequences, simply a necessary if undeveloped neighbourhood of the canon. Jules Verne's *The Purchase of the North Pole* predicted global warming as a result of an alteration in the Earth's axis. More recently, J.G. Ballard in *The Wind from Nowhere,* Ian McEwan in *Solar* and Margaret Atwood in her trilogy of novels – *Oryx and Crake, The Year of the Flood,* and *MaddAddam* – presents a dystopian perspective on a world that has been altered by human negligence and a refusal to heed the warning signs that nature sends us. These authors have pointed out that the greatest human failing is our refusal to view nature as a place rather than a conversation.

The ancients listened, but somewhere between Virgil's writings on agricultural management and the present, the conversation broke down into silence. The earliest and perhaps the most telling stories of climate change can be found in the story of the Flood in the Bible's Genesis and the plagues of Egypt in Exodus. In these ancient narratives, the point is that Man should listen to God who, when not speaking from a burning bush, is the author of the world itself and the artist behind an environment that continually wants to tell us what it is doing. We have forgotten that the Israelites realized that the world is speaking to us and that it is our duty, if not a covenant, to listen to what it has to say.

Canadian literature, by virtue of its thematic matter, should offer some hope. Canada has produced a literature that is conscious of its setting. The ramifications of nature are omnipresent in the works of Canadian writers; yet for all the wilderness musings of snowfalls or even hard-scrabble Dust Bowl farming, climate change has not been a major concern, until now.

This anthology was an answer to a call that was made by Margaret Atwood in April of 2015. Atwood came to Barrie, Ontario, to speak at a high-school literary festival. The evening had a theme: our relationship to the world and what we can do to save it. During her address to the audience, Atwood reminded everyone of the warnings former U.S. Vice-President, Al Gore, had sounded in his film *An Inconvenient Truth*. The film went into theatrical release and roused considerable international discussion. As a topic, *An Inconvenient Truth* fuelled a number of national governments to reach international accords on how to battle climate change. Canada, alas, under the Harper government refused to sign the Helsinki Agreement to limit carbon output in Canada. In the middle of Atwood's discussion of the impact of climate change, she paused and put a question to the audience: "Where are all the Canadian writers who should be addressing the greatest crisis of our age?" There was dead silence. No one knew how to respond. Several of the writers who were there that night said afterwards, "I have no idea how to respond to her challenge."

Atwood had been doing her part with her trilogy of novels, but the idea of Cli-fi, the fiction of climate change, had not entered the Canadian imagination as a convenient topic. It remained an inconvenient truth.

The absence of a subject in a national literature is the perfect challenge for writers not merely because the topic has not been addressed, but because it pushes a writer to test the limits and the bounds of language, subject, and imagination. Exile Editions understood and appreciated that Cli-fi was not merely a momentary trend among ecologically inspired writers, but a subject that would loom larger and larger in the future. The imaginings of today could well become the cold, hard facts of tomorrow. As the subject grows in its importance – as climate change presents its ugly face and alters our lives, our economies, and our futures – we will, as a nation, be forced into not merely examining the consequences of our indifference in our narratives, but in our daily lives.

What Cli-fi suggests is reminiscent of a statement made by Stephen Hawking to the effect that ultimately, over time, imagination and truth arrive at the same conclusion. The term Cli-fi was new to me. After an initial call for submissions, I received an email from the American ecologist, writer, and filmmaker, Dan Bloom. He had invented the term "Cli-fi." I wrote back to him immediately and asked if he would write the Afterword to this anthology of Canadian climate change fiction and he graciously accepted. In his message to me that accompanied his Afterword he noted that the greatest challenge for a writer is to imagine the unthinkable with the certainty of expressing it as the probable.

I would like to think that this anthology is not just a collection of short stories by Canadian writers in response to the challenge that Atwood issued. I believe these are the opening words of a much broader conversation about what we are doing to the world we live in – the only world we have – and why it is necessary to foresee the consequences of what we are doing to that world. From that I pray that readers and writers will foresee solutions to the greatest crisis of our time. At this point in that broad discussion, this book is only the first chapter of a larger work that must and will have many authors. I also see this book as a barometer that measures our imaginative weather to point the discussion toward ways we can avoid the grim prophecies that many of these stories pronounce. I am relying on authors not only to warn, but to seek imaginable and real solutions to the damaged air, the melting ice caps, and the rising seas.

The German Romantic poet and playwright, Wolfgang von Goethe (he who authored *Faust*, an epic play about man's overreaching determination to exceed himself at all costs), invented a liquid barometer, a simple device, for measuring high and low pressure weather systems. The device is simple. It is a glass teapot, filled with coloured liquid, that is sealed except for the end of the spout. When the pressure is low and stormy, the liquid retreats into the glass bulb. When the pressure is high and the weather forecast is fair, the liquid moves up the spout. I have one in my front hall. It foretells the coming of migraines and storms better than any of the mechanical barometers I own. Whenever I look at it and read what it tells me, I cannot help but feel that there is a profound connection between writers and scientists and the conversation with nature that needs to resume, and that the imagination is our human barometer. That barometer can, if we listen to it, forecast what is coming in order for us to prepare for the challenges of winter blizzards and flooded cities or the fair days of the world we dream of inhabiting.

MY ATLANTIS

SEÁN VIRGO

The picture above my head seems to be the new fashion for airport hotel rooms. It's ironic, the primitive, innocent land, nostalgia twice removed. It's a scaled-up version of what we used to call airport art, the kind of scene that people brought back from Nairobi or Dar es Salaam, last-minute gifts – plaques, coasters, placemats – for friends they might have forgotten.

Three figures stand in an African landscape, herdsmen or hunters, their red capes vivid against the bleached savannah.

They don't have actual bodies, just the scarlet folds of those capes, with limbs black and sticklike as the spears or staffs held upright at their sides. From behind, the heads are plain black ovals – a swift, looping brushstroke would do it – and the rest is almost calligraphic: a domed hut to the right, two goats conjured with the barest of lines, and at the left a thorn tree in silhouette. Once you'd mastered the style, you could knock off something like that in twenty minutes.

Yet if you came upon those figures on a rock face in deepest Sahara, three ghosts from a teeming, fertile time, half-erased by the scouring winds, you would not think them slick and inconsequential – they would be mysterious, sorrowful, haunting.

They were what I saw first when I switched on the light and closed the door behind me, and then as I set down my bag by the desk they appeared in the mirror above it, behind my own face. I went to look out through the half-drawn curtains and as I watched a late plane, its wing light pulsing while it circled, they were there again, reflected in the dark glass – not the picture itself but the mirror, a reflection at two removes, back and forth – and in a moment of vertigo, as though trapped in an infinite regression, I reached for the back of a chair to steady myself.

At my age, when the deck tilts under you for even a second there's a sudden reduction of mind to brain, of psyche to biology, the most simple of terrors. I sat down in that chair, breathing, as I have so often instructed patients in disarray, just breathing. The runway lights were an avenue, floating out there in the darkness as a plane – the same one? – came in from behind the hotel, crushingly close for a moment, dim portholes along its great fish flanks hinting at other lives.

I am tired, of course; after such a day, I have every reason, and unreason too, to feel drained, but the same disembodied feeling came over me as earlier tonight on the dark highway – that I was a watcher, detached, perhaps already dead. Between worlds anyway as, of course, I am, in a room seven stories above the earth, and my flight back to the New World mere hours away.

Will I sleep now, I wonder; the fitful sleep of these last few years? And if I do, what dreams may come, what scraps of memory and accusation from this rudderless day? As I undressed, my eyes were drawn back to the three herdsmen; my face came close to them, reflected on the glass, as I climbed into bed. They stare off towards the horizon, a line of low hills and the pale, sandy distance between.

My face on the pillow looks back at me in the mirror across the room. I am eighty-three years old, the age at which both of my parents died, and the scale of things has changed.

I came prepared for that, or so I thought, but a path can feel so unfamiliar when you retrace your steps. And sixty-five years is a long about-face.

I set out this morning, lighthearted, relieved – a pleasant sense of escape and truancy.

My brother's funeral, an era closed I suppose, though I had played so little part in it. I owed it to him to be there, but I was a stranger in that correct, perfunctory ritual, and his children afterwards were indifferent to my presence, concerned only to get back to their lives. Perhaps with their mother – her tense, polite hospitality – there was a veiled resentment for their responsibilities during my mother's last years, as though my paying for it all had been an abdication. As perhaps it was.

Her relief this morning when I told her I was leaving a day early, to revisit my childhood haunts and stay the night near the airport – just a few hours' detour in this small land. It was an impulse to escape, nothing more. How could I have guessed that by midday I would be entering the country of signs that I have spent my life helping troubled souls to navigate?

The sky, when I left the highway and took the narrow road towards the moorlands, began to seem as wide as our prairies, and as the fields and hedgerows gave way to bracken and drystone walls, it felt closer too. Fifty miles here is like three hundred in Canada, and more various: you can pass through three different landscapes in an hour. There were stone outcrops now to each side, and patches of heather. I was edging towards memory, and when I crested the hill and the grey moors unfolded before me, every cell in my body responded.

For Cicero, memory was a villa and garden – rooms, corridors, niches, patios, pathways, pools, statues: knowledge arranged by precise and elegant design. I have used that model with patients over the years, but always to guide them on through, towards the back gate, the hidden door in the wall that opens to wilderness. Fugitive memory waits in the weather out there, in hollows and thickets and ruins too, the haunts of outlaws and anchorites, worlds within worlds that may open inwards, as scale reverses itself.

The moors were my childhood's horizon, the hinterland where travellers might perish in winter storms and where you could conjure the howling of long-extinct wolves. Yet in summer the larks sang overhead there, the air smelled of honey and distances, harebells and cotton grass nodded in the constant hill wind, and you could shelter in a heather dell, a miniature world with the sky vault and clouds above you and the earth's rumours close to your ear.

There are no walls out there, the road is an alien thread on the land's ancient contours, the scraggy sheep live as wild creatures for most of the year. I rolled down the window and at once heard the two-note cry of a curlew, a plaintive legato that will still haunt the moors, I imagine, when our own race has vanished.

And it was easy enough to imagine myself the last person left on earth, driving that one-lane road. Not a single vehicle the whole journey. At every turnout, signs warned of extreme risk of fire, no picnicking, do not stray from the roadside. The moors were not themselves, except to the eye, and even there some essence was missing – instead of a purple wash across the whole landscape, the heather was blooming only in scattered hollows. And where were the sheep? I saw just one the whole way, a gaunt, stunned-looking creature, staring off into nowhere. It began to seem desolate, under that cloudless sky.

Yet there was life there still — some small birds looping above the heather, a rabbit darting across the road and evidence of its brethren further on, two or three carcasses flattened and dry on the asphalt. I heard a curlew again and then, across a ravine to my right, two brown hawks were hanging motionless against the sky.

That is such a familiar sight near my home, that I had driven on quarter of a mile before I realized what a marvel they would have been in my childhood, the excitement and wonder I would have felt, the urge to rush home and share it —*Buzzards! Two of them! No, I'm not making it up, honestly!* I stopped and backed up to the nearest turnout. I suppose I wanted to see through those innocent eyes again, but as I shut the car door a grouse burst out of the heather below me — its wings a loud blur of alarm before it went gliding off, crying *Go back, go back*. That's how the old people heard it: *Go back, go back, go back,* and I remembered Billie, a girl called Billie. I whispered her name to the hill wind and my hand reached for my touchstone.

It's a commonplace in our practice — the moments where the synchronistic intersects with the causal and conscious. Those are the crossroads, the gateways, we're always seeking, the best chance for integration, for healing even — but a psychquake is different. Causal realities are obliterated.

I was not thinking and remembering as I am now; I was lost in a moment neither there nor faraway. Yet it was decided. Half an hour down the road I would turn off, and take a right fork towards the drowned valley.

So, I found myself coasting the long slope that Billie and I toiled up on our bicycles, past places where we lay in the springy heather, down to the humpback stone bridge. Were our young ghosts there, hands on the parapet, watching the stream below and the little trout darting through the shallows? The stream itself was a mere ghost now, a scant trickle between the white stones, catching the light as I crossed.

I was driving very slowly, I think, assailed by atmospheres, images, echoes, scents, that were not quite memories. That must be what time travel would be like, not at all as in fantasy novels; and what is memory, anyway, but time travel – spasms and islands of unreliable fiction, surfacing with the logic of dreams? And all at once, I was over the next rise and driving through forest. It should not have surprised me – I was part of the student crew that planted the first trees the summer before I emigrated – but I had forgotten.

The road through the trees was dappled with sunlight, strewn and in places adrift with the tan needles. The trees we had planted, Canadian spruce, were harvested long ago – you could see the rotations of plantings and clear-cut, geometrical strips on the hillsides, what the poet Wordsworth called timber factories. The trees looked foxed and distressed at every stage, and the most recent plantings had evidently failed altogether – they stretched in lines on either side, like ten thousand dead Christmas trees, like a battlefield cemetery.

I remember now the forester telling us about the ancient forest, oak, thorn and birch, that once covered those hills. We turned up peat-stained, waterlogged roots and limbs in the drainage ditches between the ranks of saplings. Bog oak, he called it, spongy enough to take the imprint of a thumbnail. He whittled a little manikin with his jackknife and propped it on the dashboard of the bus. After two weeks, it had become light as balsa, hard as stone.

But driving away from that desolation my memory was of the crew bus passing Billie's house, and how I'd ducked my head and looked away each time, afraid of embarrassment, which was of course shame. The feeling stirred in me again.

When I came to the village, though, everything was changed. The house at the crossroads had new bay windows, dormers set into the remodelled roof, an imposing rock garden instead of the privet hedge, and an immaculate emerald lawn. The old stone houses had all been transformed, outbuildings converted to garages, garden statues on the lawns. It was the colours – the lawns and bright flower beds on every side – that shocked my eyes. At my brother's house, they saved the bathwater, to keep the rosebeds alive. It was the same everywhere. Rationing. But that little farming hamlet has become an outpost of privilege and denial.

I drove as far as the graveyard, and the stone-walled plot where they'd moved up the graves from the valley when the dam was built. The road stopped there, with a gate across it and a stile with a footpath sign. Beyond that, the asphalt had been torn up, the old valley road was a memory.

I take pride, even vanity, in my physical condition and appearance, but I had neither boots nor staff, and the old joints protested as I eased my way over the style. The path ahead was uneven, but the valley's edge and the reservoir were no more than a half mile further. I would pace myself.

And so I did, but it was so very hot out there. Mid-afternoon in October and it felt like July back on the plains. Or how July used to be. The irony of the drought here, while at home crops are late, or have failed, the arctic air hovering, yet the rivers in spate, their waters green-tinged from the shedding glaciers.

And then a rush of cool air all around me, and the valley ahead brimming over with mist, a white expanse between the terraced crags that was like snow at first sight, or like the clouds that you see from the window of an airplane. It was breathtaking. It was time travel. There have been three lakes in that place, three at least. The first when the ice sheets melted, thirty thousand years ago, and then, after ice had returned for ten thousand years, another melting, another lake, until the great moraine that contained it collapsed and the lake rushed away. Then another ten thousand years for forests to grow and a thousand more for them to be cleared and the farmers to settle, till the valley became the world of my childhood. And then, in my eighteenth year, they built the dam, just where the moraine had been, and the waters filled up again.

I sat down on the ground there and looked out on the mist, almost lapping at my feet. This was just where the road had dipped down to the derelict mill village. Below the mist, I knew, were the memories that had been waking and quickening in me through the afternoon. And I thought of Philip, my captain of industry, in his middle years, widowed, estranged from his children, a grandfather now, his voice crying out in my consulting room, a tremulous wail from that heavy frame – *Where do the memories go, where do they live?* He had been to psychiatrists, but neuroscience holds no answers for the spirit – it does not explain, it explains away. I helped him a little, I think, but he had become, like old Job, "a companion to owls." Perhaps Jeremy, my gentle, distraught ex-rabbi, could have answered his question.

The mist was stirring like a cauldron as I watched, tearing loose at the edges in long, raggy shreds. There were glimpses of what lay beneath, but no water, at least not at first. I began to make out the scoop of the valley's sides, with bands of white, like chalky tidelines. There was a boat dock, just to my right, with a peeling *Sailing Club* sign above it, and two boats on their sides below in a thicket of bracken. It must have been years since the water was at that level.

The mist was mesmeric. It seemed to condense towards the centre, with movement at its heart, like beating wings. And they *were* wings, a great bird hovering, black and white, as if it were the mist's distillation, and then the mist was gone. The valley lay open before me, the water so far below, and that bird plunging into it, then struggling aloft again, a fish gleaming in its talons. Osprey. They were extinct in this land when I lived here. Another wonder. And then I saw two tiny deer browsing at the second tideline. Roe deer – I had never seen one in the flesh. What should I make of this?

Loren Eiseley likened us to a slime mould, colonizing the planet, but I have come to see the cities, everywhere, as monsters, hypertrophic, insatiable, their tentacles drawing people and communities away from the land; the cities bloating, all interconnected and waiting unknowingly for the plague, the hive collapse, the entropic thunderbolt.

But as the countryside empties out, the wild things may repossess it, damaged though it is. Like the creatures that thrive in Chernobyl Forest, their life spans too short for the poisons to kill them, but evolving perhaps, all the same, adapting for a new Earth era in which we may have no part. King David in old age sang that the meek would inherit the land, and Jeremy told me once that "meek" was much better translated as "powerless," and the promise he said, with that high woman's laugh of his, was that power would be restored.

Everyone in my profession who deals with adolescents encounters the fantasy of an earth swept clean, a post-catastrophic Eden, a dream of leapfrogging the unthinkable, getting it over with and starting afresh. In my fiftieth year, there was Josie, brought in by her parents to my partner, Gillian, who passed her instead to me. The wonderful defiance of that fifteen-year-old, whose slashed jeans and spiked hair and black lipstick gave nothing away. "You just want to steal my secrets," she said, but she lay on my magic carpet and told me lie after brilliant lie until we both almost wept with laughter.

If there is actual human magic, it will be found in the solitudes of particular girls as they fend off the encroachment, within and without, of womanhood. Through communion with books, or horses, or the whisper of birch leaves in safe summer woods, it is ancestral, paleolithic and sadly, perhaps, ephemeral. It is forgotten, but truly it does not forget. It chooses, though few indeed are chosen these days. All I could be for Josie, all that she needed from me in those weekly visits, was an old man who understood. My parting gift was Grimm's' "Brother and Sister," the Rackham edition, telling her how I'd dreamed of her in that story, not telling her that I was the brother in those dreams, in my roe deer skin. I loved that child; knowing that I would remember what she would forget.

It was Billie I was thinking of, though, as I sat looking down at the shrunken reservoir. The past was surfacing – the long mill roof like a crusted whale back, the bell-gable of the church where I could see that the ospreys had built their nest. For that was our playground, our secret, our Atlantis – we would be the last inhabitants ever. A mile downstream they were building the dam. German POWs who had opted to stay when the war ended, and Polish servicemen who had made the same choice. There were rumours of summary justice in their camp, executions by the edge of a spade, and bodies dug into the earthen heart of the dam.

The echoing mill hall with the great ore pounder like a petrified pterosaur, the church loud with sparrows and swallows where fishes would soon be swimming. The row of tumbled-down cottages where the smelters had lived. And the graveyard, the pits where any recent burials had been exhumed and moved to the village above. Billie's favourite place to make love was in those empty graves; I think we lay in them all, the earth crumbling down on us, her eyes laughing up at the sky.

I have not thought of her for years. Perhaps the young girl who lurks at the edge of my dreams might be her. I wonder. Remembering now, I marvel at her afresh — she would have seemed a free spirit even in our day and age. We thought of ourselves as fraternal twins, two halves of a single person, with a language of our own, our sexuality as much a part of exploring the world as books, music, ideas. But she was wiser, and wilder, than I was. I feel sure that she would have outgrown me.

I do not know what possessed me to set off down between the tidelines towards the limestone terraces; I will pay the price for it tomorrow. Old limbs fare worse on the downgrade than climbing, and the going was tricky. Though grass and weeds had grown thick in places, the ground further down was dry mud that stirred into dust, but it was slick too, treacherous. I am not used to hiking without my staff. I could hear my breath growing ragged, my heart thudding at my ribs. Old fool, I thought, and stopped at a grey boulder, caked with dried waterweeds, and leaned back against it, catching my breath, looking across the valley.

There used to be water everywhere, flowing down from the moors in the ravines over there, the sound of it, and now a flat silence. The tidelines marked the retreating years like the rings on a tree stump.

It is hard to describe a parched humidity but that is what it felt like down there. It was stifling, as though the valley walls were closing in. The sun is not kindly anymore, everyone senses that; I knew I should not stay long. My mind drifted whimsically – I imagined the lake emptying like a drain in slow motion, Santorini collapsing again into the blue Aegean, gondolas in Singapore and Vancouver. I saw myself as a Mayan farmer, walking through withered cornfields. *This cannot go on*, he said. Or did he say, *We've survived such things before*? Or was it, *The gods are angry with us*?

Were we at war with ourselves? Would anything save the walrus?

I came back to myself, with the feeling that something was watching me. There was a figure above me on the highest terrace. Not a bird, not the osprey, it was too big for that. *Canute*. It was Petra's bronze sculpture, unmoved since I last was here. A great eyelid winked in the hillside and memory snatched me away. Canute, Deep Time and Betrayal.

Billie and I were searching for amethysts. She was leaving for France the next day, and wanted them as presents. We climbed in the hush mine's gully where the millworkers, and the Romans and Norsemen before them, had sent freshets of water from the dammed-up stream to strip the rocks down to the lead seams, the silver, the gold. And an old man looked down at us and laughed, and told us it was fluorite, not amethyst, and invited us to come up and join him.

Markus. She called him Marco. I say "old" but he was many years younger than I am now; lean though, grey haired, with a keen humorous face. And she, when she came out to meet us, much younger, and oh, I was smitten. The sculpture stood life-size on the terrace in front of their house – a seated man, leaning forward, his left hand outstretched, palm downwards. *Canute*, Markus told us. *Petra can tell you about him.*

She'd had a piece in the Venice Biennale, and a millionaire had commissioned her first large-scale sculpture for his island estate in the lagoon there. She'd made Canute, but when the islanders learned that he was a king who had failed to hold back the sea, they had rioted. It was shipped back to Montreal, and they'd brought it by train and installed it here. Markus laughed – *We're hoping he'll keep the waters from our door when they've finished the dam.*

Billie said, *He's got your face, hasn't he?* And Petra said no, it was the face of Toscanini, she had thought the Italians would like that. *But they are quite similar,* she said, and rested her hand on Markus' shoulder. *Good bones, what I like in a man.* I could not keep my eyes off her. I'd never looked at a mature woman like that before. I was actually in awe, but offering the kind of challenge that a young man will. Her eyes were amused, but without contempt.

She went back to her studio, and he took us along the terrace, pointing out places around and below where there had been settlements through the millennia. *They put us in our place, don't they?* he said. And he told us to look at the strata of rock in the crags, some level, some heaved up. *Deep Time,* he said, *that's what a Scotsman two centuries ago named it. He said it made him dizzy* – "*No vestige of a beginning, no prospect of an end."*

You must come again, he said. *We're too much alone.*

Halfway back down the gully, Billie said, *He's kind of sexy, isn't he?*

But he's old, I said. I remember the look in her eyes as she said, *So is she.*

My life has been spent healing secrets. Yes, it is the secrets that need healing, not the unhappy souls who have cast them out. My practice has been to work through the brambles and underbrush, and to coax the wild things back into the garden through that moss-covered door. But mine was a sea wall. An ocean had stretched between myself and the Old World, and now the wall had been breached. I fled from that place, with Billie's voice in my head, though "fled" is a light-footed word for an old man toiling up through the tidelines, with Petra's Canute looking down from the terrace, like Rodin's *Thinker* or *La Stryge* of Notre Dame.

And so, when I'd recovered myself, my arms trembling with fatigue as I slumped back inside the car, I drove through the village and turned right at the crossroad towards the county road, past the lights of the dam and then, through the fading light, on down to the motorway.

I stopped to eat at one of the modern truck stops. Sitting there, as people came and went, I felt as though the cold, bright lighting was shining right through me, a ghost, invisible as an old man at a corner table would be of course.

But they were invisible too, those travellers at their way station.

I was playing a film in my mind. I must have sat there for an hour, more than that, forcing myself, permitting myself, to remember. If I was to confront and heal the secrets, I wanted it to be here, in the Old World, where they belonged.

Billie went off to France, and two days later I came back to that house on the terrace, and found Markus alone. *I'm preparing lunch,* he said. *You must join me.* Their house so full of light, the view across and all down the valley. While he made sandwiches in the kitchen I looked at their pictures, at a sculpture of a huge cowrie shell, with its dimpled, vulvic lips, on their dining-room table, and at the glass case of flint blades, arrowheads, bone chisels. *Petra and I had the perfect arrangement,* he told me. *She was a kept woman for ten years, and now that she is established, I am a kept man who can indulge all the things I forewent as a lawyer. Gardening, reading, fossicking; writing a little book as it happens.* He handed me a string bag with the sandwiches, apples, two bottles of cider, and took down a storm lantern from a shelf by the back door. We went out behind the house, along another terrace and up onto an overhung ledge. *Now,* he said, *we shall share our picnic with some old friends of mine.*

He patted the rock face. *Take two steps more and see what you see,* he said, *while I fire up our lantern.* There was a cleft there, wide enough to slip through but invisible unless you stood right before it. *I saw a jackdaw fly out one day,* he said, *and I came up to look. I like to believe that I was the first person to go through this doorway in thirty thousand years.*

I followed him, as he edged through the cleft, into a shadow play on the sloping rock walls. *Watch your head now,* he said, his voice already changed in that space. *They were shorter than we are.* The floor was like dry prairie soil and the air, I thought, smelled of chalk. It was so still, too, as though the cave was holding its breath. We sat, with the lantern between us, away from the faint slit of daylight. *Does it go any further in?* I asked. *I expect so,* he said. *There's what might be a crawlway back there. But I'm grateful to have been allowed here. I should leave them some secrets.*

He set down the lantern and took the bag from me. *No need to talk now,* he said, and reached for a sandwich. And we ate for a while in silence, though the slightest sound was magnified there, even our chewing, a bottle top ringing. Then, *Thirty thousand years,* he said in a cathedral whisper. *Almost inconceivable, isn't it, when you think of what two thousand years mean to us? They'd have had no more sense of the ice returning than we might have.* He rolled an apple across to me and got to his feet. *Now look at this.* He held up the lantern, above my head. *See – there, and there. Freshwater mussels, perfectly fossilized; are we in Deep Time now? But let me show you their hearth.*

There was no mistaking it – the cracked, baked earth in a little cove of its own. Its sides were dark, stained by ancient smoke perhaps. He pointed. In a half-circle before the hearth was a band of the fossils, three or four wide, pressed into the floor in a herringbone pattern.

He scooped his hand through the loose earth beside him, sifting it through his fingers as he held it out. He laughed. *Freshwater mussel shells, it was a staple food, the whole floor over here is a midden. I took pailfuls out to feed Petra's roses.*

The shells on his palm were like dark pistachio husks; they could have been gathered yesterday. *What did they make of that, do you think? What did time mean to them? A joke, I would guess.* Lit from below, the smiling Toscanini features were almost scary. *At any rate,* he said, *they were living in a pun.* The bite he took from his apple was loud around us. *They must have got some amusement from that – we sometimes forget that we're the species that invented laughter.*

As I cycled home I saw her car, parked by the roadside. She was closing the gate to a field.

Hello, she said, *where's your little friend?*

I told her that Billie was on an exchange in Lyon.

I've been listening to the larks, she said. *Singing at heaven's gate. They're the voice of this land to me.*

There was an insect on her hair – a green and emerald creature, gleaming on the dark blond waves. I picked it off and showed it to her. *A rose chafer*, she said. *I wonder what she's doing up here.* She held my wrist and took the beetle off my palm. *It was like a jewel on your hair*, I said. *Your hair is beautiful. You're beautiful.* She threw the beetle aloft and it zigzagged off on the wind. Her hand touched my cheek before she turned away. As she opened the car door she called, *You should come and see my studio. Come on Friday.*

That studio, the smell of wet clay and the flowers that stood in small vases in every corner. They had converted the old mine office beside the gully. A big window overlooked the hushing pond, full now with fish, gold and silver. Her huge work table was at the heart of the room, with a figure in brown clay, half-shrouded in cloth.

It was almost human, what I could see of it – the curves and hollows that suggested flanks, ribs, thighs. *She's the valley*, she told me. *All the land around here is female, don't you feel that?*

Perhaps I did. I was tense with desire. *You're very young*, she said, *but then we're all so young in her eyes.* She ran her hand along the clay and drew the sheet over it. She smiled at me – *There are seven ages of woman too, you know. I'm in the fourth age, seeking the bubble ambition, but...* She pulled off her smock and laid it across the figure, then went to wash her hands in the oversized sink. *Come now, I'll show you*, she said.

There was a carpet beside a low table. It was dark red, with a deep-blue border, and lozenge patterns in purple and orange and tan. *My grandfather brought this back from Bokhara*, she said. *When I was a child I used to sit on it, reading or dreaming, and travel through time and space. I still do, you see.*

She sat down, cross-legged on the rug, and breathed in deeply, and exhaled. *I am only as old as you are now,* she said, and reached up her hand to me.

She gave me far more than she took. In my first year of practice I tracked down a Turkmen rug, as much like hers as I could find, and laid it in my consulting room. My magic carpet; it has wrought some miracles over the years.

For a month, I was intoxicated by her body, her knowledge, her passion, her art. Yet perhaps she allowed me to spend ten days with her, no more than that. I was at her command, I suppose, yet I felt so important, potent, mature.

Markus must have known. Of course he must. Perhaps it was part of their arrangement. He treated me no differently and I look back with shame at the way in my heart I belittled that quirky old man. And in truth, I remember him more vividly now than her. She is famous of course, dead many years now, her work in collections around the world.

So, Billie came back from France, full of life and discoveries and gaiety. We went up on the moor road and made love in the heather – and of course she could tell. I confessed, but with more pride than shame, alas. *You're vile,* she said. *You're just vile.* I watched her get dressed and go off on her bicycle, her back straight, her legs pumping fiercely as she went down, out of sight, towards our bridge.

Tears come too easily in old age, but the ones I shed in the sterile hall of that truck stop came from my young heart.

They call them arteries, the motorways – city to city, the dizzying complex of systems that arrange our time on the planet. The flyways, country to country; the radio waves, never still. Paracelsus saw each of us as an entire small world; both the Torah and Hadiths say that he who destroys a man, destroys a world; yet those of us who tend to those little worlds and their troubles know that the scale has been overturned.

We are becoming fused into one great brain: brilliant, restless, inventive, making and making and making, crowding the villa with knowledge and forgetfulness, planting the garden with bright, scentless flowers of our own invention. And out in the shrinking, occluded wild spaces, there is silence, and starlight and dreams, and the last of darkness. But the darkness wells up from deep time and will not be denied. The little door is sealed up and forgotten, the walls will breach, the stroke must come.

I drove slowly towards the city, overtaken by constant, fast-moving traffic, the lights of oncoming vehicles flashing across the median. There was nothing to recognize, just night and the lights, and the pavement ahead of me. I drove on and on in that membrane of metal and glass, and then came a lull, no cars either way, and I felt I had forgotten the last few miles, wondering if I had died somewhere back there, if this road might go on forever.

I felt for my touchstone pendant, for the comfort and sorrow in it, the green stone *zemi* with its three quiet eyes. I was, at any rate, in the company of the dead, travelling through the night between worlds.

It is all that I have of Gillian, my colleague, lover, confidante for thirty years. No one was like her. On the wall of her office room the quotation: *As soon as we'd chased the bear from the forest, he turned up in our minds.* And at the head of the couch, her embroidered cushion: *In your heart, you know that it's flat.*

She was sick, she told me, of trying to heal the damage we've done to ourselves. *I want to take it all back, all this "progress" – its diminishing returns; worse than that, its delusion.*

And she left. She had no wish to be a saint, just to be a simple person, helping in simple ways.

And in that benighted, mountainous island where the forest had been stripped and the earth washed away in the aftermath, she worked, casting aside all the skills of her profession to be, as she called it, "useful." Badgering corporations and mining companies for money, supplies. In a string of mountain villages, planting saplings, building terraces, hanging nets of plastic rope on the hillside to glean moisture from the fleeting clouds at dawn.

Keep this for me, she wrote, *this* zemi, *ancestor of a peaceful, vanished people, that I found in a vanished forest.* I can only guess why she sent it to me. By the time it arrived, her head had been battered in, all of that knowledge and wisdom and gentleness erased, for a wristwatch perhaps, her shoes, a necklace. There would have been nothing more.

I came to the city after midnight, dropped off the car and checked into the hotel.

I have been lying here, worrying my way back through the day, seeking coherence. The electric clock at my bedside says 2:47. If I can sleep now, I will have to be up again in three hours.

When I turn off the lamp there are no stars through the gap in the curtains, just the orange glow of the city, and the dull red perimeter lights below, like the flares of a thieves' encampment.

I finger Gillian's stone, my faithful ritual for sleep and untroubled dreams, and close my eyes, imagining Billie's white limbs in that vacant grave, an old man's nostalgia for lust and innocence, the black-earth smell, our laughter. But I'm sinking through her, deeper into the earth, the cave walls dimly lit, an old man beside me raking mussels from the embers. The fire plays with our shadows, water laps at the terrace. We hear the splash of a fish jumping, and smile at each other.

Canute sits brooding outside at the tideline. Toscanini's hand coaxes the woodwinds to life, and across the valley, in a mirage of savannah, three herdsmen stand in silence, entreating the sands to recede.

CHILDREN OF THE SEA

RATI MEHROTRA

The full moon brought with it two bad things every month: high tides, leaping above the crumbling seawall, and Katyani's howls, piercing the dark.

The sea had taken everything I loved and would swallow me in the end. But while I lived, my granddaughter's fate was what cleaved my heart. Even if the green-suits were telling the truth, even if the hope of my people lay in such as her, it was too late for Katyani, and too late for me.

I pushed aside the reed curtain at the entrance of my hut and breathed in the humid air. The sea roared and stars winked in the sky, dimmed by the fat, silver moon.

One of those stars was not a star, but a ship. Like Noah's Ark, the green-suits had said, escaping the drowning world with the genetic heritage of the Earth intact. Perhaps one day, thousands of years later, it would find another home. But for those of us who remained, there was no escape.

"Auntie Benita, are you all right? Why are you not asleep?"

A thin, middle-aged man, his face creased with worry, stood near my hut, just behind the mangrove stick fence. It took a moment for me to identify him – Elhad, my younger sister's son. My sister was dead now; her other children had long since fled the flooded West African coast for higher ground. Elhad was one of the few men left in our village.

"I'm all right. I just want a walk." I climbed down the stairs to the parched earth. White, hard and salty. Not the way I remembered it – green shoots pushing through the ground, rainwater flooding the paddy fields. These were all paddy fields once, before storm waves breached the sandbar that protected the coast and salt water invaded our home. The mangrove forests were long gone by then, killed by drought. No matter how hard we tried, we could not resurrect them.

Elhad came up to me and grasped my elbow. "Please, Auntie. You should go to sleep. It's not safe for you, wandering about at night. You might fall or get lost."

I shook his hand off, annoyed. "I've lived on this land and fished its waters since before you were born."

"The land is changing," said Elhad. "Every day we lose some of it."

I walked past him. "I won't be long," I said. "Isn't it too late for *you* to be out? Go, before Mariamma comes after you with a skillet."

His face twisted. "Mariamma's gone. She took the children and left for Touba three months ago. I didn't go with her because she'll have a better chance of getting out if they think she's a widow. Don't you remember, Auntie?"

"Of course I do," I said. "I was just teasing. Sorry. Why don't you boil some water for tea? I'll join you in a few minutes."

Elhad nodded and left. I exhaled and continued walking. There were gaps in my memory of the past year or two. Whole chunks of time vanished, as if I had never lived them. But I'd die before admitting it to Elhad.

Katyani called and my heart lurched. Why could no one else hear her? She was crying out for help. She longed to be back home, safe and sound. When she was little, I used to sing her to sleep. When her eyes finally closed, I'd plant kisses on her cheeks, nose and forehead. My perfect, happy little girl. How did I lose her?

And thinking of this, of everything that had gone wrong, I tripped on a piece of driftwood and fell on my face. A wave crashed over the seawall and water seeped under me, soaking my kaftan. I tried to get up, but my limbs felt too heavy. The side of my head hurt and I opened my mouth to call for help but…

"Close your eyes," says Ibnar. "No cheating now, it's a surprise."

My sister and cousins giggle and nudge each other. I scowl at them and close my eyes. Ibnar and I have been married six months, but they still behave as if he is courting me.

Ibnar takes my hand and I step away from the shade of our hut. The sun burns through my eyelids, but the earth is cool and wet beneath my feet. I follow Ibnar without hesitation. I trust him to lead me, and I will not open my eyes. Behind me, my sister and cousins follow, still giggling.

Beneath my feet the earth changes. We walk now on soft sand. Overhead a gull cries, and the smell of raw fish hits my nostrils. Ibnar is taking me to the beach. But why?

At last he halts and says, "See what I have made for you?"

I open my eyes and gasp. In front of me is a beautiful new pirogue. The sides are painted red and white, and it gleams in the sun like a thing alive. How many dawns did Ibnar wake before me to build it?

He scans my face, anxious. "Do you like it?"

I restrain the impulse to throw my arms around him. That will have to wait until later. "I love it," I tell him. "We will catch many fish this year."

And we do. The pirogue moves like a dolphin through the waves. We catch mackerel, anchovy, sardinella – piles and piles of them. The rice harvest is abundant and we have more than enough to eat. It is a good year – the best of my life. It is the year I give birth to my daughter, Aila. So beautiful she is, with her fat brown cheeks and questioning eyes.

No, I will not think of her, not yet. It is a good year, a year of plenty. Let me remember that and be content. Let me not remember what comes next.

"Auntie Benita! Please wake up. Auntie?"

I blinked at the man bending over me, feeling disoriented. Where was I, and who was he?

A wave crashed over us. I spat salt water and tried to heave myself up. He put his arms around my shoulders, but I pushed him away. "I can manage," I told him, but my legs felt numb, and it was a few minutes before I could stand without leaning on him.

"Let's get you home," said the man. "Looks like the sea will break through the wall this time."

That's what he said every full moon. I wished I could remember his name. He had called me "Auntie," so he must be related to me. I followed him up the beach, past boats tied to mangrove sticks dug into the ground, until we reached a hut.

"Why don't you change into some dry clothing, and I'll get you a cup of tea?" His voice was soothing, as if he was talking to a child. But I didn't object; my throat was parched and tea sounded like a good idea. I went inside, switched on my battery lamp – a gift from the green-suits – and dried myself.

It was coming back to me now: the beach, Katyani's cries, the full moon. And Ibnar, showing me the new pirogue he'd built. Ibnar, my beloved, dead these forty years. It had felt so real; I couldn't have just dreamt him. It had felt like going back in time, before everything started to go wrong.

If I could, I'd live in that time forever. The time before foreign trawlers appeared on the horizon, stealing all our fish. The time before drought took the mangroves, and storms pounded the coast, and Ibnar had to go out further and further to feed his family, until the inevitable day when he simply did not return. The time before everyone began to leave or die.

"There's nothing for me here," says Aila. "Nothing for you either." She stands at the doorway, my slim, beautiful girl with a shiny red suitcase in her hand. I wonder who gave her the money to buy it. She catches me staring and juts her chin out. "I can make enough in Europe in one or two years to buy a house inland. You can retire then."

"I'll never retire," I say, "and neither will you. Don't trust those men. I've heard about these gangs; they smuggle African women and sell them to brothels in Europe. Those who don't die in the Sahara Desert or the crossing are nothing but sex slaves for the rest of their lives."

"I'll be working as a maid," she shouts. "Or maybe in a shop. Why do you think the worst? It was a woman who approached me – Sesha's auntie, in fact. A girl I was at school with. Sesha came back from Spain in three years with more money than she knew what to do with."

"Money is not everything," I say, trying to keep my voice calm. "Give it another year; this will be a good season, I'm sure."

Aila shakes her head. "You say that every time. It's like you're living in a fantasy world. Look around you. This place is dying. There are hardly any families left. I'm wasting my life here. Don't try to stop me."

But I do try. I tell her about the newspaper articles, the horror stories of young women being raped and left to die in the desert.

She doesn't listen. I block the door, pleading and arguing with her. At last, she pushes me aside and runs past as if she cannot wait to be gone, gone from me, and gone from this world.

"I'll write," she calls. "Don't worry."

She does write. I receive three cheerful letters in jerky handwriting that is not like my daughter's. The letters are spaced several months apart, and describe the good things Aila is getting to eat, the new friends she's made, and the nice boss she has in the Madrid hotel where she works as a cleaner. The letters are full of lies but they are all I have, and I read them again and again, trying to believe in the words, as if my belief can change reality.

A year and a half later, the letters stop coming. After months of agonized waiting, I go to the police. It is several more months before I find out what happened to my daughter. Aila tried to run away from the men who held her captive in a Spanish brothel. She was caught and shot dead as a warning to the other girls. It is enough to kill me, this news.

But I don't die. I cannot, just yet. For Aila got pregnant before the crossing to Spain – a tactic to ensure compliance, one of the detectives tells me. A pregnant or nursing woman is less likely to be deported, and less likely to fight her captors. Men use access to the child to control the mother.

But Aila tried to fight. She tried to run away from them. And for her sake, I will stay alive and look after the light-brown little stranger she brought into this world. *Katyani*, I name her. Slayer of demons and epitome of feminine power. May you live long after their flesh has rotted away, those evil men who broke your mother.

"Please, Auntie, don't cry. Look, I brought you tea."

I wiped my eyes and took the proffered cup. I remembered his name. "Elhad," I said, "I miss them all so much."

He sat down opposite me, his face drooping. "I also miss them. If it weren't for my work, perhaps I would have left too. But someone has to do it: gathering the data, taking care of the instruments, measuring the changes in sea and land. Not that there seems much point these days. Geoengineering has failed to reverse global warming, and all our adaptations – floating villages, vertical farms, underground cities – will not be enough to survive."

"You work for the green-suits." How could I have forgotten? It was Elhad who introduced me and Katyani to them. Not that he could have foreseen what would happen. But anger rose within me all the same. "She wants to come home," I said. "Bring her back."

He raised a placating hand. "You know nobody can do that. She wouldn't survive on land now. She's absolutely fine where she is. I check the data from her implant every night. Heart rate, breathing, digestion – everything's working perfectly. The experiment so far is a success."

"That experiment is my granddaughter," I said. "And she's crying to come back to me. Don't you hear her when the moon is full?"

"I'm sorry, Auntie." He twisted, looking uncomfortable. "But last I checked, Katyani was several miles away, beyond the reef. You could not have heard her."

"Maybe she's really fast," I said. "Or maybe something's wrong with the implant."

"I pray nothing is wrong with the implant," he said, "given the news." He paused, as if debating with himself. "I did not mean to tell you until later, when the gestation period was complete. But perhaps it will help you to know, to understand. There are two heartbeats in Katyani's womb. If all goes well, she will give birth to twins in twelve weeks. The first aquatic humans in a million years!"

I stared at him, unable to process his words and their import. But wasn't this what the green-suits had promised? Healthy descendants, perfectly adapted to the new world. The start of a new race. *Twins*. I should be happy. I should be jumping for joy.

Instead, I felt spiders crawl up my skin. I imagined what they would look like, these descendents of mine: slick, rubbery-skinned pups with blowholes on the back of their heads, expanded lungs, and webbed fingers and toes. Chimeras. *Monsters*.

I twisted away from Elhad and vomited the tea.

"I don't want to! You can't make me." Katyani jerks herself from my arms and runs outside the hut.

I rise to go after her, but the green-suit restrains me. "Let her go, Benita. It's a lot for the girl to take in. We have plenty of time."

Three weeks, I think. That's all I have before they take her away. *What have I done?*

"You know it's for the best," says the green-suit, as if reading my mind. "Without our intervention, she will die in less than two years. If we succeed, she will not only survive, she will bear the first children of the sea."

"How many times have you failed already?" I ask, my mouth acrid. "How many lives have you lost?"

He pushes the spectacles up his nose, frowning. "I would not call them failures, not really. We've learned a lot in the last few years. And you know all our subjects are terminal."

Terminal.

That's what the doctor told me at the hospital where I took Katyani. She was in so much pain by then, screaming and crying every night, unable to do the simplest activities. We waited days for the specialist to see her, sleeping in the corridors because there were no empty beds. Then there were tests, and the brief, terrible words: bone cancer. *Incurable.*

If nothing else, the green-suits have taken away her pain. And if they take her away too – well, that is the price I pay for her survival. I won't let her die. No matter the lightness of her skin, it is Aila I see in her fierce eyes. My daughter's daughter. I have signed my soul away for you.

The green-suit continues to talk, explaining the series of genetic and surgical enhancements they will make on Katyani. How, if the enhancements succeed, they will impregnate her and manipulate the Hox genes of her embryos to produce a new race. Katyani, for all her modifications, will never truly belong in the water, but her children will.

I stop listening to him. I get up and push aside the reed curtain at the door of my hut. I can see Katyani walking down the beach, bending now and then to pick something up: a seashell, perhaps, or a bit of driftwood. After a while she comes back and shows me her treasures – just the way she used to when she was small, before the sickness ate into her body. She has forgiven me and accepted her fate. Or, more likely, her mind has pushed it aside, refused to believe it.

I count every day as it passes. I make Katyani all her favourite dishes. I tell her stories at night, even though, at thirteen, she is too old for stories. I watch her run on the beach, knowing she'll never run again.

When the green-suits arrive to take her away, I think at first they will have to sedate her. But Katyani goes with them without a murmur. She does not take anything. She does not say goodbye. She doesn't even look at me.

How many times can a heart break before it finally stops?

When I came to, I was lying in the dark. A faint, sour smell of vomit hung in the air. I could feel jute strings below the thin mattress I lay on. I pushed myself up, and the bed creaked. My bed, empty these many years. My hut, bereft of anyone I had ever loved.

I groped my way to the basin and rinsed my mouth, splashing water on my face. I felt better, clearer in my mind than I had done since the day they took Katyani away. I knew what I needed to do. I had known it a long time, perhaps, but it was Elhad's news – *two heartbeats in her womb* – that brought it home to me.

My time was done. For good or evil, I had played my part. Like the wicked witch or the fairy godmother, I could bow out of the story, and no one would miss me.

Katyani called and I whispered, "I am coming, little one."

Outside, it was the fleeting grey light of dawn. The moon had gone and the sea was muted as if it waited, expectant, for the sunrise. One or two minutes at most, and the sky would flame red and orange, and burn my resolve to ashes. How many dawns had I woken with Ibnar to watch the sun rise over the sea?

Please forgive me, darling. I tried my best.

"This? This is your best?"

I gape at the tall young man standing before me, blocking my way to the beach. "Ibnar!" I cry. "You're alive?" And I think of how I must look, a decrepit, seventy-year-old woman with scanty white hair and wrinkled face.

He laughs and pulls me into his arms. "You're as beautiful as the day I met you," he says. "Come, they are waiting."

"Who?" I look behind his shoulder and see a pirogue dancing on the waves, just as the sun slips its first noose of light across the sea. I blink, again and again, but the visions stays: Aila and Katyani waving at me from the boat. Mother and daughter arm in arm, the way I have never seen them before.

It is too much, after too long, and I sink to the sand, hugging myself. Ibnar grasps my shoulders and helps me up. He wipes my eyes with one callused, dearly familiar hand.

"Shall we go?" he says, gentle.

I am barely able to speak. "Yes, please."

The waves lap around me, but they do not wet my skin or clothes. Ibnar guides me to the boat, and Aila helps me in. Katyani throws her arms around me. I hug her and Aila both, wordless with joy.

The boat leaps between the waves and the shore recedes until it is nothing but a smudge on the horizon.

YOU NEED ME AT THE RIVER

LINDA ROGERS

Sometimes curiosity is way overrated. Rats, for example, why would they investigate the possibility that rat traps might be sun-beds that raised and lowered? Why, when surrounded by glorious windfall – apples, pears, peaches and plums – would they have given in to the temptation to sniff cheese milked from a cow and contaminated by humans?

Now that methane-producing animal protein has been banned and rats have devolved into coli monitors on isolated islands, that's an academic question. Still, one would have to ask, Why *did* Claire look at the sun?

The short answer is, she knows better than to count sunspots, but the long form would include the burning questions: how many, how far apart, the same reason she measured the distance between stars, and, in the time of many trees and telephones, the spaces between power poles. That was a nervous habit involving fossil fuel and wasteful travel – Sunday drives. Then she would lean out the car window and weave her fingers, knitting trees, all my relations.

"Let's get together and be alright."

Now it's the world anthem, or what is left of it, all these islands in the sun. When Claire and her neighbours lined up for selection on their hill surrounded by water, "Some go left, some go right," she sang the Marley song and a right-brained officer sent her left, *à la sinestra*. Left is good, a place where lateral thinking is prized, not like the old days when everyone thought in unison, and that was their downfall.

Now the mantra is, "Discipline the body and free the mind." Random thought is the paradigm and wasteful living is offensive. *Da capo!* Now, every move is measured, a necessary nuisance because things are getting better.

The pollen rating this morning is over the top. It's a good day for her to be outside, no direct sunlight, many involuntary orgasms clearing her brain. She thinks better away from so many human noises hurting her ears; and it *is* a special thought day, the Beeversary, ten years since the resurgence, the first successful colonies, to which she is thrilled to have contributed, *à la sinestra*.

It's the spring equinox and the bee nation is ecstatic. Never in new bee memory have there been so many blooms: clover, buttercups, dandelion, daisies, woodrush, fireweed and chickweed, a crowd in her mind now accustomed to single digits, one nervous anemone. When she was a child, she was rewarded for plucking out weeds, stars on her chart. Then they were poisoned, and that was the end, but not quite, because, if humans are stupid, some plants are hallelujah stubborn, like the poppies that break through concrete.

This is a day to celebrate. Today the workers will all get extra honey in their tea and she will ride on the carpet of sexual freedom.

No one minds when Claire excuses herself to walk outdoors, a think ramble. Allergens make her sneeze; dust pollen, perfume are all on her do-fly list. She's fine with it; they clear her mind, but her reactions distract other alpha thinkers, her cohort.

Everyone thinks about sex when a worker sneezes, and usual sex, sex between two or more workers, is forbidden without a licence, punishable by banishment to a less desirable colony.

She's wearing her usual smock and sandals. Because of the golden haze, there's no need to suit up in her sun-block overalls. Her respirator hangs around her neck, but she won't be using it. Breathe it all in, she tells herself, the pollen, the scent of new grass.

She calls her think rambles around the garden "sound walks," taps her cane on the wooden boxes, listens to the gravel as she feels her way to the very centre of the colony and sits on the throne hive (her words, her chair), listening for the queen in her brood box: her waxers, pollinators, jelly makers and fanners.

It was her idea, after hearing workers beating their wings to cool down the hive, to fan the first poppies that came back after End Days. Now fanning is standard practice. Now, wherever there are fields and flowers, there are row upon row of fanners with gossamer sleeves, working in shifts, all day long, cooling the bees. The sound is delicious, vibrating wings, harmony, key of bee, eh, so Canadian! And everyone has a job, not like the old days of post-industrial unemployment.

Charlotte, working at the station beside her, doesn't get the "eh" joke when the others laugh. She started out French.

"It's like '*n'est-ce pas*,' or 'uh huh.' The Americans say 'uh huh.'" Now there are no borders, no countries. Talking nationalities is anachronistic, not encouraged. They are all islanders now, islands with numbers, officially. Claire calls their island The Hive. Of course she does.

Charlotte is here by accident, the accident being attendance at The Eagles of Death Metal concert at the Bataclan in Paris, November 13, 2015. November 13 is code for End Days, but it's rarely mentioned. That is too painful, especially for survivors like Charlotte. She was found under the bodies of her mother and father, who piled on to protect her from the bullets and shrapnel. Her mother, shot through the eye, stuffed her hand in Charlotte's mouth to keep her from crying. First responders had to pry it out. Her father's entrails spilled on her dress. She remembers that. She was carried out box perfect, not a scratch on her, but her dress was blood-soaked. She was six years old. She was sent to Canada on the first flight out, and Claire got her ten years later after Charlotte whizzed through her apprenticeship.

Sometimes Charlotte cries almost silently, but Claire hears small noises escape from her balled fist. Charlotte mews like a kitten or a small baby. Her bones rattle inside their tiny bag of flesh. During those infrequent meltdowns, Claire rolls her desk chair over, crushes her friend in her arms and feels her heart beating hard.

There is a heartbeat in the morning too. It is strong and fresh, the sound of ants marching, bee lips sucking and a raven clearing the rattle in their throats. Claire closes her eyes and listens. Inside the hive, things are busy, dusting and cleaning, waxing and cooking, the waggle dance.

She hears the queen sneeze and she sneezes in response. She crosses her legs, just in case. Sneezing leads to incontinence, not the end of the world, but she'll be wearing the same pair of pants for another three weeks, until the next washday. They are only allowed to go to the river to do their laundry once a month, always awkward at the very least because she could fall in, especially during floods, and has to wear a rope tied around her waist, the other end tied to Charlotte.

Once, a rogue whirlpool spun her and smashed her against a big river rock. She was bruised and she lost her clothes, but she didn't complain. People like her should not complain. Disability can mean diminished value. She has had to prove her worth. As the blind gospel singer said, "We have to sing twice as well as the white guys." In a world where singing stopped, every whole note counts.

Claire sneezes again. The queen must be having wonderful sex feelings. Her right lobe retrieves the time warp dance, human variation on the waggle dance. *Jump to the left. Step to the right. Hands on hips. Knees in tight. Twerk/twerk/twerk. Achoo!* She releases a cloud of germs and a trickle of urine. That was a good one. Shook her to her core.

There is a name for her disorder, *orthorhinosomethingorother*. In the old days, before the medicine ran out, she was given a prescription for a nasal decongestant. Now she alternates between controlling her thoughts and going with the flow. Today is a flow day. One good idea could earn her a jar of fireweed, spoonfuls of sunshine, her very own to take home.

She can taste it.

Charlotte's scent, lavender, tiptoes up and catches her by surprise.

"You got me!" Claire laughs, even though she hates surprises, hates it when her ears let her down.

"I cheated." Charlotte took the longer way, over the grass, avoiding the noisy gravel.

"Shouldn't you be inside?" Claire follows the rules, her survival map.

"Shouldn't you?"

"I enjoy my pollen reactions," Claire laughs. "But…"

"I'm fine. I'll put my mask on."

"Good, and don't say it, 'You are not my mother.'"

"That is and is not true." They *are* a generation apart.

"Sit down." Claire wiggles over and pats the top of the hive, which alarms the bees.

"Now they're mad." Charlotte has phobias and Claire knows she is entitled to them.

"Don't worry. The homies are stuffed with nectar, too sticky to come after us. Do you have a pass?"

"You mean, to be here?"

"What else would I mean, Charlotte?"

"Short answer. Yes."

"Do you want to listen with me, or play?" Claire welcomes her company; either would be fine.

"Let's play. I have fifteen minutes," Charlotte says in a way Claire knows will stretch time for as long as she will let her.

"You choose. What will it be, memory or desire?"

"Memory."

"Category?"

"Food." Charlotte always chooses food, the treats she does and does not remember.

"OK. Are your eyes closed?"

"Yes."

"Imagine you're sitting beside a beach fire at sunset in Monterrey, California. You are drinking a glass of Napa Valley *Pinot Noir* and the beautiful half-naked man beside you is prying open a shellfish he caught this morning."

"Continue."

"When he pounds the flesh on a rock, all his muscles contract. You can't take your eyes off his ass."

"So, you could still see then, Claire?"

"Oh yes, clever girl, that was before the trouble. We'd been warned but we didn't pay attention. That was the last time. I think it was already endangered.

"After he pounds the flesh, he dips it in an egg and bread mixture and cooks it over the fire. It smells gorgeous, like fruit of the sea, sweet and warm. You pick it up and eat with your fingers, right out of the frying pan. The taste defies description, somewhere between scallops and *foie gras.*

"When you finish eating, he licks the butter off your hands and your chin, then passes you a pearl in a mouthful of wine."

"And now we make love." Charlotte says this in a way that triggers something in Claire. It sounds like it belongs in the memory category.

"Of course."

Charlotte opens her eyes. "What happened to him, Claire?"

"We were so careless."

"I've never had wine. Not that I remember."

"You may yet. I've heard some vines are returning. Can you guess the mystery food, Charlotte?"

"Oysters."

"Close."

"I don't have a clue."

"I'll give you a hint. I'm wearing the pearl around my neck." She touches her purple teardrop, so Charlotte will see.

"I've never seen another pearl that colour."

"It's abalone! Your turn."

"My choice is good for you, feeds your mind with oxygen and turns your brain on like a light bulb; but you can't swallow."

"That's easy, Claire responds. "Chewing gum."

"I only had it once, on my sixth birthday. They said I had to wait."

"Imagine all those trees destroyed so people could chew like cows."

"Flatulent cows, a double insult." Charlotte saw cows on a holiday in Normandy with her parents, before her world exploded in gunfire.

"Oooh, a negative note. How are you doing this morning?" Charlotte is amazing, but fragile. Her parents were scientists, and her double helix radiates brilliance, but the storm clouds gather quickly.

"Breaking even." Charlotte laughs at her ambivalent answer. "I had a dream last night that I ate meat, a filet mignon, medium rare. I don't remember eating beef, but I must have. I woke up choking on blood."

She shivers, and Claire puts her arms around her. She missed that. There is nothing to be said. Charlotte will always taste blood, as would her children if that were her job description. Thank God it isn't.

"We should focus on sweet things."

"Candy forests."

"Yes. They are making progress with pine cones buried in the great tsunami. I heard a report from the silviculture lab this morning."

"Who told you that?"

"The Candy Man."

"Sugar-coated propagandist." Charlotte does not like him. He has tasting privileges and a zeal for busting rule breakers.

"Could be."

"Back to the candy forest. Fill me up with jujube bushes and chocolate fountains. My stomach is growling."

"I hear it." Claire puts her hand on Charlotte's belly and waits for the next clap of thunder. Instead what she feels is a strong kick, a little foot.

"What is this?" she asks, as if she needs to.

"It's mine." Charlotte answers simply, putting her hand over Claire's. "It's ours."

"Ours?" Claire pulls back her hand, imagines the dark shapes of predatory birds as this morning's yellow fog crashes to the ground. The noise is horrific, infants screaming, their flesh tearing off bone.

"I mean we're family."

"But you know the rules. How did this happen?"

"The usual way, Claire. I hoped you'd support me."

The silence is stunning. Claire's mind dials back. Were there signs? Yes. Charlotte has been sleeping more. She had the flu, or maybe not. She's been moody, hormonal, more than usual.

Exhaling punctuation, maybe a question mark, maybe an exclamation point, not a period, Charlotte stands up and walks away, leaving a tunnel of lavender-scented air. Claire should follow her, but where? She is needed at work. They are all needed. That is the point. They all have jobs to do. She gathers her untidy thoughts.

Privacy is an anachronism. There is no way to hide a child here. Children are raised on Mother Island. Charlotte might qualify for selective breeding, but she has not requested a permit. She would never give up a child, and her family is here. Claire is her family, and to a lesser extent, the others. What are her choices? She will have to leave.

"What were you thinking?" she asks later, in the commissary. Tonight, the Beeversary, there is a special meal: dandelion leaf and bitter-cress salad with sumac dressing and whipped June berries in milk rowed over from Mother Island. Charlotte doesn't answer.

"Mother Island is not so far." She pushes her own dessert across the table.

"It might as well be the moon," Charlotte whispers, digging in with her spoon. They have been roommates ever since she was brought to the colony as a sixteen-year-old aspirant and Claire was assigned her mentorship. For a year, Charlotte climbed under Claire's blanket every night. She sucked her thumb. She had nightmares. But she was an inspired student and, to be honest, her seeing-eye girl.

"Is it someone here? Do you imagine you are in love?" Claire asks.

"No to both questions. I want a child and I used a visitor."

"And of course, you're not telling."

"What's the point? It's not his fault."

"Of course, it's his fault. He would have needed a permit, or he could have chosen to be sterilized. That's the reality, Charlotte. We can, until things get better, only sustain a few humans."

"I know."

Claire hears her tears gathering in storm clouds. "We'll think of something."

"I was so careless."

"Yes, Charlotte, you were."

Claire is afraid. Charlotte, so thin, so vulnerable, is not a reed that bends in the wind, and is, to be honest, her window.

Tonight, for the first time in years, Charlotte returns to Claire's mat on the floor. They sister-spoon under the blanket made of plastic bags fished from the ocean, shredded and woven like most of their textiles, and Claire waits for the baby to kick again. "Tell me what today looked like," she says, and Charlotte talks her unquiet mind to its rest.

While Charlotte trembles and dreams about tidal waves of blood sweeping her and her child out to sea, Claire fishes in her sleep for answers, and there are none except the obvious and the unacceptable.

They do not speak of it for a few days. "You need me at the river," Charlotte says, and Claire's heart twists in its cage of bones.

"I think I have it," she says finally. "Now I am clear." She rarely makes mistakes. That is why she is so valued in spite of her disability, the wild curiosity that cost her eyesight. She has learned her lesson.

"We will tell them when it is obvious. If they want to know who helped you, tell them you were in the parthenogenesis project and sworn to secrecy. No one knew, not even me. There is no trail. No one knows who was selected and no one will tell. They will send you to Mother Island. That is for certain. You will go and I will follow."

"How?"

"I'm still fertile. I will find a donor and join you there." She puts her finger on Charlotte's lips and kisses her forehead, sealing a remembered holy image, the Madonna and Child with St. Anne.

Charlotte asks no questions because Claire will not provide answers until she is ready. She will move the earth on her own. She has done it before.

Solstice passes, the full moon, the intolerable sunshine. They spend a few weeks working with cracks of light in the shade room, a large Hogan dug in the earth with a woven ceiling. No one notices Charlotte. She is a little thing and so is her baby; and the workers are preoccupied with the drone surge. Now that they have no cyber records to refer to, all labour is time-consuming, slow research. They work from pre-dawn to evening with meal breaks and it is dark when they return to their quarters. Water workers bring tubs for bathing, one per unit, once a week, a godsend in Charlotte's case, because no one sees her naked.

"Say lovely things," Charlotte asks in the dark.

"Toothpaste, razors, soap, toilet paper, books," she answers.

"Tell me about ice cream." Charlotte remembers but she wants to hear Claire describe all the flavours: chocolate, strawberry, vanilla, pistachio, maple walnut, butterscotch ripple, green tea and orange.

Meeting day arrives with a bump. A messenger orders them in early, before the workers. They hold hands on the short walk to the lab. Charlotte looks up at the sun as if it is her last chance. Claire feels her jerk her head and tells her not to do that. In movie times, she saw condemned men look at the sun on their way to the scaffold. Luckily there are clouds in the way, clouds Charlotte describes as baby lambs, but they are mute, confused, bereft of lamb radar. When did the lambs fall silent?

There are three jurors in lab coats, all co-workers. They do not look sympathetic, but they do give Charlotte time to make her case. She explains about the parthenogenesis project, which is partly true, and it does not sound rehearsed. Her bit, she says, involved regeneration among nearly extinct insect species with only female survivors. She was curious, and when she admits it, the jurors perk up because "curious" is a golden word, the key to discovery and survival. Her curiosity led to self-experimentation and self-experimentation led to this pregnancy, believe it or not.

Claire most certainly does not believe it, and she controls her body language to convey susceptibility. Charlotte almost convinces the jury that they ought to buy her story.

They wait while the jurors confer. It doesn't take long, and their decision is inevitable.

"There is no way of confirming your story and there is no evidence that you used conventional methodology to reproduce," Alice, the head of beeswax by-products says to Charlotte. "We are curious about the outcome of your pregnancy, but we have no provisions for child care on our island. Your work is valued and so we are giving you the option. Go to Mother Island for your confinement and return afterward, or stay there until your child is sustainable."

"What does 'sustainable' mean?"

"Until the child presents suitability for work. If it is with bees, then you could return together. We do appreciate that you have been traumatized by separation, but who here hasn't? That is the reality. We all agree to abstinence or sterilization and those qualified must apply for sexual permits. Those are the rules."

Charlotte's hand in Claire's grows icy cold. "I choose to go," she says. "I will raise my child."

It was over in under an hour, and the workers waiting outside for the meeting to be over stand back as Claire and Charlotte, with her few things already packed in the old suitcase she brought from France, walk hand in hand down the path to the dock.

"I won't be long," Claire says, kissing her, wishing it was true. She has no idea if or when they will meet again. As of now, that is only a dream. She is glad she won't see Charlotte leaving, a forlorn figure in a small sailboat boat rowed by eight, four at a time. It will take them all day to reach Mother Island, unless a Westerly comes up and blows them there.

"You didn't say who…" Charlotte whispers in her ear.

"You didn't either." Claire forces herself to laugh, and pushes Charlotte off her. "Go, God bless." She hears her step into the boat. She hears the oars in the water. She thinks she hears a seagull crying in the distance. Wouldn't that be lovely? A sign. She must get to work. Charlotte must complete what she started. It's all about survival now. Claire and Charlotte will, as a poet from the time of trees and paper wrote, live their way to the answer.

THE FARMER'S ALMANAC

HALLI VILLEGAS

The hot sun slanted through the bedroom windows and tangled with the bedclothes where Elisabeth lay chewing the ends of her hair. Only four more days until school started and summer was done. She lifted one tan leg into the air and pointed her toes to and fro while her teeth snick snick snicked on her curl. Even though it was almost September, the sun blazed relentlessly on. Elisabeth slept with only a sheet covering her and even then it was almost unbearable. She dropped her leg and let the strand of hair drop from her mouth. She closed her eyes and tried to use the self-hypnosis instructions that were printed in the back of her book, *A Child's Guide to Meditation*. The book was really stupid, but Elizabeth liked the idea of being able to imagine yourself anywhere you wanted whenever you wanted. *Imagine you are at the lake. Imagine you are in the cool pine woods beside the water.* She conjured up the metallic whiteness of the water creeping among the Christmassy scent of the trees. In her mind, she wandered down towards the lake's edge. Then her memory took over and it was early summer again, and there were her father and her sister squatting down at the edge of the beach, peering intently at something in the water.

"What is it?" she called, as she scrambled down the slight incline to the little beach.

"Dead fish," her sister, Cassie, yelled up at her, waving excitedly as if Elisabeth had come home from a long journey. Elisabeth wrinkled her nose in distaste, but she joined Cassie and her father beside the water. Masses of tiny silver fish floated on the edge of the lake. From far away they looked like a patch of light on the water. Closer, they were starting to give off a slight whiff that reminded her of the fish-and-chips truck they always stopped at on the way up here to the cottage.

"Look how many. And they're all dead!" Cassie pointed to the silver mass.

"Not all," Elisabeth said. She saw that a few of them still opened and closed their minute mouths trying for a last gasp of air, but every one of their flat eyes looked panicked, whether they were dead or not.

"Daddy, can't we save some?"

Her father stood up and looked down at the lake. He crossed his arms and shook his head. "No, Elisabeth. It warmed up too quickly, there wasn't enough oxygen at the bottom of the lake for them." He turned to go back to the cottage, calling over his shoulder, "Don't play with them. They could be diseased." He disappeared into the pine trees up the rocky path that led back to the cottage. Cassie came and stood beside Elisabeth and put her arm around her waist. Even though Elisabeth usually pushed Cassie away, for now they stood quietly together looking at the dead and dying. Cassie picked up a stick to try to prod a few off the shoreline into the water, but Elisabeth held her back.

"No. Cassie. Daddy said not to touch them."

Remembering the silvery fish and their empty eyes, Elisabeth shivered. She opened her eyes, not wanting to remember anymore. And now Daddy was at that stupid conference in Ohio, though he was supposed to be back tonight. Late tonight so they couldn't wait up, but back before they started school on Tuesday. They'd have the whole weekend together like at the cottage. They could pretend it was the beginning of summer instead of the end.

Elisabeth pulled on some shorts and a wrinkled T-shirt. Her mother's and Cassie's voices floated up from downstairs in the kitchen along with the rattle of dishes.

"Nothing comes clean." Her mother's voice, frustrated and puzzled.

"What's that brown stain, Mom, there, on the plates?"

"I don't know, Cassie. Don't touch them. I'll have to run the whole load again."

In the small bathroom she and Cassie shared, across from her bedroom, Elisabeth peered hopelessly into the mirror. No overnight miracles had occurred. Turning thirteen hadn't changed anything. Even if she was a teenager now. Her long brown hair still straggled down her back, the bangs an uneven chop where her mother had tried to cut them for her a week ago. Her eyes weren't emerald green, or sapphire blue. Instead, they were muddy-water brown and small. How could someone have such small eyes, she wondered, leaning over the sink and staring intently at herself. When she tentatively smiled, there was a space between her two front teeth that her mother kept telling her would close up when the rest of her teeth came in, but so far there it was, wide enough to drive a truck through. How could anybody be so ugly, she wondered in despair, ugly and stupid. With a sinking heart, she realized school was going to be just as hateful this year as last year, that her friends would be few and capricious, prone to going off into corners and giggling without her, and that she would be tired from the moment she got in the front doors of the school with its smells of crayon wax, dirt, warm milk and the industrial cleanser the janitor used. Her nose pinched just thinking about it. She turned on the water to brush her teeth, looking away from her image deliberately. With a funny rumbling, the water sputtered, finally coming out in a thin brown stream and then stopping with a shudder she could feel through the pipes. Experimentally, she turned the handles on the hot and cold a few times, and nothing. She ran her tongue over her teeth, which felt slightly furry as they weren't brushed since last night. But there was nothing she could do now. Maybe she could use the downstairs bathroom.

Down here it was a little cooler than upstairs. The walls of the house were thicker on the first floor. In the kitchen her mother sat at the table, staring down at her cell phone. She looked up when Elisabeth walked in.

"I can't get a signal." Her mother banged the phone down on the table. "I told your father to get us a better plan. These damn cheap plans get no service anywhere."

Unable to help herself, even though she knew it would make her mother even angrier, Elisabeth added, "There's no water upstairs. It's all brown and the pipes are making funny knocking noises."

"Wonderful, just what I need. Your dad is going to have a hell of a time when he gets home tonight. Try getting a plumber on the weekend." She looked Elisabeth over. "Come here." She pulled the girl's hair back into a ponytail and secured it with an elastic from the dish of pennies and various junk in the centre of the table. Elisabeth winced. "I'm not hurting you. It's too hot to go around with your hair hanging down like that. God knows why it's so hot. It's the end of summer and it feels like mid-July."

She held Elisabeth at arm's length. "If you don't keep your hair out of your eyes, I'm going to cut it short."

Elisabeth squirmed away. She hated her mother. Her mother picked up her phone and started fooling with it again. Wandering into the dining room Elisabeth saw that Cassie was playing with the dollhouse. The dining room was the only room big enough for their dollhouse to be set up and they never had anyone over for dinner anyway. Cassie manipulated the dolls intently, making voices for the little family, high and low. The dolls argued about who was going to make dinner and who was going to wash the dishes. "No, don't touch that, it's dirty!" In Cassie's hands, the dollhouse mother shook the daughter, who flopped limply back and forth. At age ten, Cassie could lose herself in the imaginary world, but Elisabeth felt self-conscious now whenever she played with her old toys, as if someone was watching her, laughing behind her back. It wasn't the same anymore. Elisabeth slouched her feet into her scuffed white Keds and went out the front door to see if there was anything better to do outside. She didn't think there would be. Hot and boring, just like every day this long summer.

The sun a bright gold eye, wide open and indifferent, made Elisabeth's head begin to prickle as soon as she stepped into the yard. Hot, hotter than at the lake. Pansy, her cat, sat under a forsythia bush, as low to the earth as possible. Elisabeth knelt and called to her. She looked at Elisabeth impassively, squeezing her eyes shut and turning her head away, the tip of her pink tongue just visible between her lips. A cat panting, something Elisabeth couldn't remember seeing before. Was Pansy sick? Maybe she should tell her mother. Pansy might have eaten something poisonous. Elisabeth reached out her hand to the cat, but Pansy slunk off away from Elisabeth, still crouching low, her tail almost perpendicular to the ground. It was too hot to chase after her. Elisabeth sat and ran her hand over the dry grass. The tips of the blades needled her palms and made them itch. The neighbours were mowing the lawn, she heard the obnoxious kids two doors down calling each other "motherfucker" over and over until they collapsed in maniacal laughter. A car went by, and then another. Human sounds. No birds, or whirring of cicadas, not even an annoying fly to land on her hot knee. So still, despite the people on the street rattling through the usual late summer routine, as if the sounds were in a vacuum.

"Elisabeth, Elisabeth, look what I found!" Cassie tore around the side of the house, something cradled in her cupped hands. "Oh look, oh look. " She knelt in the grass beside Elisabeth and opened her hands. Cradled in Cassie's grimy fingers lay a dead robin. Eyes half-lidded, its feathers were dull and unruffled. Even the red feathers on its chest were leeched of colour, now they were just brown. Elisabeth screamed.

"What, what is it, Elisabeth?"

"It's dirty, drop it. Birds have lice, Mom said!"

Cassie dropped the bird in Elisabeth's lap and quickly wiped her hands on her cotton skirt.

"Pick it up," Elisabeth shouted, the dead bird in her lap, claws curled as if trying to grasp one last branch. She imagined she saw the movement of almost invisible insects among its lifeless feathers, dirty lice that would get in her hair and stay there. "Pick it up right now!"

"I'm not going to touch it." Cassie broke into tears. "It's dead, isn't it?"

Elisabeth jumped up and the bird fell from her lap. She began to run as far as she could from the spot where it lay, still clutching at nothing in the crisping grass. Cassie followed hard on her heels. They ran, ran to the end of her block, five houses down and stopped, panting in the heavy air. Cassie's cheeks were flushed and her hair plastered wetly against her forehead. She reached out to take Elisabeth's hand.

"Don't touch me. You better wash your hands."

"Don't tell Mom I picked up the bird, okay? Okay, Elisabeth?"

She shook her head. She wouldn't tell their mother. It would somehow become her fault for letting Cassie play by herself or something. Cassie drove her nuts. At school, Cassie with her loud voice and good humour was always the centre of a group of friends. Always having a sleepover or going to birthday parties, but at home Cassie was treated like some baby that Elisabeth had to look out for, make sure was entertained and out of trouble. When really, Elisabeth thought, it was Elisabeth who needed looking out for. Needed someone to make sure she had friends and didn't spend too much time alone.

They walked back to the house in silence, both too hot to run. The rubber of their tennis shoes slapped along the sidewalk, smeared a hopscotch pattern that someone had optimistically drawn. It was much too hot to hopscotch.

Back in the cool dark of the house, Cassie hurried off to the downstairs bathroom. Elisabeth heard the pipes shudder with the effort of providing water. Cassie sang a show tune from *Oklahoma* while she washed and the words came faintly to Elisabeth sitting on the couch. *"Old Judd is dead, old Judd Frye is dead, he's looking oh so purty and serene..."*

Elisabeth felt the still house around them. Her mother must be out. Probably left a note on the kitchen table. She levered off her left shoe with her right foot and then did the same with her right on the left. She noticed her grimy toes, remains of chipped red polish on the nails, but she didn't care. Sometimes in the summer she took a perverse pleasure in getting as dirty as she could before her mother noticed. She ran her nose along the skin on her arm and smelled the outdoors, the dirt and the grass, and the pong of her own salty sweat.

"Old Judd is dead, a candle lights his head!" Cassie sang dramatically, twirling into the living room with her hands waving.

"Oh, shut up."

"You're not supposed to say 'Shut up.'"

"Who cares? S-h-u-t u-p."

"I'm telling." Cassie swung around and headed for the kitchen, "Mom, Mom."

There was a moment of silence. "Hey, she's not here."

Elisabeth sighed and pushed herself up off the couch. "Isn't there a note? Did you look on the table?"

In the kitchen, Cassie stood in the middle of the floor, hands on her hips. Elisabeth pushed her out of the way and scanned the surfaces in the room. Cassie stumbled against the counter but made no protest. There was no note on the table. Or stuck on the refrigerator with the magnet made to look like sushi. Their mother's phone still sat on the kitchen table, its blank black face showing no signs of life. A tiny, the tiniest of all time, tremor of fear shivered through Elisabeth's chest. "Mom?" She walked around the house calling her mother, Cassie right behind her. Through the dining room where the dollhouse dolls lay flung about on the house's roof, staring at the ceiling uncomprehending, through the living room where her Keds sat like two small white animals hiding deep in the shade of the couch. In the den, dust motes floated in the air and the television reflected the La-Z-Boy and beanbag chairs. Empty.

"Mom?" Cassie called out now, her voice high and thin.

"Shut up," Elisabeth said, afraid now of who might answer. Cassie took Elisabeth's hand. This time she let her. They looked into their parents' bedroom where the bedside clock blinked 3:00 over and over. *It must have come unplugged*, Elisabeth thought. They started up the narrow stairs to the second floor where their bedrooms were.

A jumble of stuffed animals and papers and clothes hid the floor of Cassie's room. A red-striped sock curled just out of the doorway like an unfurling tongue. Elisabeth kicked it back in and shut the door. They walked down the hall to the bathroom where a thin trickle of beige water now ran silently into the basin.

In Elisabeth's room the sheets, pillows and books held their lifeless places. As the girls stood and stared, the light grew dimmer and dimmer. Elisabeth knew a storm was coming. All summer long there had been storms; great rolling ones, with hail and lightning. Trees knocked down, sewers overflowing. The last one had only been a week ago and they had watched it coming across the country on their television, even as the wind outside had been pulling at their own windows, rattling them in their frames like dry bones shaken out of a cup.

"Never seen anything like it," her father said again and again.

"It's El Nino, I'm telling you," their mother said as they watched the weather channel spin out pictures of tornadoes and hurricanes over a tiny map of the US and Canada.

"El Nino?" Their father laughed. "That was years ago."

"Well, then?"

"It's just weird weather. I bet they had this kind of thing back in 1865 or something. If you were to look at old *Farmer's Almanacs* from the turn of the century or something, I'm sure there were at least one or two years when they had this exact same kind of thing." He took the remote from their mother's hand and switched the television over to *The Bachelor*.

"I hate this damn show," he said, fumbling with the remote again.

"No, leave it," their mother said, taking the remote from him. "I want to see if he finds out about the other girl."

"Christy? The one with the big tatas?"

"You're sick." Their mother slapped him lightly on the arm. "Now shut up so I can hear."

The family sat in silence watching the man pick his favourite woman from the group of women, while outside the sky grew darker and rain pelted the windows with furious intent. The bachelor gave the woman he liked a rose. Elisabeth couldn't remember the name of the one he chose, even though her parents argued about it afterwards, both passionately defending their own choices as the storm raged outside.

◦◦◦

Now the rain had begun again. It sheeted against the window, blown by a wind that pulled at the house, as if it were trying to get inside, trying to get to them. Elisabeth reached out a hand to turn on the lights but the switch did nothing, her room remained dark. They ran out of the room together. Cassie began to cry as she ran alongside Elisabeth. Downstairs, Elisabeth wrenched open the front door, struggling against the wind. She called, first for her mother and then for Pansy. Her voice tore out of her throat and spiralled away down the street with the leaves and the driving rain. A garbage can rolled down the sidewalk, gaping open and empty. She pulled the door shut with both hands. Outside, the crash of the first tree – the one in front of the house next door – shook the floor of the living room. Their mother always bragged about those trees along their street, how they made the neighbourhood so nice, really gracious.

"Come on." Elisabeth pulled Cassie along by a sweaty hand, stumbling through the kitchen to the basement stairs. "We've got to get into the basement."

"I don't want to go down there." Cassie twisted her hand in Elisabeth's grip. "That's where the ghosts are!"

"It's the only safe place. There's no such thing as ghosts." She gave Cassie a sharp jerk. Cassie looked at her and pressed her lips together, but she didn't try to wiggle away again.

They passed by the kitchen window and there was a dull thud, then another, and then a sharp sound, and another thud. Elisabeth glanced briefly.

"Oh, Elisabeth. Oh, the birds!" Cassie jerked to a stop again, pointing at the window. Birds dropped from the sky, spun, plummeted and hit the window, as if their wings were useless. The window glass cracked in a crazy web, marked with drops of blood and feathers.

Elisabeth pulled her hand again. "Don't look, Cassie. Just get down the steps."

From the basement, the odour of wet and mould floated up. They hesitated on the landing, then plunged down the steps, bracing themselves like swimmers diving into an ice-cold lake.

Feeling their way through the dark, junk-filled basement, they stumbled toward an old velveteen sofa with ugly oversized orange and brown blooms printed all over, that had been shoved into a corner. Their grandparents had given their mother the sofa when they moved to Florida and their mother hated it. "My fabulous inheritance," she'd said after they left, and kicked the sofa's base. "The friggin' family jewels."

Cassie and Elisabeth clung to each other on the damp cushions. Relegated to the basement, the fabric absorbed all the moisture and now smelled strongly of mildew. It seemed as if the unnatural flowers printed on its ungainly curves breathed out rot. Elisabeth felt Cassie shake against her and thought, *It's just like in a book. People really do shake when they are scared.* She couldn't control her own tremors no matter how sternly she talked to herself. As if she was far away, she felt her body shiver ridiculously, dramatically.

A snake of water slithered past the couch. Then another, coming faster. That meant the sewers were overflowing, and her daddy would be mad when he had to clean up the basement again. Elizabeth pulled her feet up off the floor. Cassie did the same and hid her face in Elisabeth's shoulder. Elisabeth watched as the two runlets joined, like a small stream. She closed her eyes. *Imagine you are anywhere. Imagine you are not here. A small stream running through a magical forest. It winds past a small house where brown and orange flowers bloom on the lawn, and Pansy sits on the front door step washing her face carefully, one paw flicking over her ears, her eyes shut in contentment.*

"Elisabeth?" Cassie's voice, faint and far away, called across the stream that ran under Elisabeth's feet. Silvery fish filled the water and twitched past, alive, on their way to some fish place.

As she watched, a bird skimmed the surface of the water and rose again with something struggling fiercely in its beak. Something that wanted to live.

THE HEAT WAS UNBEARABLE

FRANK WESTCOTT

NOTE TO THE READER: Read as pregnant pauses the irreverent placing of periods and commas. To YOUR heart's content. No aborting punctuation planned as it is written. Ah… the blessings of the high-tech texting world transveresing skies and *sigh-burr-rr-rr*, cyber zones to destiny anew, renewed, de-glued after all was said. And done.

Now to my story: THE HEAT WAS UNBEARABLE

RALPH:
The pigs are reeling, wigging their butts in extremes of pancakes and bacon, shaking and bake-on-ing their ribs in time to moving jagged patterns across his, the writer's, screen. The pigs are winging it, flying like no other pigs he's ever seen. They are in my space too, but invading his inner and outer lives where he would like to go, to either or both, and beat the heat or get his feet cooled, moving in air like the pigs, cooling their hooves. When flying.

THE WRITER:
They said it would come. The heat. Neither they nor I knew when. But it did come. Sooner than expected. It looked a bit like a glacier of chocolate melting.

When it did, the thermometer outside my shell broke. Glass shattered. Temperature rose. Red steel became redder. Like it was cold. But it wasn't.

On TV I saw one bridge sink into the earth, melting the sand it was so hot. My sanity fell away. I slid into some other universe like I was in Wasaga Beach and sliding to Toronto. Then back. I watched more sand melt, then harden. Then fill Lake Ontario. A beach without a lake.

I watched the TV for news. My shell's window fogged up. The shell got warm. Warped slightly. Time seemed to warp too. Air streaming through the universe. My shell universe. Streamed and de-streamed inside then out. Digitized air control.

A poet once said, "It is in the air we breathe we find ourselves." It might have been Ralph. Not sure. I hoped I kept breathing. I wanted to find myself. Somewhere. When all was said and done. Heard a poet mutter one time too, "The life we are living is the most important one." That might have been Ralph too. Not sure.

I wished I could time travel forward or into some future tense. And Off-Earth myself early. Before the future came. And was present.

RALPH:
The pigs are climbing staircases without wings now. The staircases can't fly. But the pigs do. So the staircases think they can too.

THE WRITER:
I see a blue tube coming from my TV. The heat expands inside my shell. Everything staggers. Even the heat in the sun which I am not supposed to see. I realize I am seeing this on

TV. I watch. The sun melts icebergs, fridges and chocolate. People kept their fridges outside their shells. Small shells. I had a deluxe. Kept my fridge inside.

RALPH:
This heat came. It was number two. Or three. Can't remember.

THE WRITER:
Damn.

RALPH:
The pigs are real. Now. They are wiggling. Doing yoga curls and looking like bacon frying in a pan. There are screams. Destiny emerging. Being released. I wish this was a future tense for the writer's sake. At least this, his point of view, would be over. The density of space in his shell is becoming overbearing. It is increasing. He is finding it hard to breathe. I sing softly. No breath too deep. To conserve air.

THE WRITER:
Everything is metric now. I have trouble reading metric. I wonder what wild, wonky-eyed number system will exist in my future, when, if, I get there and I am not just past. I think of wild-eyed numbers. A mix of ones. Twos. Threes. And their cousins. Change shifting things. Even the counting system. Heat rising inside my shell reminds me the thermometer is broken. I remember back to the 70s, or thereabouts, and how the government way, back in Prime Minister Pierre Trudeau's day, changed Canada to the metric system. Secret files released before the first melt said it was all to make the heat seem less when the heat came. Fahrenheit has higher numbers. It was getting hot no matter which way you looked at it.

I watch the heat swirling on TV, surrounding everything like swords of fire heating, raging itself on the original anvil's flame.

RALPH:
I watch monkeys in a soup commercial. They become pigs. They escape their moment. Like musicians fine-tuning their instruments in the hallway, missing their turn. The pigs the monkeys become are decadent. Manifesting a sparkling odour out of the soup. It comes out of the TV. I smell soup. The odour. And the sparkles tickle the writer's nose. Something is burning. The writer tries to turn off the TV. It does not shut off.

RALPH & THE WRITER:
Resurrect yourself in the the daylight of the night before when the heat comes." Who said that, I wonder, hearing it again. *"Resurrect yourself in the daylight of night in climate change, when you know it is too late, and change has already happened. Tragedy in change is the metamorphosis occurring when you rely on nothing else... but what is."*

I wonder more who is saying this.

"Or more..." I hear, added to the previous, still not understanding.

Then I hear... *"It resonates and knows itself, you are yourself, in the more of heat exchanged in energy out of control, especially when you rise into your future tense. There is no climate button to control the outcome. Or shut off the outcome. Or your TV, for that matter. Or push the button of you to the you, you seek in your tomorrow. Time's button is released. It has been pressed."*

I Off-Earth in my mind, escaping and wishing for a climate change stop button. It is hopeless. In my shell, it is already over. I have to wait it out. Feels like fragments torn from time, dancing into some other existence I cannot see or want to. I am hopeful to manifest life, now, itself, now. I am living in a past, yet it seems like a present I wish could be a future so I would be happening then, now. Not yet gone.

"We – do – have – a future – if – we – only – allow – it," a robotic voice says. "You – do – not – have – to – live – in – a – future – passed – or – a – present – futured – only – now."

It is always this way, I think. It is like when a miracle happens and my blood swims in my veins faster, as if dripping my very heartbeats onto a canvas of solace and soul I cannot fathom. Fully. I cannot see it. But I do. I pray for the mother and father of gods to Mary-Joseph themselves and Jesus out of aborting bastardizations to canonize themselves. Pretending to be saints who walked among us. The past cannot move forward, regardless its hold on you, just like the future cannot backtrack to now, to set you free. A child out of wedlock, even if you call him Jesus and make a god out of him, is still a bastard. And I remember how they called Barabbas Jesus. Too. He was Jesus of Barabbas.

The heat melts across time, melting chocolate crosses at Easter time and chickens hatch out of brown worn eggs, so we can eat in the cannon thrusting us into space, our shells intact and our destiny mortalized. Immemorial. I know I am not. I wait for the second coming. Of the heat. And realize it is the third I am waiting for. I remember it is. The moment between two and three I want. The one I want to be back for. I am no longer scared. Or sacred. Melting gold crosses have already occurred outside my shell. They call them churches. Albatrosses around necks until the last melt when people adorn goats and false gods, and seem to walk out of cheese boards and cheese. And knights' light candles at round tables in historical moments, flashbacking to then, themselves farther back in time than anyone ever realized, out of context with what, who and where we are, and what is happening now. The heat.

I think knighted, sainted or tainted... it is all the same. Adornment of one kind or another. Redemption bastards in heat. Time ticking. Now. In seconds, replete. And the TV blinks and smokes. I know what is burning. The wires. Rubber coating. That is what is smelling.

The heat gets to you in strange ways.

Good thing for the wafers. Else, I would go hungry. They are brittle. I think I see religions floating in Time's carcass in front of me. But it is only Lake Ontario blistering Hudson Bay, and flashing it on and off my flickering TV screen. The Fraser River bolts. Boils. And redeems itself. And so does the TV.

RALPH:
"Well, would you look at that?"

THE WRITER:
I recognize the voice now. It is Ralph.

I long for the days of penny stocks and haypennies, imagined in haystacks when you can't find any needles, but have a penny in your pocket. It is like reading cereal boxes when there is no cardboard or box for that matter. Just the cereal in a bag. Only the memory of the box. As you look at the bag and try to read it anyway. There are no words on the bag. I chew on the wafer. I offer a piece to Ralph.

RALPH:
"Don't eat," he says.

THE WRITER:
"I forgot," I say. "You seem so human…"
   The heat is making my thinking unclear now. Not that it ever was. Clear. Things too. Fuzzy. And it is foggy in here. Transitions required. Translations required too. Of some kind. From what to what I do not know. Maybe I am looking for a conversation conversion like metric to imperial, or Fahrenheit to Celsius and back again. I would like to convert from pre-heat to post-heat. My liftoff is not working. I have got to get separate the cups for my half-full ones and my half empty ones. They are hard to see when your brain gets heat and water-loss wobbly, and you to try to put litres into cups that measure ounces and *cups* too, and everything gets very scary confusing.

RALPH & THE WRITER:
"Your milk and honey is on the other side," Ralph says.
   "Hope so," I say, hoping to get fresh cups there too, full ones, that hold a litre or a bunch of ounces no matter what language I want to count in.
   "Time passes out of honeycombs of hair and rinse brushes, brushing back follicles of sound, when you REALLY want to drink the honey that bees make in their honey tomb combs. Shells," Ralph says.
   I wonder what he is getting at now that I know who is speaking. And wonder how he got to be such a poet.
   "Destiny is but a morsel in time," I hear Ralph say. *"The happening will happen whether you are William, or Tell or even Shakespeare, shooting arrows at apples on foreheads, or on barrels you want to shoot fish in."*
   And Ralph has become a philosopher too.

RALPH:
There are pigs shaking now, glued onto dough-like cookies. They seem to want to make money in restaurants in capital cities, shaking too now, and baking franchises in ribs and Glory Syrups. Syrups from Canadian maples drip onto pancakes flooding where water used to be. No dikes present or thumbs poking holes. The dough is hard now.

THE WRITER:
"All get out! The heat is coming. Everyone out of Earth's oven," I hear someone call from outside my shell. I know it isn't Ralph because he is in here with me.

I move across my own screen and look like a pig wiggling, winging itself, wobbly in the air, flying to Certainia, like no other pigs have ever flown before. I wish the heat would go away. It won't. And I think I smell bacon cooking.

The BIG picture comes. I am glad they didn't take the seconds out of clocks, even though they talked about it. I want to know when the last second comes.

RALPH & THE WRITER:
Ralph starts singing. "*Goats are on a cheese spread ~ Spreading time and destiny ~ With no monkeys in sight ~ They are climbing trees ~ You would not know if they were ~ They are not in sight ~ They are flying pigs ~ The melt comes ~ The people stop measuring ~ Distance ~ Everything comes together ~ It is a Vegas spending spree ~ Melting my everything ~ And shortening things ~ Ratcheting time ~ And tables rouletteing foreign destiny ~ All numbers covered ~ Balls bouncing off wheels to floors ~ Wiping everybody out ~ Wasaga Beach comes to Toronto ~ Again ~ The Prairies slide to New Brunswick ~ The CN tower is in plain sight ~ Where Niagara Falls falls*

now ~ From rooftops boiled over ~ Fleeing back to Ontario-on-the-Lake ~ Spinning Huntsville over to Winnipeg ~ And Sudbury nickel-belts a melt to silver lining ~ Plate-ing mushrooms in wild soups ~ For molten pleasures ~ Monsters Science-Fiction-Flicking realities ~ In the melt of chocolate ~ Morphing into cellophane dolls ~ On sightlines lost ~ Where poets read trademarks and tread-waste ~ On E-lines lost ~ Morphing been gone and went ~ Outta here's and there's ~ To laughing moments ~ Gone awry ~ Nobody is there to tell a joke ~ All listening grown deaf ~ Growing wheat out of chaff chaffing on the St. Lawrence ~ River ~ Bubbling porridges in heat ~ Destiny wanting and awaiting a changing world ~"

I waited for the after-melt, after the second one, before I came back. I saw how it, the melt, moved train rails making distance disasters on shorelines and drying up diverse rivers. Lots of water got stored for the melts.

"Chickens crossed the egg to get to the road on the other side, and Jack and the bean stock monster fell out of the sky and a two-storey building wanting to be truth, but became monsters instead, sound and heat mixing film vibes in the melding (not melting) together, creating flicks to Off-Earth in or go to L.A.," Ralph adds.

Ralph is being Ralph again.

The pigs are flying in a rare formation now. They are holding court in clouds of time before it is all over. I see them spread their wings. They are out of fry pans now. They are cooking in flight, it seems, baking penance moments beyond angels singing, wings golden again, blowing remorse signals out of whole moments, returning to dog-shells as whole-angels resurging out of disasters awakening, to sever destinies' connections, so they too, can fly in formation now, and into their own lives. Steel wings work well together too. Dancing in their flap-flap and wishing they were not wings with pigs, but could be pigs with wings.

And I see I am poetick-ing too.

"It is all in the figment of the perception flap," Ralph says.

"Huh?" I say, and ignore him… it… So much evaporated in the first heat. And the second.

The pigs are still flying that rare formation. Geese are trumpeting, wailing like a dizzy Gillespie wall of sound making their horns play loud and louder still. Their mouths blow as they fly to new heights, their bills breathing nose holes singing everlasting songs, joy moments winning one more time. Joy sounds like that when it comes from a goose and out if its mouth called bill.

I feel the leftover heat between the second melt and the third. My memories cloud. Recompensed poetry makes songs out of words sung in a future I cannot see, but want to. And my TV is off now.

Ralph says, "And the chorus rang true. If pigs could really fly and do it horizontally too, they would be able to move sideways in the air above the sky, blue, but they can't. So, I wonder if pigs can really fly. Sideways. Or front ways. Or any other ways."

My empty glasses are not half-full or half-empty. They are just empty. Wholly-empty. They rock and rattle on tables shaking and tipping, and melting in the heat. They melt hot under my fingers.

"Running bees wax springs eternal under fingers of time, melting too, in the paradox of memories' hearts' beatings, and half-full glasses aren't reality either-or, they are betwixt and between, and it isn't Valentine's Day yet, but Earth will be massacred, everything melting. Better get off. Earth," Ralph says.

I ignore him. It. Still. Tired of his poetic new-found ways.

The heat is climbing now as I speak. Write. Sweating now. Back to Fahrenheit in my brain. No Celsius conversions. Direct to Fahrenheit.

They said there were three heats we could live through. There would be the first. Then the second. The third, if we were in our shells or Off-Earth. They said the last one would be the sixth. We would either be gone or dead by then. Hopefully, we would have Off-Earthed to Certainia before or between two and three. I got two round trips because I was a writer. I wanted to see the melt from two to three. And tell about it. Write about it. Then fly in my shell back to Certainia.

You had to stay on Certainia a minimum four days before you went anywhere else. But they let me leave after two, since I was going back to Earth to write about it. Before leaving Certainia, I jogged so much in my shell, I lost enough water to *not* boil back on Earth. That is why they let me go back after two days, too.

I thought I was returning to now, but got then instead.

Ralph laughed in the density of distance I travelled in time and out of time, all the while in step and out of step, with the step of the universe, wanting to be on Earth one more time, but avoid the melt that time. And live on in my future. Tense, I was.

I was amazed. My TV still worked when I got back. To. Earth. I just had to plug it in and wiggle the wires a bit. My old residence shell worked. My transporting shell got me there. I called the TV spot my Rabbi-Zone. Had rabbit ears for reception. Reminded me of rabbi-ears.

"*Ecumenical viewing,*" I think I hear Ralph say. But it sounds like it is outside my shell.

"I guess," I say, not knowing who I am saying it to. For sure.

There is a knock on my door. Shell. It is Ralph. It *was* Ralph's voice I heard.

"Hi, Ralph," I say.

Ralph is a robot originally programmed to be whoever I want him to be. Got screwed up in the first melt. Now he is whoever he wants to be. Talk about having a screw loose. I guess he is an it, but if you hang with Ralph long enough, he starts to seem like a he.

I look around my shell. It seems to be moving. Rolling. I feel like I am rolling. A rolling doughnut. As if my axel is spinning wobbly in its hole. I wonder if I am blob-streaming to another existence.

"Nope," Ralph says. "Heat does that. Heat does that to you,"

"On the verge of a melt, I think," I think and say. "So, what's up, Ralph?" I add asking.

Ralph is built not to burn until at least the fourth melt. I'll be Off- Earthed permanent-like by then.

"How much time we got?" Ralph asks.

"Lost my seconds, hand, watch after the second, second minute clock evolution. No minutes left counted in seconds. Got me when it comes," I say, Ralph bringing out the friendly in me.

"When will it all end?"

"Don't know. I told you that. When it does, I guess," and say too, feeling happy for some reason.

"Do I get to stay?" Ralph asks.

"Where?"

"Here."

"Don't know," I answer, waiting for his next question. I wait while he programmes himself a bit.

"It's gonna melt. BIG," Ralph says. "I can tell."

"How?"

"Like chocolate."

I think I see Ralph grimace. I am not sure. It is hard to tell if a robot grimaces. Or if one, he, it, can do it. Not sure what he programmed.

"To melt or not to melt," Ralph says.

"That is the question," I say.

"Or could be the answer."

"Could be the answer, too," I say. "You are right. Not bad for a robot."

"Chocolate bar?" Ralph asks.

"Sure," I say, wanting one.

"Everything is going to melt like a pawn in a chess-chef's breakfast," Ralph sounds like he has hiccups and says. "Why are you writing this? About this?"

"Somebody has to…" I answer.

"That is not the question," Ralph says.

"It is the answer. Again. Somebody has to…" I answer and say and wonder why I am talking to a robot who just offered me, asked me, if I wanted chocolate. And I think of melting in a sea of chocolate factories melting themselves out of or into Lake Ontario. I wasn't sure which. Getting bleary-eyed now. Heat getting to me. As it is rising.

"Why did you come back?" Ralph asks more.

"To write about it," I say. "Like I said."

"But if nobody is here, nobody can read it… And if you Off-Earth and take it back with you, nobody elsewhere'll know if it's true or not, so you could'a just made it up. Are you going to take it back to Certainia? They'd never know if you made it up or not!"

"Yes, I am going back to Certainia. As for your making it up thoughts, I do not want to be like a Chopin trying to do yoga, instead of play the piano. That is why I had to come back to write about it."

"I've got you in hand," Ralph says. "Here, have a chocolate bar and step outside for a bit. I don't want to smell it or watch... it... you... the melt."

I step out.

Ralph takes over writing.

RALPH:
"Pigs don't fly, you idiot," Ralph writes.

THE WRITER:
I hear a pig fly by.

RALPH:
"Looks like an angel," Ralph says inside my shell and to himself as he writes.

THE WRITER:
"Only if they have silver wings," I say, and watch a gold one fly. Pig, that is.

RALPH:
Hi, reader. This is me Ralph. Now. Writing without hesitation. Except where I put the periods. The writer, the Frank guy, lost his way outside when he got into the chocolate.

I watch from the window. I see light bowling itself towards the porch. I watch him melt. Chocolate too. Hands go first. Then feet. Extremities. Lips. In mid-chew. Lake Ontario starts to bubble. He thought he was returning to Certainia. Was so relaxed about it all. But he was going to an afterlife. A destruction destination holiday. I push his shell button and bounce him

Off-Earth where even a robot can live forever. A full moon bays at a dog.

I think in robot-think and ponder wagging my last lever-tail, ejecting myself to another planet to watch Earth burn and the heat get everything. I see the writer floating belly-choc-o-full-up in Lake Ontario, eating chocolate still and wondering what all the fuss is about. I watch the writer-guy rising like a New Testament starting to write itself, and the writer puts himself back into the story. He writes me out of it.

THE WRITER:
"Hi," it's me, the writer. Robot's gone. I turned his page with a flick of a finger. I am floating in destinies less travelled now. The prevailing winds of time are blowing stars out of dancers' routines, where destinies cannot really meet, but only shine together. Water boils in the heat around me. But I am close to waterless and not boiling. Everything else is gurgling itself.

```
        I
    F
        E  E
           L
    L  I
           K  E
        I        A_M
         M_E
                L_T
              I_NG
```

THE WRITER
I see there is a pig that looks like a fly in the oinkment. It flies by out of these words and destinies. I hear the command,

"Bake on!" It becomes bac-on. I am in an afterlife. We all eat together, reminiscing about flying pigs in a time where stories and heat came together under a one-lit candle, in a one-bake oven's kitchen. Between mouthfuls the chef says, "Amen to that." A robot named Ralph goes on rewind to get the story right. He says, "Grace." And George Burns comes out of afterlife retirement and past performing days and says, "Gracie, look-itt… a flying pig!" "Pigs can't fly," Gracie says. "That's kinda what I thought, but that one is," George says.

The robot laughs. I laugh too. You do too. We are all in this. One and the same.

A pig sits down to dinner, burps, dung-drops and digs into a beef meatloaf, looking chocolate-ee and taste-ee. The pig is glad it isn't a cow, otherwise it might be eating itself, and it had already chewed its nails to the bone, and didn't like the flavour. The writer passed on and out of Certainia into worlds unknown. He would write about them when he was gone long enough to get it right. They, the pigs, they say… pigs have wings wherever he went. And some are even learning to fly.

ANIMATE

KATE STORY

Laurie makes the nine-hour drive from the city in seven. St. John's to Gros Morne: *great sombre*, mountain standing alone.

The land slips by. Standing stones of the Avalon barrens and rolling terrain of the east flatten out; Deer Lake; farms, fields of hardy wheat, unthinkable even fifteen years ago. Finally, the land pushes up into dark peaks, a cast-off far-flung northeastern arm of the Appalachian range.

They are lucky to live here. In some ways, things in Newfoundland have become – Laurie admits it – easier.

The road winks in and out of shadows, and Laurie watches Daniel sideways. It seems to her that he becomes magnetized. His thick, shiny hair, combed back from forehead to nape, pulls into lines like iron filings dragged across paper, and his lazy eye pulls further to the side.

The immense boreal forest – stretching from Alaska to Siberia, to Japan even – you can feel it watching. It's slowly dying, the forest, in many places, but not on this island. The forest watches. The car slides through the old, worn mountains, beneath hard green eyes.

Daniel sleeps. Signs for the national park begin to appear. Laurie turns on the radio. There's a news story about an inexplicable outbreak of pulmonary edema among the millions of Bangladeshi people resettled in India since their country succumbed. "They're drowning in fluid inside their own bodies," a doctor explains. She says in her lilting English that they can't explain how or why the condition has spread through the refugees, but a geo-pathologist is interviewed. He posits a psycho-geographic effect, an intangible link between people's bodies and the risen ocean's submergence of their land.

Daniel wakes. He doesn't speak, and as for Laurie, she gave up trying to make conversation as far back as Grand Falls. Daniel is a wreck of a human being, so word goes, and she is newly divorced; they should have everything to say to each other. Silence seeps into the car from the land around them, like water through the timbers of a raft.

They enter the park through a construction zone; they're re-routing the road due to persistent flooding. Replacing asphalt with solar panels. That's good, she thinks, we're finally catching up. The guy holding the SLOW sign jerks his head as Laurie drives past him, and she nods in return.

Daniel speaks. Laurie jumps.

"That sideways thing," he says, "that oblique sort of head jerk?"

He's talking about the construction worker. "It's a bay guy thing," Laurie says.

"What does it mean? Hello?"

"Hello, and a bit of a flirt." She glances over at him. He could be handsome, if he wasn't so knotted around himself. "But to you, because you're a man and we're obviously from St. John's, a bit of challenge."

"I'm not from St. John's."

Daniel's the veterinarian from the mainland. He grew up somewhere in Ontario – it's vague, it's just "the mainland" after all – and later practised in Vancouver. Then the San Andreas finally heaved. He was one of the few survivors of that terrible event. While everyone knew it was due to go, there's a school of thought linking the planet's increased seismic activity to the melting glaciers. Earth's crust bounces back in "isostatic rebound" as the ice thins, seeps, falls, lightens. That makes Daniel another climate refugee.

He aroused a lot of interest in her single friends: new man, *with* a job; and clean, nice manners.

Then his personal fault line cracked. He's been in hiding since.

He needs to learn how to be human again.

One of her friends from work, Karen, suggested Laurie take Daniel on this trip. "We dated, you know, he was nice," she said a touch wistfully. Karen, with her perpetually broken heart; she picks the wrong men – youngsters and drunks and disasters.

She should know better. We're social workers, Laurie thinks, and then remembers that the snug cocoon of her own marriage has split. It opens in her gut, a pit, a piece of her that Jesse took and the hole he left is festering, getting bigger. Laurie closes it over. She's getting better at that. She pictures a pile of stones filling up the hollow putrescence. Stones, one then another, like rocks worn smooth on a beach. They sit heavy in her body. She prefers insensate weight to the hole.

Just before sunset they pull into a site just in view of Kildevil Mountain. It rises like a shoulder on the other side of a bay, trees patchy, rock shrugging through torn fabric. The rain that's been spitting on them all the way across the island suddenly clears. They set up a tarp over the picnic table as a shelter, tying it to the convenient overhanging branches of a spruce tree. The sites have been crafted to look natural, but the National Parks gravel lying under the grass makes it hard to sink the tent pegs. Laurie hurts her hand. Daniel is awkward, alternately pulling with too much strength or drifting off. She has to call him back to task three, maybe four times; he keeps staring up at the sky, or at the bay, or at the mountain, still visible as the sun slips under.

The rain comes back as light dies from the sky and so they huddle under the tarp, sitting on the picnic table. She pulls up her hood and hugs her knees. They had stopped at Pizza Hut in Deer Lake, so they're not hungry. It hardly seems worthwhile to light a fire. And she didn't bring any booze, of course, not with Daniel's history.

A mistake – it was a mistake to come.

Vague shouts and singing come wafting from someplace down below. Or across the bay, maybe – hard to tell.

"You hear that?" Daniel says, head cocked. His yellow raincoat is torn, she sees, at the armpit.

"Probably the Christian camp at Kildevil." More and more of them of late; they come here from all over the world to sing down the end of days.

"Did they name the mountain?"

"No, the name's older… I don't know where it came from."

She's rubbing her hand, not even knowing she's doing it, and Daniel takes it between his palms, massaging it.

She freezes.

He drops her hand.

"I'm going for a walk." His figure disappears into the drizzle, the twilight, and she listens to the crunching of his feet on gravel until that disappears into the rush of wind across the bay, through the spruces over her head.

She sits for what seems like a long time. More singing from the Christian camp wafts on the breeze.

She wonders when Daniel will come back. She needs to look after him; it helps her build her stone walls. She's honest enough to admit it; and she is hoping to bring him out of his exile too. Waste of a good human, that. The accident wasn't his fault, he was addicted. You have to allow for that sort of thing although Jesse would say that even an addict holds responsibility for—

Rocks slide in her chest, and for a moment it's hard to breathe. She builds herself up again, here, now, woman on a picnic table under a tarp in the rain. When it feels safe again she slips off the picnic table and crouches to pee. Rain rattles on her hood. She heads for the tent; the hell with trying to brush her teeth or anything. She wriggles from her clothes and changes her socks to dry ones, zips into her sleeping bag. Empty one next to her, old one of Jesse's, *shut up*.

Daniel will come back. He's not that deranged.

Stories she's heard from Karen: he hid in his house for months after it happened, drinking and pissing in corners, on the furniture. Behaviour that would have led him, were he an animal under his care, to put himself down.

The wind rises and the trees around the site creak. Laurie lies under the rattling synthetic tent in the rain.

A dream of a creature in a house, howling in the basement. The basement is an empty theatre: rows of old, red velvet seats, a theatre set of painted ocean waves on the back wall. The creature hides among them. The theatre's leaking, water is coming in from all sides and she doesn't know what to do. She goes upstairs, and Karen comes over for tea. They talk over the howling. Trees push up through the floor, hard, dark-green points. The dream devolves into formless emotion that works her jaw, even in sleep.

No telling how much later it is when the tent unzips and something wet and breathing hard rolls inside.

"I hope that's you, Daniel," she says.

A grunt.

Daniel lies down on top of the sleeping bag, muddy boots and wet coat and all. Then he says, "I'm sorry."

Within moments he is snoring. Annoyance; Jesse's sleeping bag will be ruined, all that wet and dirt.

She has to pour rocks into her chest again. She lies there, weighted and suddenly cold, wondering why she thought she could save this wreck of a man snoring and breaking next to her all night long.

She wakes and the light is orange inside the tent, the rain has stopped scratching and rattling. She's alone. Mud streaks on Jesse's sleeping bag though, she didn't dream that. And she smells wood smoke. Laurie rolls out of the tent, struggling into boots she left under the fly. It's overcast but not raining. Daniel has gotten a fire going.

"Good morning."

"Hey." Bacon too. He's gotten stuff out of the car and is making breakfast.

No, just bacon. The whole package of it in the pan.

A flash of camping here with Jesse two years ago, and the terrific eggs he used to make, even over a fire.

This enters her. The force of the anger that follows catches inside, a physical pain.

She mutes the feeling, stone by stone, walking toward Daniel across soggy grass. A thought – that this trip feels like some sort of penance for not having been able to keep Jesse – slithers out from some gap in the rocks.

"You want to go for a hike today?"

Daniel nods, pokes at the bacon with a fork. Jerks his head in a passable imitation of the bay-boy nod. "That way." She catches his eye and they both almost smile.

After bacon and instant coffee, Laurie hauls out the park map from her glove compartment. "The Tablelands. You want to go there?"

"Tablelands?" His brown eyes are startled, vague. She wonders now if he managed to bring some kind of drug with him. Some of the horse tranquilizer they found in his veins the night he killed that boy with his car.

"They're in that direction," she points. "Where you said you wanted to go. I've never been on that trail before, but I hear it's nice." She's babbling.

"Nice." He stares through the trees as if he can see the Tablelands from here.

Laurie cleans the pan and then comes back; he's still staring. She puts together a daypack with water, food. She gets in the car. "You coming?"

"Where are you going?"

"To the Tablelands, Daniel. God. Get in the car."

"I thought we were walking," but he uproots himself and clambers into the passenger seat.

"We are. But it's a drive away; the trail starts in Trout River." She looks at him, still in his torn yellow raincoat. "It's a, maybe, seven-kilometre hiking trail in, and then you come out again; it doesn't loop." She rattles the map. "You up for that?"

He nods, staring out the windshield.

Trout River is gone now. Too much tidal flooding, too many storms. Many communities have been abandoned in what the government calls "a managed retreat." The example of Florida haunts them; the U.S. waited too long before admitting the rising seas weren't going back down.

She doesn't miss it, Trout River; it was always a bit of a hole. Houses, half-built and peeling, the broken windows.

It's a relief to see the Parks Canada sign, all very civilized, in the parking lot outside the old town. They head into the woods, following the markers. Daniel doesn't offer to carry the daypack. Well, what did she expect, a knight?

After a bit the sun comes out from behind clouds and it's unexpectedly hot under the trees, humid and stifling. She stops to drink water, ties her coat around her waist and stuffs her sweater into the daypack. The path meanders up and down: tree roots, slippery rocks, small waterfalls that tumble across the trail. She remembers climbing Gros Morne with Jesse five years ago, and how they almost killed themselves doing the Snug Harbour trail. "Park staff chronically underestimate the difficulty levels of these trails," Jesse used to say. She remembers that she hasn't reminded Daniel that they need to watch for ticks – that's new – hadn't had any ticks here, not before, the winters used to be too hard… Why can't she stop thinking of how things were before? But the remembering is softer than it has been; the going's hard enough that it hardly hurts to remember, it's a jumble of footsteps, past and now, past and now. Seven kilometres, but the elevation is making it a bit of a challenge, the long slow climb up to the Tablelands.

"Daniel, do you mind slowing down?" She has to call out, he's gotten so far ahead. He turns.

"Sorry," he calls. He bounds back toward her, almost running. "Sorry."

"It's okay. You want some water?"

He takes the platypus water skin and drinks deeply. He looks along the trail. "There's something…" and he trails off.

"What?"

He lifts his head. "Over that way." He shifts. "Do you feel it?"

"The rock?"

"The watching."

That feeling of being watched, yes. She nods warily. "The forest or…"

"In Ojibwa," he says, "in the language, things are animate or inanimate. Not masculine or feminine, just… wood is animate. And stones."

It's the longest utterance from him this whole trip. She wants to ask if he has any Ojibwa blood in him, but you don't do that. "Animate," she says, looking down, rolling a pale, smooth stone under her foot. She wonders if the Beothuk people who used to live here thought like this too. "What's inanimate?"

"People," he says.

She hopes he is kidding.

His eyes focus on the daypack she's carrying. "Let me take that. Sorry."

They continue. Trout River Pond opens out to their right, too huge for its name, like a fjord. Pure, pure water in there. The trail begins to climb more steeply. Laurie sees caribou scat, and bear. Through a break in the trees she spots two eagles wheeling above the water. Ravens, hidden in the trees, cackle and roll marbles in their throats at the two damaged humans toiling below. If she were hiking with anyone else she'd point all this out, it'd become part of the story of their hike. But with Daniel there is no making a story; his desolation pulls words apart.

They are coming out of the woods, now. Trees die, then bushes, even grass. A vast hump of land soars above them, painfully bright against the blue of empty sky.

Orange rock, weeping rust. No birds here, no animals. The silence is terrible.

Daniel has stopped walking, he stares up at it.

"It's really old," says Laurie, catching her breath. "Some of the oldest rock in the world." She's just saying this to fill the silence.

"Why is it... why does it look like that?"

"It's poisonous."

He looks at her now. That thing she'd noticed on the trip across the island, it's happening again: his eye pulls to the side, his hair strains back over his head in lines, neat as if he'd just combed it, iron filings on paper. How dark his eyes are.

"The rock's from too far below, or something. It doesn't have any nutrients. It's full of heavy metals, or toxic, or something."

"Toxic."

"I'm not a geologist or anything but that's what I remember Jesse telling me." She's said his name.

"Your husband." This slowly, coming from inside him, a memory of meeting at a dinner party maybe, that one at Karen's.

She wants to say *ex* but her tongue is thick.

There's a look on Daniel's face she can't read.

Maybe this is what it's always like for him. Maybe everything is thick, slow, walled up. She imagines kissing him.

He has turned and continued walking. He's got a prowl that is somehow sexual. Attractive. She lets him get quite far ahead before she follows.

The trail climbs up over the Tablelands. It reminds her of Iceland, some of the volcanoes she climbed on that trip with... yeah, with her *ex-husband Jesse*. She wonders if she'll travel alone now. She wonders if she'll have the guts. No, she can't think ahead, the thoughts will fester in that ripped-open place in her chest. One step, one step, one step. Walking on stones. Daniel far ahead again, she lets him go.

The trail climbs, levels out. They're on top of the Tablelands and she sees the reason for the name. It is flat, level as if a god sheared the top off. The water far below is blue, and on the other side, startling, a hill mounds up as high as the Tablelands. It's a normal hill, covered in green – tuckamores and spruce. Waterfalls tumble down it, far, far. Like Earth next to Mars, the fjord a starry space between.

Daniel's lost to view. She walks. There's something about following a trail: you will go, keep going, because there's a destination. She wonders what the end will be. Maybe there will be something – a look-out, a view. She wishes she had the pack with her still; she's thirsty.

Finally she sees a blot of yellow up ahead. He's sitting on a rock. Waiting for her? No, it's just that the trail has ended, petering out in the wilderness.

There's a sort of vista, no grander than anything else they've seen: green land and water where the Tableland drops off into air, the red rust of barren rock all around them. Daniel sits staring at the green across the void.

She makes her way to him and sits down, taking water from the pack he's tipped off his shoulders. She drinks, watching as he picks up a red, poisonous rock, hefts it in his hand. He throws the rock; it bounces, tumbles down the slope. "I hate it here." He picks up another rock and tosses it high in the air. It falls out of sight in a pit.

"The Tablelands?" Well, what the hell, she's done her best to please the creature.

"No." He looks her way. "This island. This whole goddamn island."

"Why?"

"It's too cold in the winter. The wind. Goddamn cold."

"Yes." She feels inexplicable laughter bubbling up. "Yes, it is cold in the goddamn winter."

He throws another rock and when this one lands it splits, showing its deep green inside. Daniel stares. "Look!"

"They're all like that. Green inside." Green, like jade, like a secret.

The silence, she feels… It passes, he shifts away again.

She bows her head, rifling through the pack to find the food she brought. She fills her mouth with chocolate. If Laurie were on death row, this would be her last requested meal: fair trade organic, dark.

On the way back, when the trail meanders down to the vast, pure pond's edge, she steps off the trail onto the rocky shore. She unlaces and kicks off her boots, intending to go wading. Instead, she finds herself walking out and out; feet hurting as stones slip beneath her, sliding like the stones in her chest. The water wicks up her clothes, to her waist, to her chest where the rocks are. The cold insolence creeps into her body.

"You going in?" Daniel's standing on the trail, a poisonous red rock in his hand.

"If you are," she says.

"I'm already in." A smile pulls at his mouth. He cocks his arm, throwing the stone far out into the water, almost boyish. They both watch it disappear, slipping below the surface. "I'm already in."

The ripples from his stone spread, fading. But there's a resurgence, ripples becoming small waves. Laurie feels her hair standing up as if electrified, pulling, back toward the Tablelands. The ground shifts beneath her feet. She laughs, spreads her arms to keep her balance. Daniel looks back the way they've come. Rocks are sliding down the slopes. A tree begins to walk.

Still laughing, Laurie says, "Daniel, I think it's an earthquake!"

Isostatic rebound.

She feels her hair coiling like a Medusa's, and as for Daniel, his head is a Sputnik, a straining halo. Daniel too begins to laugh. He does a half-spin and falls spread-eagle into the water.

Laurie doesn't wait to see him come up. She crouches down, lungs shuddering, gulping air. Her clothes are heavy. She lets the water close over her head. Cold. She crouches like an animal on the bottom of the ancient lake, ground shaking, water surging. She feels her weight.

The silence of the sky above and the water below meet inside the shifting earth.

DEGAS' BALLERINAS

LESLIE GOODREID

Dust devils be spinning over the dried lake bed. They twirl like Degas' ballerinas, dancing on a grave. Seen that art in a book once – blue girls all shiny in their misery. Degas' canvas ain't got nothing on this heap of dirt. Cracks split across the caked mud like scars on withered skin. Don't remember a time when the water flowed, or the ground was giving up its greenness. This land be full of ghosts, and I be one of them. Can't barely see me no more.

North of Toronto there be bog clutter, birthing mosquitoes with their malaria. Them little death soldiers come on paper wings, no matter the weather. I can barely walk from the lake to Front Street. The air be heavy with heat, and my bones weary. Hunger be driving me into the danger place. The city ain't got no safe shelter, but there be food. Two-legged vermin hunt there, too. I be a tasty morsel to them.

I rub my belly and ignore my pasty tongue. Water be scarce. Them pirates at the un-Market trade bottles of Dasani like they be made of gold. Shoo. I avoid that canker government store. It be full of armed guards, all fatty in their purpose. They dress in black uniforms, with a map of the world wrapped up by two olive branches on their armbands. This be a twisty truth. Ain't nothing peaceable about charity doled out from the barrel of a gun. The poor be squatters on the guards' good will, and there ain't much good left after they take care of their own.

An American drone whines overhead – a bug of the daytime. Pulling my bandana over my nose, I take shelter under a skeleton tree. The fly-bys be more frequent since they closed the border to refugees. That spybot rise on a swath of blue sky, like an eagle all hard in its metal. I imagine it covered in feathers. When the climate changed, birds been the first to go. Now they only be seen in paint-can scrawls on the crumbling tenements. The city streets be a jungle without green. Cobwebs cling to the sandstone and brick. Wish I could creep into the cracks and disappear to a droneless land – a garden with a pool of cold water. But all the lands be the same. They only be growing bones. There ain't no escape, 'cepting back into the earth.

Flutters come in my belly again. Been four full moons since my courses flowed. I feel my body changing, like it ain't mine no more. Don't want to think 'bout what might be growing in there – if it be aching with my hunger. I press my hands against my temples, trying to squeeze the fear out. Shoo. This be wasted thought. Need to find food for them that's already here. The Elders in Tent City be loud in their grumbling. If I bring no meat back, we be dining on tree bark. That be like eating dirt.

Front Street be hopping with the Yankee settlement. I cling to the back alleys, avoiding the protesters. Their rage fumes like tar on a hot summer day. Seen the Stars and Stripes painted on the building face of Union Station yesterday. Them damn Yankees have claimed it as their own. Molotov cocktails and balaclavas fill our news feeds. The government wants to send them back home, but America be a wasteland now. Nothing grows there, unlike in my belly.

I pull at the folds of my T-shirt, trying to hide the swell. The Elders ain't figured it out yet. They think I be getting fat. A babe ain't in their consideration. Been no live births in almost twenty years. I be one of the last whelped, a hundred years into the *Age of Drought*. Rumours swirled something was in the water to stop the babes from quickening. And then there was no water. People be sad the playgrounds stand empty, but also glad a new generation ain't been born to suffer. Until now. There be suffering in my belly. Don't want to bring this babe into the world, but the choice ain't mine.

My boots feel made of stone, as I step careful 'round the putrid offal. Already the sky be bleeding to azure. The mosquitoes be coming under cover of dark – and the others. "Badgers" we call them, lost souls given over to a kind of madness the subway breeds. When the trains stopped running, the Badgers took hold of the tracks. Some whisper they run contraband through the tunnels for the un-Market. Can't say for sure. No one who worships the Sun goes down into them dark places. I am in the Sun Clan. The Elders call me Little Kat. Don't know why. I ain't little.

I catch a hint of movement, black on black in an unlit doorway. Small and stealthy, Mr. Rat's head pokes out from the bricks, his whiskers testing the air. My slingshot be ready, but that faulty stone clinks against the brick. My dinner scampers into a crack in the mortar. Fuming, I call down the God of Thunder himself to smote that sneaky rodent.

I be so caught up in my rant, I don't see a bigger rat in the doorway. When he speaks, it startles me to silence.

"Cray, cray, Kitty Kat. You gonna send me to my maker with that aim." A boy steps out from the shadows, his palms cupped as if he be praying. My mouth falls open wide enough to eat the stars. "Shoo. Who you praying to, Bra? Ain't nobody listening up there."

"Maybe I be praying to you." Cast in shadows, that boy's face looks like he be wearing a death mask.

"You waste your breath, then." I lean back against the bricks and mop my sweaty brow. My heart pounds so hard I feel the blood rush between my ears.

He turns his face into the faulty light, and the mask falls away. I know this boy. Goes by the name of Raver. He be a turncoat, sleeping in the Badger camp now. No one in the Sun Clan be trusting him, even though he once pitched his nylon in Tent City. Defectors ain't seen kindly by the Elders.

"What you want, Raver?" I wiggle my finger through a hole in my khakis. "Ain't got nothing but misery in these pockets."

"Don't want your misery. Got 'nough of my own. Just want to talk."

He wraps his long black hair into a ponytail. His ruddy skin be dewy and taut, his lips curved down in a pout. Pale hazel eyes nestle between furrows of pain too deep for one so young. He be beautiful in his suffering.

I look at him wary. I know what men can be. Pointing to the wall behind him, I scuff my boot on the asphalt. "You talk from over there."

"Big temper for a little girl." He shrugs and steps back against the wall. I spy a bone handle peeking above his jeans' waistband.

"Ain't so little. Can take you down." My hand tightens 'round my slingshot, feeling the new stone in its cradle. Don't want to hurt this boy, but I can't be showing weakness.

A streetlight sputters and flares to life above me. The moment that light finds my skin, so does a mosquito. I swat at it, forgetting my fierce pose. Raver laughs at my awkward dance.

"They be coming in for blood." He watches the bug fuss above my nose. That mosquito be joined by another and another until they swarm like a living blanket. Raver's pupils be wide as a tunnel.

"Shoo. Why you all pasty? They ain't coming for you, Bra. No blood in your veins. Just vinegar."

He pokes his fingers through his suspenders and snaps them tight. "Don't taste so bitter, Kitty Kat. Come take a bite. Find out for yourself."

"You know that ain't my name. Why you use it like a warring word?"

" 'Cause you got your claws out half the time." He sniffs, and pushes off the wall, his shadow stretching towards me over the cobblestone. Hunger burns in his eyes, but not for food.

"Why you be sniffing at me? Those Badger girls ain't got no teeth?"

"Ain't got no vision, Kitty Kat. Them trollies be happy to burrow in the dirt. I want more from this life. I want the sun." His hand taps my shoulder. "I see you bursting with it."

"You only be seeing your own need." Slapping his fingers away, I sidle down the wall. I cover my belly, worried he be guessing about the babe.

His eyes fill with strangeness, fixing on the path of my hand. "When you ate last?"

"Been two days. Ain't got nothing to trade at the un-Market but my smile." I feel his heat sink into my skin as his calloused fingers slide over mine.

"Cray. Cray. You gonna starve then. You ain't never smile." Folding my hand in his, he pulls me down the alley. His steps be springy, like he floating over the asphalt.

"Don't need no government handout. Can eat rats."

"Only if you catch 'em." He lets go of my hand and pats my back. The gesture be more snub than comfort. "Pride ain't gonna fill your belly."

"Don't need your lecture."

"Got something you do, though, Kitty Kat."

"Food?" I catch my reflection in a window. There be dirt on my face, but I ain't got no spit to wipe it off. I pull at a matted tendril, suddenly concerned with my look.

"Can get. You stick with me and that belly be full soon." His hands talk as he pats his stomach. "How you get so fat with no rations and a bad shot?"

I grind my boots against the stones, waving my finger under his nose. "Shoo. Your sweet talk be as sour as your blood."

"You like. Don't lie." He skulks off, waving for me to follow, but these boots ain't moving. Noticing my stillness, he slows his pace, his face grown soft. "Ain't enough kind words these days. Too much talk of war."

"Men get mad when they be thirsty."

"That why your face all sour?"

Digging in his pocket, he pulls out a half-drunk bottle of water and tosses it at me. I watch it spin end over end. My hand moves too slow. The bottle slips through my fingers and skitters across the pavement. I scoop it up like a treasure, cradling it to my breast.

"Don't remember the last time I seen this much water at once." Unscrewing the cap, I sniff at the liquid. It smells like life. "Where you get it?"

"Badgers got contraband." His eyebrow starts waggling. "You come down to the trains and see for yourself."

I walk cautious towards him. "I hear stories of Sun Clan going in, and never coming out. Badgers get meat this way. Long Pig."

Laughing, he slaps his thigh hard. "Youngun's stories. Ain't no eating humans down there." He holds up his hand and wiggles his fingers. "Still got all my toes and fingers."

"Can't see your toes in those boots."

"You want me take them off? You need proof?" He tugs at his boot, hopping up and down like he be on a bed of hot coals.

"Not the kind you be offering." I screw up my nose, and he stops his fumbling. "Probably smells like skunk anyhow. Badgers don't want that meat."

"You be hungry enough, you eat my smelly toes."

"Ain't never be that hungry." I raise the bottle to my nose and smell its goodness again.

"Ain't you gonna drink that?"

"Once I take this liquid into my belly, the hope in it be gone."

"Won't go down to the trains for water. Won't drink it when the trains come to you."

"You make fun of me, but my point be sharp. There be many ways to prey on others. Don't want to be a trolly for the Badgers' need." I tip the bottle. "No water worth that."

Raver grabs the bottle out of my hand before I spill its prize. "Cray. Cray. Ain't never force you, Kitty Kat."

"It be the nature of a Badger to force."

"Ain't Badger nor Sun Clan. I belong to the land." He shoves the bottle back into my hand, face scowling. "Drink."

We walk in silence as I sip from the bottle. Ahead, Union Station sits like some mirage at the end of the street. Heat vapor be rising from the pavement as the night brings its cools. The building face be newly whitewashed, like some drunk man had hold of a paint roller. Can still see the blue and red from them Stars and Stripes bleeding through. Picketers stand out in front, yelling their rage to the night sky.

We duck down a side street, away from this hotbed of protest, winding through the empty alleys until we come to the un-Market. The marquee above the entrance flashes bright, but all the skyscrapers 'round it be dark. Lines queue down the sidewalk, trapped meat for the mosquitoes. Desperation hangs thick in the air. Under the marquee, newscasters speak their propaganda on a large screen. Armed guards patrol the line, waving their guns in the air like it be the First of July.

Raver points me down an alley beside the un-Market, away from the guards' notice. There be a halo of mosquitoes 'round his head. He slices his hand through the buzzing mess. It reforms as soon as it scatters.

"Don't know what be worse, running from the Yankees or the un-Market guards."

"We all the same in our skins, Raver. We all fleeing the same thing." I flash him a twitchy grin. "The mosquitoes."

He laughs, draping an arm over my shoulder. This ease between us feels natural, like we be co-conspirators against the world.

We sneak down the path, hands covering our giggles. In a few steps we come to the back entrance and all gladness disappears. I see two armed guards standing on either side of a freight door. Their skin be pale as tropical sand. They ain't wearing uniforms. These men be Badgers. A truck idles in the bay, black smoke belching out its exhaust pipe. I stare at that plume like it be some magician's trick. Fossil fuels been outlawed since before I was born.

"Shoo. They be burning oil. Men been killed for less." I snatch up Raver's hand and squeeze. "What you get me into, Raver?"

"This be the way of the world, Kitty Kat. Laws made to be broken. Can't have no un-Market without Badgers to stock them shelves."

"What stock? The shelves be near empty inside."

These Badgers hear our noise. Their hands stiffen 'round their guns.

"Don't shoot." Raver raises my hand with his and waves at the first Badger. "We be friends."

The glowering man steps to the edge of the ramp. He lowers his gun, but the murder don't leave his eyes. Dressed all in red, he be the splitting image of Santa Claus, if that old elf had tattoos and no teeth. "I have all the friends I need."

Santa speaks in proper English, all hoity-toity like he a member of the Royals from across the salty waters.

Raver pats at his chest. "Be from the trains, just like you."

Santa scratches his white beard. "What's your name, lad?"

"Raver."

"Have you come to barter, Raver?" Santa speaks the boy's name but ogles me. He tucks the gun in his waistband and rubs his hands together like a housefly eying a tasty treat.

"Not flesh trade." Raver steps in front of me, his voice edgy. "Something better."

"What are you carrying? Water?" Santa jumps off the ramp. His huge belly bounces up and down as he stomps towards us.

"Drugs." Raver says the word like he be singing the gospel. He digs in his pocket and pulls out a white bottle with red letters on it. As he flashes the plastic, the alley echoes with the sound of rattling pills.

Raver plunks the bottle onto Santa's palm, grinning wide. The letters on the plastic spell Amoxicillin. This be gold in a world where cuts kill.

The fat man unscrews the cap and looks inside the bottle. He grunts satisfied and calls up to the other Badger, "Let them in. Whatever food or drink they can carry."

I hold Raver's hand as we sidestep Santa and climb up on the ramp. The other guard stares at us with unseeing eyes. A light switches on behind him, sputtering like it be ready to shine its last. It shroud the man in a criss-cross of moving shadows. When I walk past him, my skin puckers.

Inside the receiving bay, I see boxes stacked to the ceiling. The plastic wrap be dusty, as if the cargo been sitting in a warehouse for years.

Clambering up behind us, Santa pulls a box cutter from his back pocket. He pushes the blade against the truck side like he be performing surgery. The top cutter pops off and skitters to the ramp, leaving a shiny new blade ready for its work.

He marches to the first skid. It be piled high with cans of Chef Boyardee Ravioli. The box cutter slices through the plastic. Tin cans clatter to the floor, sending up a plume of dust mites. They glitter in the faulty light. Reminds me of the Niagara Falls' snow globe I got hidden in my tent. The water be all gone, but sometimes I shake it to watch the snow fly. Never seen real snow outside of books.

Raver scoops up as many cans as he can carry. He shoves them in his pockets and his waistband. Santa jokes 'bout all the Badger girls Raver can buy with this booty. The boy looks at me nervous. I turn my face away.

Walking to the back of the storage area, I feel ill humour fast on my heels. Dust covers most of the bounty. I look down the narrow pathway between the rows. The stacks seem to go on forever, piled to the ceiling. "There be so much food. Why this, and people starving?"

Santa's face grows redder than my sunburnt arms. "Have to have something to trade. Good feelings aren't currency."

"It ain't right."

Raver's voice cuts through the tension. His words don't ease the ache in my heart. "Right don't matter in this world. Only power."

Anger coils inside me. Something I know well – this sense of violation. "World belongs to all of us, not just them that can pay."

"Says you, girl?" Raver tugs at my hair. He grins in his cruelness. "How you gonna change it?"

"Oh, I change it, alright. You watch me." I step back from him, not liking this version of the boy. Walking over to a skid, I wipe the grime off and peer through the plastic. There be boxes of medicine inside. In tiny blue print I see the word Mifeprex. "What be this?"

Raver shrug his shoulders. I know he can't read. My momma taught me how when I was a youngun, from stolen paper books. Raver's momma didn't have nimble fingers. Been a time when the libraries be open to all, not just the rich. I would have liked to live then.

Santa comes over and laughs throaty. He cuts open the skid and tosses me a box of medicine. "You can have that abortion pill as a special bonus, not that you'll ever use it."

I feel the heat on my cheeks and turn away, but not before I stuff the box into my pocket. It feels like a wrongness in there, pressing against my belly. I know what abortion be. Santa thinks he be funny in his words, but he don't know the twist of this gift.

I stride over to Raver and stare at him baleful. Pulling out my T-shirt, he frees more cans from the skid. He drops them into my jersey, tying a snug knot.

"You take your trolly and have fun now." Santa clutches his gun and spins it on his finger like some wannabe gunslinger. He scratches his beard with the barrel. I hope his finger be trigger tight. Let that bullet free his grey matter all over this hoarded cargo.

"She ain't no trolly." Raver's smile be brittle as he pulls eight large bottles of water from a skid. He tucks them under his arms.

Santa scowls so deep it looks like cuts across his face. Raver pays him no mind. Strutting to the door like a big old peacock, that boy leaps off the ramp. He seems to hover in the air, body framed in halo before he lands light on his feet. He sets his precious cargo on the pavement and holds his hands out. When he lifts me down, I feel like one of them dust devils, spinning lighter than air.

We walk cautious back out on the street, careful to hide our loot. The queue be longer now, with people shoving at each other. Their lips be heavy with curse words.

I stop, moved by their plight. Ain't no different from mine. I call out in a voice made for riot: "There be food in back. Only two men with guns, and all of you. Go take what be rightfully yours."

They look back in disbelief. I wave a shiny tin, and their eyes fill with hunger. Raver and I start running, but the crowd don't give us chase. I hear their angry clamber down the alley instead. Seconds later there be shots, then nothing but boxes moving. The food be free now. We all be free.

Raver and I slow after a few blocks, panting heavy. My hands cradle the cans as I lean against the brick wall. He squeeze my arm. "You make me homeless, Little Kat."

I secretly be pleased he use my proper name, but that happiness don't live long. I see the fear in his eyes. This be my doing.

"We all homeless, Raver." I lay my hand on his chest. "You come with me to Tent City. I share my nylon with you. Be Sun Clan again."

We move toward the lake. Raver be silent, boots heavy in his trudge. He don't speak until we come to the lakebed. Tent City looms down the shore, quiet in its promise.

"The Elders gonna run me off," he says, all breathy.

"You be bringing more than apologies, Raver. You be bringing hope." I hold up a tin, and he grins in his sadness.

We stare at the lake, watching the sky leech from indigo to black. A growing breeze tousles our hair. The air be charged with static. Lightning arcs across the sky. In the flash, I see a black feather spiralling down. Raver catches that feather, and sticks it in his ponytail.

"What strangeness be this?" I touch the plume. The stiff feathers prickle my skin.

"Gift from the sky. Be a sacred thing." New fire gleams in his eyes. He stands stoic, like a living tree taking root.

We gather twigs and dried moss on the lakeshore, and weave through the tents to my nylon. I hear coughing as we build the fire. Malaria be here. Taken four people this week. Elder Crats' chest rattles as he sleeps, a wet sucking sound that makes me inch closer to the flames despite the heat.

The villagers come out of their tents with our noise. They watch Raver with mistrust in their eyes. Ain't want no traitor in their midst. I jut my chin out and challenge their frowns as I smash stones for a spark. The moss takes quick to the flame. I stack branches in a pyramid, and soon the whole fire be crackling.

Raver takes the knife out of his waistband and punches it through the tin lid. He sits the can on the fire. Sparks shoot up the side as the tin blackens. Can smell tomatoes and spice mixed in with burning moss. My mouth waters as hunger rattles my bones. Several villagers creep closer, their bones rattling, too. I take all the sealed tins and sit them in the dirt. The villagers scurry in, eyes pools of empty need.

Raver cocks an eyebrow at me. Picking up two water bottles, he thrusts them toward the crowd. Though meant to be a kindness, it comes across hard. A woman limps in wary, wrapping her shawl tight 'round her shoulders. She snatches the plastic out of his fingers. Raver laughs. He picks up two more bottles and walks them to Elder Crats' tent. The old man's nose pokes through his zipper. Raver slams the bottles in the dust. The two men eye each other. Elder Crats grabs the water and shakes his fist at Raver, but there ain't no anger in it. These men be playing a role, finding their way to forgiveness.

Raver struts back to me, all proud in his gift. He squeezes my hand in knowing. We got to share, otherwise the government wins. They treat us like we ain't human no more. We got to remind ourselves we are.

Fires pop up 'round Tent City as our loot makes its way to hungry mouths. The night air be full of the smells of life. Raver drags the tin out of our fire with a twig, nodding for me to take the first bite. I dip my fingers into the can and pull out a juicy ravioli. My skin complains with the heat. I nearly drop the pasta in my excitement. Raver giggles as I pop it in my mouth, juices flowing down my chin.

We sit by our fire long after the food be gone, watching the sparks waft up into the blackness. Raver fingers the ashes and paints war stripes on my face. "I be calling you Little Warrior now."

"I fight for you, Raver. I fight for us all." Taking his hand, I pull him to his feet. We dance 'round that fire like we be possessed. Others join in, laughing in their prospect.

When our bones be weary from dancing, I bring Raver into my tent. We sit on the sleeping bag, suddenly shy. I lie back. Raver watches me pat the bag. He props himself up on his elbow and kisses my shoulder. It be a gentleness I ain't known since my momma. Tears well in my eyes.

"Don't need to," he whispers throaty, his eyes unsure.

"Shoo, boy. Be needing your lips more than food." I hide my burning face behind my hand. He pulls my fingers away and kisses my tears. His tongue probes my mouth gentle. I feel the moistness come between my legs.

"You can love me, Little Warrior?"

There be loneliness in his words. I cup his cheek. "Already do."

He sings the song of a lover, gentle in his timbre. Gives me peace while our bodies find each other. In the heat of the rut, I feel my heart beating whole. Hope spills its seed between my loins. We collapse in each other's arms, happy in our union. When sleep comes, I dream of water.

I wake to the sound of Elder Crats' hacking. Burying my face against Raver's chest, I try to hold onto the dream a moment longer. He pulls his fingers through my hair, sending tingles along my scalp.

Spying the corner of a book tucked under my head roll, I pull it out and hug it to my chest. Those pages got memories between the letters. "Been five years since Momma's gone, but I still smell her on the paper. You want I share this with you?"

He nods, lying back.

"Don't know all the words, but the truth lies between 'em."

"Tell your truth, then."

His eyes be mystified as I crack open the book. I prop it on his chest, and speak the stories my momma once spoke to me. I let him hear my joy and pain. Raver knows this loss. His momma's been gone a decade. He closes his eyes and lets the magic roll over him. We talk of elves and dwarves, and fields of green.

When Raver opens his eyes, I see the fire lit there. He pushes himself up to a sit, and takes the book from my hands. "You teach me to read?"

"Shoo. I teach you to dream."

I show him the letters and name them. He be raptured in his learning.

As the sun grow hot outside, we dress each other. Our hands be tender. His fingers drift over my belly.

"You know?" Pain crushes at my chest.

"Was guessing. Saw the way you was holding those pills, like they be some kind of salvation."

I blush, feeling naked in my truth. "Ain't no salvation. Just a choice."

"You gonna keep?"

"Don't know." I look at the abortion pills, hating their promise. "Be a hard world for a babe."

"I help you raise it, if you want. Keep it safe."

"Ain't enough to be safe. Need a future." I turn away, ashamed in my talk.

"We make our future." Raver pulls me back to face him. "You show me this."

Shame stops me from seeing his eyes. I look at the bottle of pills again. How I be human if I take them?

My guilt turns to anger. I stare accusing at Raver. "Why you want to raise a babe that ain't yours?"

His sadness gives me pause. My breath catches in my throat. He sees this, and folds me in his arms. I feel his spirit through the hug. "Belongs to us all, if you give it. Maybe more will come."

I bury my face against his shoulder, confusion making noise in my head. "Won't take no pills today."

"Today belongs to life." He guides me to the door flap.

"Can't say what tomorrow brings."

"Don't need to." He motions me through, his smile steady. "I be here no matter what you choose."

I crawl out into the sunlight with Raver right behind me. The Elders be sitting 'round a campfire. A cast-iron pot bubbles on a fire, oats brewing in their sauce. One of the water bottles lies empty beside it. Elder Crats stirs the porridge with his second wind. Though his skin be tinged yellow, his eyes sparkle. Ain't no death in that face today. He scoops out two mugs of porridge and hands them to Raver and me. One by one, the villagers join us. There be happy talk with full bellies.

The sky looks different this dawn. The sun be shining like a friend. Don't know what the sunset will bring, but this morning, the village be family. For the first time in my short years, I know hope. Cradling my belly, I think of songs my momma used to sing. Dust devils spin across the cracked lakebed, merry in their movements.

"Dance, little ballerinas," I whisper. "One day there be water."

INVASION

PHIL DWYER

Davo leans forward and grinds the butt of his cigarette into the concrete parapet. He feels the dry, stuttering rasp of the filter through his fingertips. He grinds harder and notices how the still-moist tobacco leaves scrunch over each other. He's never noticed that before; how they catch and release, catch and release, like the scrunch of fresh snow. He wonders what the right word for that would be. Everything seems different this morning, more real – the air vibrant and chill on the back of his throat, the call of the crows in the distant treeline clearer and more resonant in the still winter air. His last cigarette. He stares down at it for a long moment. It cost him a month's wages. He was saving it, but there's no point now. The taste of tar and nicotine is still sharp on his breath, but it's already fading. He runs his tongue over the inside of his mouth and his front teeth to savour the last of it. He won't be tasting it again for a long, long time. Maybe never. Atoosa used to nag him about the habit once. "Think about the children, the money, your health," she said. Concerns that seem futile now.

You can't get them any more. They shut down the whole industry, said they couldn't afford to waste valuable natural resources growing a non-essential crop. A man can buy bootleg cigarettes if he's prepared to spend the money and run the risks. Davo wasn't. He has a family. But when it looked like things were going to blow up he relented, dipped into his savings for one last smoke – a packet of vintage Winston, hoarded by profiteers in the early days of the crisis. The price was doubling almost daily lately. He was lucky to get hold of a packet when he did.

Still, the nicotine hadn't relaxed him. He eases a finger under the collar of his uniform; tries to swallow. His mouth is dry.

Once the fighting starts I'll be fine.

Who am I kidding? The fighting will probably last all of twenty seconds. I'll be a pile of half-cooked flesh and shit at the end of it. I might not even see it coming.

His earpiece crackles.

"Davo?"

"Yes, sir."

"Any movement?"

He lifts his binoculars and scans the treeline at the southern horizon. A narrow highway bisects the fields, splitting the treeline in two almost equal parts. They'd come up that road.

"Nothing, sir." The earpiece dies. He tugs at the cord to pop it out, and it dangles, limp on his Kevlar vest.

A crow rises from one of the distant trees; its lazy wingbeats tangle with the winter-stripped branches of the trees behind it. Still watching the crow's slow progress, never taking his eyes from the horizon, Davo reaches behind him. He rested his weapon against the wall to smoke. The gun's heft, as he lifts it, is reassuring. A fully loaded gun is serious: intentional. He snaps the sight into place and flicks the function switch to sniper. Davo swings the gun up and fixes a bead on the crow. For a second, maybe two, the gun is angry in his hands as he tracks the bird over the horizon. But as he adjusts the sweep of the barrel to the lazy grace of the bird's wing beats, it begins to purr with venom and purpose. These guns are wonders. They compute the distance to a target by echolocation, and correct for wind speed and direction as well as the relative speed and direction of the target. The one thing they can't do is aim and shoot. They still need a human for that. Leave it to the arms manufacturers to figure out a way around the human problem of inaccuracy though. You lock on a target: the gun vibrates. Aim wide of the mark and these vibrations are fierce, bordering on painful, like the shockwave a bat sends up your arm when you misconnect with a baseball. But when your aim is true the gun's vibrations calm to a contented purr. He eases his forefinger onto the trigger, feels a resistance that demands firmer decision. He squeezes harder. In the distance the bird erupts in a plume of feathers, blood and bone, and spirals out of the air and into the trees. It's gone from sight before the echo of the gun's report dies away. His dangling earpiece crackles angrily. He fumbles with it, twists it into his ear.

"Sir?"

"Davoodian, what the fuck are you doing?"

Damn. Forgot the head cam. "Sorry, Sarge. Thought it might have been a drone."

"It was a fucking crow, fuckwit. That'll come out of your wages."

The new army, where pay is performance-based, where kill-rate efficiencies are rewarded, and soldiers who waste valuable resources like bullets, suffer claw-backs to their pay.

"Any news, Sarge?"

"You know as much as I do." The earpiece clicks off again, and he pops it out, despite the protocols. Despite the penalties, the risks, all he could lose.

He stands, head bowed, eyes fixed on the spent filter on the parapet.

"Praying, soldier?"

He hadn't met the General – the man only arrived at the facility yesterday – but Davo recognizes authority when he hears it. He stiffens like Pedram's tension toy – the dog that can be made to nod if you gently press the disc in its base, or collapse if you push hard. His son loves that toy.

"At ease, Private, I wouldn't blame you if you were."

"Not praying, sir. Just thinking."

The General takes a step towards him and picks up the spent cigarette. He holds the filter delicately between thumb and forefinger, as if it's a fledgling fallen from the nest. He seeks Davo's eyes, his eyebrow lifts a fraction. "Yours?" he says.

"Yes, sir."

The General twists the butt between his fingers. "Winston. Haven't seen one of these in years." He looks back at Davo. "Don't suppose you've got any left?"

"No, sir. That was my last."

"Pity." He turns and tosses the butt over the parapet and they both follow the arc of its fall to the ravine floor, 300 feet below. "Didn't think you could get them any more, even on the black market."

"You can get anything if you're willing to pay for it, sir."

"Was it worth it?"

Davo smiles for the first time this morning. "Every penny, sir."

Silence settles over both men. Davo takes a deep breath. He catches the bitter tang of wood smoke, faint, but clear on the chill winter air. Somewhere out there, out in the borderlands, someone is risking a fire. It brings back memories of home: a rake dragging damp leaves across the lawn, a bonfire crackling and spitting in the corner of the yard; the children, wrapped in autumn woollens and Wellington boots, barrelling two-footed into the leaf piles. He hadn't known it then, but that was as close to heaven as he'd managed to reach in his thirty-two years.

The General reaches up to the clip on his chinstrap, releases it, lifts his helmet off and places it on the parapet in front of him. He folds his arms over his chest and stares south, towards the border. Davo considers the light-blue helmet for a long moment, stares at the two letters stencilled upon it. Stares long enough that the U and the N lose their easy familiarity – start to look foreign and slightly menacing. UN… what exactly? Unhinged? Unravelling?

He's the first to break the silence. "Should you be doing that, sir? It's not protocol."

The General's jaw tenses, the muscles flex just once. The low winter sun catches a small triangle of silver stubble at the curve of his jaw, when he relaxes.

"End times, Private." Davo shifts on his feet. The General turns to face him. "Not in a Biblical sense. Extraordinary circumstances. The protocol doesn't seem important this morning."

"Do you think they'll invade, sir?"

"They must. The General Assembly's answer was unequivocal. They can't annex another sovereign state. But they want what they want, and if they can't get it with the UN's approval they'll take it without. Men always have."

"Do you think they'll be sending tanks?"

"I doubt it. Even the U.S. can't afford to fuel them."

"Infantry?"

"No one's used infantry in a war in a hundred years."

"Then we're not expecting it. Might be a good tactic. Element of surprise."

"We're not expecting elephants, siege engines or cannons either, soldier."

"Sir, yes, sir. But you really think they'll go to war?"

"Why not? You don't believe they will?"

"I just don't see how it's worth it, sir."

The General glances down at the nametag sewn over Davo's chest pocket. "Davoodian. That's a Farsi name, isn't it?"

Davoodian nods, a quick, shallow bob of his head. He concentrates on keeping his face passive, unreadable. He doesn't want to register surprise. "Yes, sir."

"Do you have children, Davoodian?"

"Yes, sir."

"Are they worth it?"

Davo's arms tense, his fingers curl into his palms, dig into the heel of his hand. He'd trained himself out of the response lately – make himself aware of it: he'd started to tear holes in his hands where the nails dug in. The man wasn't to know. It had been three years and still the flashbacks hounded his days, and visited his dreams. The day Parnaz died. They shut down the hospitals – couldn't afford to power them, they said. So his daughter died of a burst appendix. It was agony to watch the shards of pain twist her on the bed as they tore through her body. But at the end she seemed so calm. She'd tried to console him. "Don't worry, Daddy," she said. "It will be okay. Don't cry for me. The pain's almost gone away now." She died half an hour later. Slipped away from him so easily.

How old would she be now? Seven? Parnaz's death changed everything. Atoosa barely spoke to him. She cooked their meals and cleaned their clothes and sat in silence on their small veranda, watching the city hustle by. He never saw her shed a tear. He caught her watching him every now and again. As if she was trying to figure out who this person she found herself living with was. Pedram fell silent too. He spent most of the time in his bedroom, playing with his cars and his airplanes. He stopped asking about Parnaz after a few weeks, and retreated into a space Davo couldn't enter. Atoosa went back home to her parents in the end. She took Pedram with her. He misses her, but less than he misses the child. He misses Parnaz like you might miss a limb. He's heard stories from some of the other men, friends or comrades who lost an arm or a leg, but who still feel it. Phantom limb syndrome, they call it. Sometimes an amputee even feels an itch or pain in the phantom limb. It's like that. A constant ache for a part of him that's no longer there.

The man wasn't to know.

"Well, soldier?" the General says. "Simple question, with an easy answer from where I'm standing."

"One now, sir. A son."

"Now, soldier? What do you mean one now?"

"I had a daughter too. She died, sir. Hospital closures. Resource limitations."

The General raises a hand and places it gently on Davo's shoulder. "I'm sorry, son. The death of a child is the most tragic thing imaginable."

It was unimaginable. Unimaginable and unfair. Why did they have to shut the hospitals? We had the resources. Maybe the rest of the world didn't, but we had them. It was so pointless.

He'd gone over it again and again in the past three years, trying to make sense of Parnaz's death. A simple operation was all she needed. The hospitals were standing empty, the equipment was idle, the doctors laid off. He'd had to stand by, impotent in the face of a common illness. An illness that hadn't killed anybody in the developed world for decades, until the crisis.

It happened on Sunday. He'd offered to look after both kids to give Atoosa a break. He took them to the park because the swimming pool was closed – another concession to the crisis. They flew their favourite kite – an evil demon with sharp white teeth and silver eyes – most of the afternoon. Parnaz had an ambivalent relationship with that kite. It scared her, enough that when Davo worked the strings and made it swoop low over the grass to chase her, she would scream and run to hide behind her daddy's legs. But it didn't take her long to regain her courage and sneak from between them; chasing it, shouting "Go way, monster." She seemed fine then. That evening, Pedram and Parnaz sat at the dining-room table, colouring. Davo sat with them reading the news. Parnaz coloured with tongue as well as hand, a sliver of it slipping over her top lip rhythmically as her hand rocked back and forth. Every now and again a stray strand of hair escaped from behind her ear, and flopped down over the screen. She hooked it back in place, never interrupting her rhythm. Not for a second.

Davo felt a sudden flush of love burst up inside him as he watched. It was almost overwhelming how much he loved her.

She was kneeling on her haunches, but as she shifted to one side to free her feet she winced, and held a hand over her side.

"What's up, little pea?" he asked.

"I had a little pain when I moved," she said. "It's sore." But she'd said no more and he hadn't thought any more about it.

The next morning, she was racked with agony. A few days later she was dead. Davo knows the General is right. He would have killed another man, twenty other men, to spare Parnaz her pain and keep her with him. We fight for what we most treasure; die for it, if we must. They will come.

The General removes his hand from Davo's shoulder and clasps his hands behind his back, turns again to face the border.

"We had to do it, son. It's impossible to explain it in terms of single lives. It sounds callous, but it was necessary. Hospitals were closing all over the world – in Europe and the US people were dying by the hundreds. We had to show solidarity with them. Stand shoulder to shoulder, making the same sacrifice and suffering the same consequences. If we hadn't, can you imagine the backlash?"

And yet they hadn't been able to conceal their envy of a country so rich in the resource that others had spent so totally and disastrously. The miracle liquid that had powered our civilization, made it possible. The most precious liquid on the planet. The envy of the world quickly turned sour. Some nations could barely conceal their greed and hate. Men had killed for it before. They would certainly kill for it now.

"When did your family leave Iraq?" the General asks.

"Just after the second Gulf war. My father moved to Canada. He was twenty. He wanted to get away from warfare – go somewhere safe, peaceful."

"That was, what? Forty years ago now. Is he still alive?"

"Yes, sir."

"What does he make of this…" the General hesitated, unable to define what 'this' was in that second… "conflict?"

"I don't know, sir. I haven't asked him."

The General looks back over his shoulder at Davo and measures a slow nod, as if he understands. It's not wise to try to measure the evil consequences of our best intentions.

Davo feels the low frequency rumble of a massive turbine kick in through the soles of his boots. They have opened her up. They said this would happen before the offensive.

"That's my cue," the General says. He reaches for his helmet and clips it on, fingers, deft with practice, find the clip almost instantly. "Thank you, Private."

"Sir?"

"I came out here to clear my head. Within the hour my command post will be manic. I wanted a little peace to collect my thoughts. Our little talk has helped me. So thank you."

Davo nods, snaps to attention and salutes. The General returns his salute, spins on his heels and walks smartly towards the metal staircase at the end of the walkway. Davo watches the blue UN helmet – the peacekeeper's helmet – bob out of view as its wearer goes to prepare war. He turns and gazes north, over the still, calm waters of the dam. The water he is supposed to be protecting.

At 9.30 that morning, Tuesday, December 5, 2040, the armies of the US move to annex Canada. Some five hundred UN troops are killed in an attempt by UN peacekeeping forces to repel the offensive, amongst them Private Javid Davoodian. The brief opposition was quickly overcome, and the UN surrender Canada at around 12.37 pm.

THE WAY
OF WATER

NINA MUNTEANU

She imagines its coolness gliding down her throat. Wet with a lingering aftertaste of fish and mud. She imagines its deep voice resonating through her in primal notes; echoes from when the dinosaurs quenched their throats in the Triassic swamps.

Water is a shape-shifter.

It changes yet stays the same, shifting its face with the climate. It wanders the earth like a gypsy, stealing from where it is needed and giving whimsically where it isn't wanted.

Dizzy and shivering in the blistering heat, Hilda shuffles forward with the snaking line of people in the dusty square in front of University College where her mother used to teach. The sun beats down, crawling on her skin like an insect. She's been standing for an hour in the queue for the public water tap. Her belly aches in deep waves, curling her body forward.

There is only one person ahead of her now, an old woman holding an old plastic container. The woman deftly slides her wCard into the pay slot. It swallows her card and the light above it turns green. The card spits out of the slot. The meter indicates what remains of the woman's quota. The woman bends stiffly over the tap and turns the handle. Water trickles reluctantly into her cracked container. It looks like they have another shortage coming, Hilda thinks, watching the old woman turn the tap off and pull out her card then shuffle away.

The man behind Hilda pushes her forward. She stumbles toward the tap and glances at the wCard in her blue-grey hand. Her skin resembles a dry riverbed. Heart throbbing in her throat, Hilda fumbles with the card and finally gets it into the reader. The reader takes it. The light screams red. Her knees almost give out. She dreaded this day.

She stares at the iTap. The dryness in the back of her throat rises to meet her tongue, now thick and swollen. She gags on the thirst of three days. Just like her mother's secret cistern, her card has run dry – no credits, no water. The faucet swims in front of her. The sun, high in the pale sky, glints on the faucet's burnished steel and splinters into a million spotlights...

Hilda had read in her mother's forbidden book that water was the only natural substance on Earth that could exist in all three physical states. She'd never seen enough water to test the truth of that claim. She remembered snow as a child, how the flakes fluttered down and landed on her coat like jewels. No two snowflakes were alike, she'd heard once. But not from her mother; her mother refused to talk about water. Whenever Hilda asked her a question about it, she scowled and responded with bitter and sarcastic words. Her mother once worked as a limnologist for CanadaCorp in their watershed department; but they forced her to retire early. Hilda tried to imagine a substance that could exist as a solid, liquid and gas, all in the same place and same time. One moment, flowing with an urgent wetness that transformed all it touched. Another moment, firm and upright. And yet an-other, yielding into vapour at the breath of warmth. Water was fluid and soft, yet it wore away hard rock and carved flowing landscapes with its patience.

Water was magic. Most things on the planet shrank and became more dense as they got colder. Water, her textbook said, did the opposite; which was why ice floated and why lakes didn't completely freeze from top to bottom.

Water was paradox. Aggressive yet yielding. Life-giving yet dangerous. Floods. Droughts. Mudslides. Tsunamis. Water cut recursive patterns of creative destruction through the landscape, an ouroboros remembering.

She'd heard a myth – from Hanna, of course – that Canada once held the third richest reserve of fresh water in the world. Canada used to have clean sparkling lakes deep enough for people to drown in. That was before the unseasonal storms and floods. Before the rivers dried up and scarred the landscape in a network of snaking corpses. Before Lake Ontario became a giant tailings pond. Before CanadaCorp shut off Niagara Falls then came into everyone's home and cemented their taps shut for not paying the water tax.

When that happened, her mother secretly set up rainwater catchers on her property. Collecting rainwater was illegal because the rain belonged to CanadaCorp. When Raytheon and the WMA diverted the rain to the USA, her cistern dried up and they had to resort to getting their water from the rationed public water taps that cost the equivalent of $20 a glass in water credits. It didn't matter if you were rich – no one got more than two litres a day.

Hilda and her mother hadn't seen a good rain in over a decade. Lake Ontario turned into a mud puddle, like Erie before it. The St. Lawrence River, channelized long ago, now flowed south to the USA like everything else.

One day the water patrol of the RCMP stormed the house. They seized her mother's books – except Wetzel's *Limnology*, hidden under Hilda's mattress – and they dragged her mother away. The RCMP weren't actually gruff with her and she didn't struggle. She quietly watched them ransack the place then turned a weary gaze to Hilda. "We were too nice… too nice…" she'd said in a strangled voice. She didn't clutch Hilda to her bosom or tell her that she loved her. Just the words, "We invited them in and let them take it all. We gave it all way…" It took a long time for Hilda to realize that she'd meant Canada and its water.

CanadaCorp wasn't even a Canadian company. According to Hanna, it was part of Vivanti, a multinational conglomerate of European and Chinese companies. When it came to water – which was everything – the Chinese owned the USA. When China finally called them on their trillion-dollar debt, the bankrupted country defaulted. That was when the world changed. China offered the USA a deal: give us your water, all of it, and we'll forfeit the capital owed. And they could stay a country. That turned out to include Canadian water, since Canada had already let Michigan tap into the Great Lakes. That's how CanadaCorp, which had nothing to do with Canada, came to own the Great Lakes and eventually all of Canada's surface and ground water. And how Canada sank from a resource-rich nation into a poor indentured state. Hilda didn't cry when her mother left. Hilda thought her mother was coming back. She didn't.

A tiny water drop hangs, trembling, from the iTap faucet mouth, as if considering which way to go: give in to gravity and drop onto the dusty ground or defy it and cling to the inside of the tap. Hilda lunges forward and touches the faucet mouth with her card to capture the drop. Then she laps up the single drop with her tongue. She thinks of Hanna and her throat tightens.

The man behind her grunts. He barrels forward and violently shoves her aside. Hilda stumbles away from the long queue in a daze. The brute gruffly pulls out her useless card and tosses it to her. She misses it and the card flutters like a dead leaf to the ground at her feet. The man shoves his own card into the pay slot. Hilda watches the water gurgle into his plastic container. He is sloppy and some of the water splashes out of his container, raining on the ground. Hilda stares as the water bounces off the parched pavement before finally pooling. The ache in her throat burns like sandpaper and she wavers on her feet.

The lineup tightens, as if the people fear she might cut back in.

She stares at the water pooling on the ground, glistening into a million stars in the sunlight.

Hanna claimed that there was a fourth state of water: a liquid crystal that possessed magical properties of healing. You could find it in places like collagen and cell membranes where biological signals and information travelled instantly. Like quantum entanglement. The crystalline water increased its energy in a vortex and light. Hanna seemed to know all about the research done at the University of Washington. According to her, this negatively charged crystallized water held energy like a battery and pushed away pollutants. She told of an experiment in Austria where water in a beaker, when jolted with electromagnetic energy, leapt up the beaker wall, groping to meet its likeness in the adjoining beaker. The beaker waters formed a "water bridge," like two shocked children clutching hands.

Hilda's mother had dismissed Hanna's claims as fairytale. But when Hilda challenged her mother, she couldn't explain why water stored so much energy or absorbed and released more heat than most substances. Or a host of other things water could do that resembled magic.

Something Hilda never dared share with her mother was Hanna's startling claim about water's intelligent purpose. She cited bizarre studies conducted by Russian scientists and some quasi-scientific studies in Germany and Austria suggesting that water had a consciousness. "What if everything that water does has an innate purpose, related to what we are doing to it?" Hanna had once challenged. "They've proven that water remembers everything done to it and everywhere it's been. What if it's self-organized, like a giant amoebic computer? We've done terrible things to water, Hilda," she said, sorrow vivid in her liquid eyes. "What if water doesn't like being owned or ransomed? What if it doesn't like being channelized into a harsh pipe system or into a smart cloud to go where it normally doesn't want to go? What if those hurricanes and tornadoes and floods are water's way of saying 'I've had enough'?"

None of that matters now, Hilda thinks rather abstractly and feels herself falling. They are all going to die soon anyway. Neither water's magical properties nor Hanna's fantasies about its consciousness are going to help her or Hanna, who had disappeared again since last month.

"I can't do this anymore with you," Hilda ranted. She paced her decrepit one-room apartment and watched Hanna askance. Hanna sat on Hilda's worn couch like a brooding selkie. Like a sociopath contemplating her next move. Waiting for Hilda's. "This is the last time," Hilda kept her voice harsh. She wanted to jar Hanna into crying, or something, to induce some kind of emotional breakdown. In truth, Hilda was so relieved to see her itinerant friend, alive and well, after her lengthy silence. Hilda went on, "It's always the same pattern. After months of nothing, you come, desperate for help... water credits or some dire task that only I can perform. Then you disappear again, only emerging months later with your next disaster. I never hear from you otherwise. I don't know if you're dead or alive, like I'm a well you dip into. Like that's all I mean to you. Where do you go when you disappear? Where?"

She dropped back in the lumpy chair across from Hanna and watched her gypsy friend, hoping for some sign of remorse, or acknowledgement, at least. She knew Hanna wouldn't answer, as though every question she asked her – particularly the personal ones – was only rhetorical in nature. Hanna just stared at her like a puppy dog. As if she didn't quite understand the problem. She could barely speak at the best of times. Hilda had decided long ago that Hanna was partly autistic. Maybe a savant even; she was inordinately clever. Too clever sometimes. Maybe she'd been traumatized when she was little, Hilda considered. Apparently, the emergence of sociopathic behaviour was created – or prevented – by childhood experience. She knew that Hanna's childhood, though privileged with significant wealth, was terribly lonely and troubled. Her parents, who both worked in the water industry in Maine, spent no time with her and her sister. Like obsessed missionaries, they were always travelling and tending their water business. When Hanna was in her late teens, her parents perished in a freak accident.

Hanna had avoided any cross-examination, but Hilda's uncompromising research on Oracle uncovered a strange story — a common one in the old water wars. Hanna never revealed her last name but Hilda guessed it was Lauterwasser, the name of a known water baron family in Maine: John and Beulah Lauterwasser owned a large water-holding of spring water near Fryeburg and sold Aqua Fina all over the world. They'd refused buy-out offers by the international conglomerate Vivanti. Soon after the Lauterwassers drowned, the holdings mysteriously came into the hands of Vivanti. Hilda suspected foul play. Not long after that, Hanna appeared in her life.

From the moment Hilda saw her, seven years ago, she'd felt a strange yet familiar attraction she couldn't explain. A bond that commanded her with a kind of divine instruction, a *déja vu* that bubbled up like an evolutionary yin-yang mantra: *You two were born to do something important together*. Hilda felt a strange repelling attraction to her strange friend. Like the covalent bond of a complex molecule.

Like two quantum entangled atoms fuelled by a passion for information, they shared secrets on Oracle. They corresponded for months on Oracle; strange attractors, circling each other closer and closer — sharing energy — yet never touching. Then Hanna suggested they actually meet. They met in the lobby of a shabby downtown Toronto hotel. Hilda barely knew what she looked like, but when Hanna entered the lobby through the front doors Hilda knew every bit of her.

Hanna swept in like a stray summer rainstorm, beaming with the self-conscious optimism of someone who recognized a twin sister. She reminded Hilda of her first boyfriend, clutching flowers in one hand and chocolate in the other. When their eyes met, Hilda knew. For an instant, she knew all of Hanna. For an instant, she'd glimpsed eternity. What she didn't know then was that it was love.

Love flowed like water, gliding into backwaters and lagoons with ease, filling every swale and mire. Connecting, looking for home. Easing from crystal to liquid to vapour then back, water recognized its hydrophilic likeness, and its complement. Before the inevitable decoherence, remnants of the entanglement lingered like a quantum vapour, infusing everything. Hilda always knew where and when to find Hanna on Oracle, as though water inhabited the machine and told her. Water even whispered to her when her wandering friend was about to return from the dark abyss and land unannounced on her doorstep.

Hilda leaned back in her chair with a heavy sigh. She always gave in to Hanna. And Hanna knew it. "Okay," Hilda said. "What do you need this time?"

Hanna's face lit with the fire of inspiration and she leaned forward. "Oracle told me something."

Hilda slumped deeper in her chair and rolled her eyes. "Of course, Oracle told you something. It always does."

Some cyber-genius created Oracle after the Internet sold out to Vivanti. The Oracle universe was the last commons, Hilda considered. It had brought her and Hanna together, bound them into one being with a common understanding. Hilda discovered one of Hanna's sites. It turned out to be a code for what was happening to water. To Hanna's obvious delight, Hilda decoded her blog and, like two conspiring teenagers, they shared intimate secrets about water. Hilda shared from her textbook and Hanna embellished with facts that Hilda's mother reluctantly confirmed or vehemently denied. Hilda never discovered how Hanna got her information, how she managed to cross the Canadian/US border or who Hanna really was. Whether she was a delusional charlatan, the itinerant daughter of a murdered water baron, a water spy for the US or something worse. Hilda realized that she didn't want to know.

"I was right but I was wrong too," Hanna said, beaming like an angel. "Mandelbrot has the last piece of the puzzle. It's right there, in Ritz's migrating birds and Scholes's photosynthesis." She lifted her eyes to the heavens then grinned like an urchin at Hilda. "…In Schrödinger's water." Seeing Hanna this way, lit with genuine inspiration, Hilda knew she would totally give in to whatever plan the girl had concocted. She wasn't prepared for what Hanna asked for.

"I need a thousand water credits."

"What?" Hilda gasped. "You know I don't have that! What the chaos do you need it for?" Hanna had inherited a hoard of water credits in the Vivanti settlement but had lost them all, through various wild ventures and a profligate lifestyle. Over the years, Hilda, who had barely anything, had given Hanna so many water credits for her wild schemes during their strange friendship. She'd funded Hanna's Tesla-field amplifier, her orgonite cloud-buster and anti-HAARP electromagnetic pulse device. Hilda had never once gotten any proof of them having amounted to anything, except to keep Hanna hydrated.

Hanna inched forward in her seat and her eyes glinted like sapphires. "You know about the nanobots that keep the smart clouds in the States from coming north over the border?"

Hilda nodded, wondering what Mandelbrot's fractals – and photosynthesis – had to do with weather control and cloud farming. It was part of the deal the US made with the Chinese, who had first perfected weather manipulation with smart dust. Vivanti owned the weather. Canada, which had been mined dry of its water, was just another casualty of the corporate profit machine.

"Why do you think water lets them do that?" Hanna said.

Hilda squirmed in her seat. What was Hanna driving at? As though water had any say in the matter…

Hanna wriggled in her seat with a self-pleased smile. "What if those nanobots 'decided' to let the clouds migrate north?"

Suddenly intrigued, Hilda leaned forward and stared at her friend. "Are you talking sabotage?" she finally said in a hoarse whisper and wondered who Hanna really was. "How?"

Hanna grinned in silence. A kind of conspiratorial withholding look. She always did that, Hilda thought: looked reluctant to say, when that was precisely why she'd come. To spill a secret. The two women stared at one another for an eternity of a moment. Hilda struggled to stay patient, understanding the hierarchy of flow.

Hanna finally confided, "Not sabotage. More like collaboration." She leaned back and her mischievous grin turned utterly sublime. She looked like a self-pleased griffin. "Like recognizes like, Hilda. Have you ever noticed how children going for walks with their mothers notice only other children? The most successful persuasion doesn't come from your boss, but by a trusted colleague… *a friend.*"

Hilda shook her head, still not understanding.

Hanna leaned forward and gently took Hilda's hand in hers. She pressed Hilda's fingers with hers in a warm clasp.

Smooth hydrated fingers that were long and beautiful; not like Hilda's selkie hands. "It's okay, my friend," Hanna said. "Just trust me. Trust me one more time…"

⚬⚬⚬

The faucet swims into a million faucets. Hilda understands that she is hallucinating. People generally stay away from the public iTap when someone in her condition approaches. People don't want to share, but they also don't want to feel cruel or greedy about not sharing. In today's blistering heat, urgency overrules decorum and they simply ignore her away. They know she is close to the end. She's seen others and has shied away herself. She feels the water guardians hovering. Waiting. If she doesn't walk away, they will come and take her – probably to the same place her mother was taken. Someplace you never came back from.

It is a month since she gave Hanna everything she had in the world. A month since Hanna disappeared with Hilda's thousand water credits – worth a million dollars on the black market. Credits she borrowed off her rent. In that month, Hilda's entire world collapsed. Her research contract – and associated meager income – ended suddenly at the Wilkinson Alternative Energy Centre, with no sign of transfer or renewal. Three weeks later, the Co-Op wiped most of her bank account clean then locked her out. She found a piece of shade from the relentless sun under an old corrugated sheet of metal in the local dump, and set up camp there.

Nothing has changed with the water. No clouds have come. No rains have come. And no Hanna has come.

This time, Hilda knows that Hanna is really gone. That whatever fractal scheme Hanna had conjured, she's failed.

Since they flowed into one another, they always seemed to know when the other was in trouble... Strangely, Hilda feels nothing. No presence; no absence. Just nothing.

Hanna is probably dead. Or worse. Since meeting her, Hilda has learned to monitor the Oracle for signs of her elusive friend. Small blips of signature code on certain sites. Anonymous tags. Like ghosts, they wisped into existence, whispered their truths, then disappeared like vapour in the wind. Even they stopped. Hanna too has turned to vapour.

Hilda is alone. Doomed by her trust, her faith and her gift... All gone with Hanna...

No. Not all gone.

For every giver there must be a receiver in the recursive motion of fractals. Everything is connected through water, from infinitely small to infinitely large. Like recognizes like. Atom with atom. Like her and Hanna. Like water with water...

She's fallen recumbent on the dusty ground. She is dying of thirst metres from a water source. And no one is coming to help her. They just keep filling their containers and shuffling away in haste. She doesn't hate them for it. They aren't capable of helping her. She squints at the massive sun that seems to wink at her and chokes on her own tongue. Perhaps her vision is already failing, because a shadow passes before the sun and it grows suddenly dark. It doesn't matter.

She's given all of herself faithfully in love and in hope. Through Hanna. To water. She is two-thirds water, after all. Just like the planet. Water and the universe are taking her back into its fold. She will enter the Higgs Field, stream through space-time, touch infinite light. Then, energized, return – perhaps as water even – to Earth or somewhere else in the cosmos.

Her mother was wrong in her angry heart. They weren't too nice. It is simply the way of water. They are all water. And water is an altruist.

It starts to rain.

Huge drops spatter her face, streaming down, soaking her hair, her clothes, her entire body. It hurts at first, like missiles assaulting her with suddenness. Like love. Then it begins to soothe as her parched body remembers, grateful.

Dark storm clouds scud across the heavens like warriors chasing a thief. She's vaguely aware of the commotion of people as they scatter, arms and containers pointed up toward the heavens. She smiles then feels her body convulse with tears.

Is that you, Hanna? Have you come to take me home?...

ABDUL

WENDY BONE

"The fate of the orangutan is a subject that goes to the heart of sustainable forests... To save the orangutan, we have to save the forest." —SUSILO BAMBANG YUDHOYONO, former president of Indonesia

The prophets of her dream vanished on awakening. For a second, Sara didn't know where she was. The vibrancy of the dream – trees laden with all kinds of unfamiliar fruits, animals that could talk, a hut on stilts in the middle of a jungle – clung to her memory like filaments of spider silk. The thud of music from the nightclub down the street tore the last strands of the dream away and lay the night bare. Outside the Glass Castle, drunks hooted and hollered like they did every Friday and Saturday night. Sara tensed up in bed, waiting for the sound of gunshots. What kind of a world was this when guns were fired on the streets of Canada? This wasn't Compton, for fuck's sake. Yet the rules of the jungle still applied. A young girl, just twenty, was shot to death outside the club two weeks ago for trying to break up a fight on the sidewalk. The screaming and crying of the girl's name chilled Sara because she had the same name. Those words like they were calling her, the drunken commotion, the blue and red lights flashing through the venetian blinds of her high-rise apartment: they replayed endlessly in Sara's mind. She twisted in her bedsheet. The clock stared with its implacable face, arms tracing circles with increasing speed. 3:00: drunks eating hot dogs at the roadside cart. 4:00: muscle cars drag racing down the road. 5:00: a woman sobbing in the next apartment, her husband hurling curses at her. At 6:00 the sky grew a shade lighter and the birds started chirping. Time for work. And there was Gary, a lump under the covers, sawing logs. Jealousy panged her heart. Gary could always sleep through anything.

On the other side of the world where it was already the next day, branches rustled. Fat raindrops fell off the edge of the dinner-plate-sized leaf, curled in her hand so it made a tube. She held it to her lips: the water was cool and sweet. She stirred in her nest. With baby latched to her side, she reached out an arm, pulled on a branch to get the fruit at the end. Just then a cracking sound came from below. Something hit her, as small as a wayward honeybee, beneath her heart. But it was not a honeybee. An explosion of warmth burst inside her, flowered in her chest. Her head began to spin, forcing her to let go of the branch. Her hand opened and released the small red fruit she held in her palm; it dropped into the abyss below. A hornbill rattled from its perch as the air took her. The mottled brown leaves of the forest floor whirled fast in a circle, coming closer and closer. In the middle of the circle was the last thing she saw: the face of a being that seemed like one of her kind, dark as an overripe fruit. Waiting for her to fall. The last thing she felt was her baby still holding onto her.

Sara put two feet on the floorboards and left Gary a snoring lump, out of a job and completely unconcerned. Eyes burning, she got ready for work and drove west, to the good side of town and her job as the art director of *Western Lifestyle*, one of Canada's top lifestyle and home décor magazines. The traffic was bad again. Her knuckles turned white on the steering wheel and she could feel her blood pressure rising to her ears. High up in her glassed-in office with a bird's eye view of the city, Sara stared into the computer screen, coffee at her elbow. Her eyelids felt heavy. Another empty-eyed model to airbrush. That same feeling of restlessness crept into Sara's veins, made her reach for her coffee. She'd studied so long, worked so hard to get this job, the envy of all her friends. Yet now she'd got what she wanted, an uneasy feeling of dissatisfaction left her hollow. She wanted more. She couldn't quite put her finger on what. But she knew it was more than this high-profile job that seemed more glamorous than it actually was. More than the baby Gary wanted so badly but was unable to support. More than a life of the same dull, boring routine day after day that left her feeling empty. It was all so safe. Once she had a baby she'd be locked in. No freedom for another twenty years.

He couldn't let go. With hands that would be as strong as those of eight grown men when he was older, he clutched at his mother. He could barely breathe. Hands pulled him away from her body. He cried, made sucking motions with his mouth. His mother's eyes were open but she didn't see him. They held treetops and clouds. She didn't move. Terror froze his belly. The hands pried him away from the only security he'd known, suspending him in mid-air. He kicked out and found nothing to hold onto. The tall brown being, familiar yet hairless, clasped him tightly but was little comfort. The arms were not his mother's. There was a sound. A tiger's roar that didn't stop. It grew louder. More of the creatures were on the ground. They held machines that bit the trees and spat them out in chunks. He smelled tree blood. He looked up at the tree where he had nested with his mother that morning. The tree groaned and swayed. It crashed into the forest, green arms waving goodbye. His world was falling down around him. But the ground was a very dangerous place to be on.

Sara scrolled down, clicking hyperlinks. She should have been working on the latest photo spread of exotic teak furniture from Southeast Asia. But her dream hovered alongside the unsettling memories of the other Sara lying on the sidewalk. It was hard, ticking off any of the tasks in her day planner, the first of which was: airbrush pimples off model's chin.

Buzzing on coffee, Sara fell down the rabbit hole of the Internet instead. With a click, a window opened: a photo of children with brown faces and white smiles. Another click: a blond bikini girl swimming with a turtle in the cobalt blue. Sara's finger lingered on the mouse. The site highlighted opportunities to travel and do something good for the planet, like volunteering at an orphanage in Cambodia or helping conserve sea turtles in Thailand. Some friends had taken such adventures and returned exhilarated, the envy of the office. Maybe doing the same thing would give her life meaning, a sense of direction. Yet the photos, however vibrant, didn't quite match what she saw in the dream. Sara opened another window, searching. Her hand froze on the mouse. Maybe it was the soft brown eyes filled with light and innocence. The gently comic face. The tuft of hair on its head.

According to the United Nations, by the year 2020, Indonesia's forests, known as "the lungs of the world," could be completely destroyed due to illegal logging, poaching, and the expansion of palm oil plantations. *Palm oil is found in an estimated fifty percent of supermarket products, including snacks, chocolate, soaps, and cleaning products. It is sold as biofuel, a clean alternative to gas. As a result of deforestation less than 6,000 Sumatran orangutans are left in the wild.*

Where was Sumatra exactly? Sara was about to check but the editor appeared in the doorway. Cute cover model, she said, edging closer and eyeing the screen. Sara's hand flew off the mouse, then she laughed at being caught slacking off. Look at those eyes, she said, pointing. So human. I've always wanted a monkey for a pet, the editor said. Actually, I've learned that monkeys should never be kept as pets. It supports illegal trafficking of wild animals. Besides, this isn't a monkey, it's an orangutan. For an infant orangutan to be kept in captivity, its mother is shot from a tree and killed, and more often than not the baby dies in the fall too. Then they're sold into the illegal pet trade. The editor gave her that look with the arched eyebrow. Um, she said. Anyway, I just came to tell you the post-mortem is starting. Sara set the orangutan pic as her wallpaper and went to pour her fourth cup of coffee. She'd need it to get through the next few hours.

The road was bumpy and full of potholes. The baby bounced around in the cage. His stomach churned and his leg hurt from the fall. The smooth metal bars looked like branches but felt cold and leafless. He stuck out his tongue. Tasted like the blood on his lips. His throat and mouth were parched. He tried to sleep, but his mind whirled and his body hurt too much. He craned his neck to see out the window. A different kind of tree, branches like bird feathers, thick with orange fruit. His stomach grumbled. Sick and weak in the heat, he gripped the cool bars and rested his head against them.

No no no. I want this photo, the editor said. Tensing her mouth, Sara dropped it in the page layout. The model's face was petulant, pouty like a spoiled child. How models are supposed to look. Smiles and laughing eyes: not cool. Sara scrubbed out a constellation of pimples on the girl's chin. She must be the perfect replica of a skinny heroin addict, minus the bumps, bruises and scars. As soon as the editor left, Sara maximized the hidden window where images of heaven had become images of hell: orangutans and fire-eyed tigers in cages, dead Sumatran elephants sprawled in the mud.

Black tree stumps.

Indonesia has the highest tropical-forest-loss rates in the world, with an average of 1.7 million hectares cleared every year. By 2000, the number increased to two million hectares, roughly the size of six football fields disappearing every minute, every day. Sara wasn't sure if she was any better for selling out and promoting a lifestyle that could not be sustainable for much longer. Hell, she couldn't even afford it on her salary. Then a thought came, unbidden: Why not go to Indonesia? Do something to help the orangutans survive. More unbidden thoughts came: You could really break free and learn how to live. Not just for a couple of weeks but for however long it takes. Sell everything and go.

The counter thoughts came: What, are you crazy? Fly away – alone – to a country, a culture, you know next to nothing about? Give up your status and everything you have worked so hard for just because you had some crazy dream?

Sara forgot her dream and returned to her work on the cover model, adding light to warm up the emptiness of the eyes. All ego where soul should be.

⸙

He watched the strange beings from between the bars. They didn't swing freely through space, up in the trees. Only walk on the dirty, dangerous ground. Their feet scuffled dust into his face. In the next cage macaques hopped up and down, chit-chitting. Cage after cage was piled up. Songbirds beat their wings against the bars and called in many languages. Bats squealed and flapped like dark moths. Rabbits slept in furry heaps. But the upright beings walked freely. They yelled at each other across the muddy path in a language he didn't understand. A small face appeared at the bars of the cage. It looked familiar, like his mother's, but smooth and blank as a river stone. The hair on her head was long and black, not red. Orang-utan, orang-utan, she chanted. Person of the forest, person of the forest. He had heard the same word when he fell with his mother: orang-utan. He understood this was the name for him and his kind, and he recognized it as similar to the name the uprights used. They called each other "orang," too. The girl reached in and took his hand. He remembered her from a dream. Small and warm, her hand held the pulse of life. He wasn't alone. Another was with him in his ever-diminishing world.

Sara read Farley Mowat's *Virunga*, about Dian Fossey's work with gorillas in the African Congo. She read about the slaying of Dian's favourite, Digit, and her own murder as an outspoken opponent to poaching. She read the work of Jane Goodall, the primatologist who brought her chimpanzees on the late-night talk shows as a way to educate people. And Biruté Galdikas, a publicity-shy Lithuanian-Canadian who established the world's longest-running research on orangutans in Kalimantan, Indonesian Borneo.

Sara was not a scientist but she wanted to do something. So she bought a backpack. She went to the clinic and got vaccinated for hepatitis and typhoid. She bought malaria pills. She gave her notice of resignation to *Western Lifestyle*. With this step she felt as if she had taken a leap off the edge of a cliff and was now in mid-air, either flying or falling, she couldn't tell. There was just one more thing to do.

What do you mean, you're leaving? Gary looked up from the football game on TV. The Broncos and the Packers, not even Canadian. Why can't you save the planet here at home, he said. There are enough people here to do that. Besides, she added, cringing at her own words, I have to find myself. What a lame cliché, the ultimate excuse of a spouse that wants to leave an unhappy marriage. Still, Sara did need to find herself. Somehow along the way, like the models in the photographs she doctored, she had lost herself in the sea of influences that told her who and what she should be. Sara needed to remake herself from the ground up. When the

Packers scored a touchdown Gary threw his beer can at the wall.

※

You are so cute, the girl chirped. Like a small, hairy person. You are my adorable Abdul. She wrapped her arms around him. That was his name: Abdul. His new orang taught him to dance to Michael Jackson's *I'm Bad*. He loved the attention of the children. When he was out of his cage he was the star. His favourite game was when his trainer taught him to play dead. The trainer cocked his finger, said Pow! That was his signal to throw his arms out, ape a wide grimace, and drop on the ground. The children giggled. They circled him in their arms and picked him up again. Most of the children were nice, but one boy pulled his fur and pinched him. Sometimes he jumped around and made faces. Hey monkey, he yelled. Oo oo oo oo oo. Abdul was confused. Didn't he do everything asked of him? Why was the boy so cruel? Over time the children lost interest and didn't come any more. He spent weeks alone in his cage. It was uncomfortable and hot. His mind wandered to the green trees that whispered secrets to the wind and tickled his face with their leaves. He remembered his mother's arms. An eagle squawked and weaved in his cage. He turned a yellow eye on Abdul, ruffled his feathers. A macaque hopped up and down, chained by the neck to a wooden pole with a house on the top, but the he didn't want to go in it. He had eyes like an orang, but small and shrewd. They darted around, looking for escape. Sometimes when Abdul was allowed out they played together, but he didn't get out often anymore. He just watched the macaque rattle at the end of his chain. Boredom stole over Abdul. It crept into his mind, then his limbs, freezing them numb. His injured leg grew stiff. He smelt his own shit in the corner of the cage. There was nothing to do but wrap his hands around the bars, press his face against them and wait. It was in his nature to love solitude, though it was solitude of the forest. Here, he shared mutual isolation with the other beings in cages. One day the trainer came. Abdul reached out to him. The trainer took his hand and held it a moment. Then he laughed and pulled his hand away.

In the rice paddies of North Sumatra, bubbles of frog-song rose and fell. Crickets rubbed their wings like bowstrings on a violin. The serenade grew louder and more fevered until it became a living wall of sound. But it was a sound that soothed. It didn't rattle the nerves like rush hour traffic, coffee or bullets. The night air breathed through the pores of the hut. It was woven of split bamboo, built on stilts over the flooded rice paddy. Beneath the floorboards, fish fanned their tails across the water. With a plosh they dove deeper. It was rainy season, and the paddies were filled with water and looked like mirrors. Sara was in her sleeping bag, awake. No need for dreams. She was here now. She wandered outside. The moon glowed between the clouds. The air was fresh, charged with rain. In the distance, lightning flashed over the treetops. When the tour guide of the Orangutan Protection Society first led her through the paddies to the organization's headquarters, the hut on stilts had appeared, just as she had imagined it would, framed by palm trees and mountains. At first she thought she had done this on a whim, but now realized her decision had been years in the making. She'd finally taken the step off the well-trodden path and onto a much smaller, more interesting one of her own. Her stomach felt giddy, as if she were still airborne on the plane that brought her here. Tomorrow morning she'd hit the ground running with the other volunteers for her orientation session, visiting the orangutan rehabilitation centre on the edge of Sumatra's largest forest and conservation area – Gunung Leuser National Park.

◦◦

More more more, shouted the children. They squealed and pushed each other, giggled uncontrollably. The trainer let Abdul out of his cage. He could barely move his injured leg and his stomach hurt from eating rice and other foods he wasn't used to. But the chance to move around freely cheered him. Swags of white cloth and balloons hung in the courtyard. It was a special day. The girls looked like flowers in their party dresses, and the boys looked smart in fresh-pressed shorts and shirts. The macaque, wearing blue pants and a red jacket with a conductor's cap, rode a monkey-sized bicycle and pulled a monkey-sized rickshaw. When it was Abdul's turn he danced a pirouette to *I'm Bad*. Then the trainer tapped his cheek, and Abdul kissed it with a smack of the lips. For the grand finale, the trainer looked at him with a sly smile and cocked his finger. Abdul staggered backward, feigning surprise, then threw his arms out and collapsed on the courtyard tiles. The children's laughter exploded around him. They surrounded Abdul, wanting to touch him. Careful, said the trainer. He's still a wild animal. The boy, now taller and lankier, leaped up and down and swung his arms. Oo oo oo oo, he cried. Oo oo oo. The children laughed and copied him. A strange feeling arose in Abdul that made him sit up. Oo oo oo, the boy shouted in his face. He grabbed Abdul by the arm, eyes glinting. Don't do that, the girl who had named him shouted. You'll make him angry.

The boy pulled harder. Suddenly a picture of his mother's body on the ground rushed back. Trees in her eyes. Trees falling. The roar of tree-eaters. Ahhhhh, ahhhhhhh, cried the boy. The girls screamed. Abdul's eyes cleared enough to see the mob of children shrink back, eyes and mouths like o's. The trainer leapt in and pried the boy away from Abdul. Blood dripped from the boy's hand as he wailed for his mother. Abdul remained motionless, the boy's blood still on his lips. It tasted like iron bars. He trembled at what he had done. He hadn't meant to do it. What did I tell you, the girl shouted. The macaque went wild, jumping up and down, yanking on his chain with a wicked gleam in his eyes. Waaahhh! I just wanted to dance with him. Drool hung from the boy's mouth in wet ribbons. The mothers rushed over and pulled the children away. He is too aggressive, they said. You must get rid of him. Led away by his nanny, the boy left a trail of blood spots on the tiles through the open door. The girl who once held Abdul's hand turned and looked at him sadly. The girl was kind, like his mother. He felt a familiar feeling in his stomach, as if he were falling from a very high place. He hadn't meant any harm, but he had made a terrible mistake.

The mother orangutan looked down at Sara briefly from her place in the trees, but she was more interested in the bananas and milk proffered by the local park ranger. Her baby is very sick, the ranger explained, but she won't let me near to feed it.

Sara caught a glimpse of the baby's face. It wasn't the sweet dewy-eyed picture on the Internet. The baby looked like a tiny old woman. Her face was pale and wrinkled, drawn in a severe way that suggested serious illness. Her eyes were closed. Sara had a sinking feeling. The baby did not seem likely to survive, especially if the mother could not trust the ranger enough to allow him to come close. What do you think it is? It could be a human disease, the ranger said. Because we share so much of the same DNA, orangutans can catch the same diseases as us. That is why we tell visitors not to touch them.

A shaggy orangutan with a comical face slowly swung his way over. He dropped to the ground and did a pirouette. The tourists laughed and peered at him through their cameras. Shutters clicked. The orangutan revealed a gorgeous array of crooked yellow teeth. Then he reached out a long arm and accepted a banana from the ranger's hand.

Who's this guy? Sara asked. Abdul, said the ranger. He arrived at the centre a few days ago. He was kept as a pet, so now he thinks he's human.

Bananas were his favourite. Now he was free, he could have as many bananas as he wanted at the feeding platform. Events had turned out nicely for Abdul since he was led back to his cage and loaded onto a truck. He had felt quite dismal not knowing where he was going. Yet when he was finally let out and prepared to meet his doom, he looked up. Trees! At first he hesitated. Maybe it was a trick and he'd be put back in the cage again. But the orang made encouraging noises and indicated for him to venture forward. Slowly he took his first steps back into the world again, dragging his bad leg. Good, fresh air expanded in his lungs. He looked up at the green roof. The orang made more encouraging noises as he moved to the edge of the forest. When he found the shade of the trees, he reached up and touched a branch. It was smooth but nubbled with leaves. He pulled it toward him and stuck out his tongue. Green leaf-blood, ants. He climbed off the ground. As he made his ascent the other orang sat in the truck, smoke coming from their mouths. He didn't look down after that. Abdul swung from one branch to the next, enjoying the stretch in his limbs and the feeling of freedom. No more bars, no more food in tin bowls. The leaves breathed. Their breath was fresh and clean. He reached up and swung again, travelling along the roof of the forest. He reached out and plucked a red flower, wrapped his lips around it. Sweet, full of nectar. He felt the tickle of ants as they escaped the flower and ran across his cheek.

Below, orang crawled on the ground. They raised their fingers and pointed up at him, faces like mushrooms on brown leaves. Orangutan, they shouted and scuttled, raised silver boxes that gave off small bursts of light. Abdul had seen these boxes before. He knew the orang liked to capture tiny pieces of themselves in them. Him too. He descended to give them a better look. It felt good to see the orang smile and go hahahaha. They made more noises like this as he came closer. These orang were different. Faces and eyes like moons. He dangled from a branch and posed for them. They chattered and crooned in their language. Their boxes like crickets. One female orang was close enough for him to touch. Hair the colour of banana. What did it feel like? She made a quick, startled movement, but her eyes caught his. She was still while the others went hahahaha. She held a silver box. She lifted it so one dark eye looked at him.

Abdul let his hand drop to his side. Then he spread his mouth wide and waited for the flash. The girl's eyes appeared again. She made her mouth wide too, and showed her teeth. He touched his fingers to his mouth. Flowers, bitter. Not bananas.

Around them the forest spoke. It breathed hot steam like a tiger and warbled in the voices of birds. It whistled and clicked with insects, rising and falling on each breath. From the top of a smooth-barked tree croaked a great bird. He swooped down, pinions pointing like fingers, rattling his yellow beak. A hornbill, the guide Aziz said. The girls looked up and followed the path of his eyes. The hornbill coasted in a circle, making an aerial survey. His kind had lived in this forest long before man ever set foot in it, and this was his domain. But it was Aziz's land, too. According to my faith, he said, it is my duty to be a steward of the land. Knowledge is dying out, kids want to live in the city. Not me.

The size of one of the fabled orang pendek, short people believed to inhabit the forests of Sumatra, Aziz was no mythical man but an educated guide able to speak and read in both Indonesian and English. A shock of curly, black hair sprung from his head and a clove cigarette hung from the corner of his mouth. His feet were nimble on the slippery terrain. His eyes studied the world around him, or one of his books he read by firelight. The information he gathered he shared with travellers like Sara. Aziz led her and group of volunteers on a six-day trek to study the orangutans and gather data on their nesting and eating habits. The information would help the team of scientists at Orangutan Protection safeguard their habitat or, failing that, provide better nutrition and living conditions for orangutans if their only home left was the zoo, the new Noah's Ark for the endangered species of the world. To get to the base camp, they crossed the river over twenty times, following it through the forest. In some places they formed a human chain to keep standing against the currents. It took five hours to walk. On the way they counted seven new orangutan nests. Aziz pointed to each one and gauged how high it was in metres, how tall the tree was and what type, and if the nest was fresh or old. Each night orangutans made a new nest and in the morning moved on. The women wrote the data in their notebooks. Huffing with exhaustion, picking leeches off their feet as they went, they climbed the steep terrain. Aziz cleared the way, swinging his machete to cut through the undergrowth and long hanging vines of strangling figs. Orangutans love these trees, he said. He grabbed a long, strong vine and swung. He crouched to touch the feathery fronds of the peacock plant carpeting the forest floor. For snake or centipede bites, he said, you can chew the leaves and put it on the wound to slow the movement of poison. Sara chewed a little. It tasted mild and green. They stopped to rest at the top of a ridge where the range of mountains intersected. On the mountainsides, layered with mist, grew such a diverse variety of trees and plants that they appeared to be a cascading waterfall of every possible shade of green. Their branches bounced with gangs of Thomas leaf monkeys, hair like punk rockers, and the excitable long-tailed macaques chattering in their own languages.

The trees rustled. A forest mango, another orangutan food, dropped on the ground. As they rested, Sara thought of

Abdul, who had reached out to touch her hair. She was told not to touch an orangutan, but not what to do if an orangutan touched her. He touched you because he has lost his fear of humans, Aziz said. But losing the fear is dangerous for orangutans. If one tries to touch you again, you should move away and keep your distance.

Ayee! Ayee! Orangutan! Orangutan! An orang in a flowered housedress came at him swinging a broom like a madwoman. Her teeth were bared and her eyes were fierce. Abdul reached for another handful of bananas and ducked the broom just in time, loping out the open door of the kitchen, past a quizzical dog that cocked his ears. He had made his escape, but received a swat on the behind from the farmer's wife. Orangutan nakal, she shouted. Naughty naughty naughty! Abdul made a safe distance, then hoisted himself up into a tree on the edge of the forest to enjoy his favourite snack.

The truck careened down the potholed road, bouncing recklessly past chickens, children, geese and goats, dust flying in its wake. Sara gripped the side of the window, bracing for possible impact. Aziz was calm at the wheel, miraculously averting near disaster. The society had set up an education program to provide information about orangutans and encourage people to call the centre if an orangutan was causing trouble in their area. Orangutans weren't the only ones creating a disturbance. Other animals were also emerging from Sumatra's disappearing rainforests, among them elephants and tigers. In the more remote areas they sometimes killed villagers – elephants by blundering through, and tigers because they were starving.

Orangutans posed an economic threat. Like people, if they saw an easy way to get food, they would help themselves. Shortly after their return from the trek, Aziz received a phone call, and invited Sara along for the ride. Past several kilometres of bare, baked earth and the charred trunks of already harvested palm oil trees, Aziz pulled to the side of the road. As far as the eye could see grew line after line of palm oil trees, trunks shaggy with ferns, crowns overlapping to create arched green corridors. They didn't appear to be an environmental menace, and to the eye of someone flying above, they appeared as an innocuous green carpet arranged in regular, undulating rows, a shade brighter and greener than the dense dark jungle clinging to their periphery. A palm plantation worker emerged, faded clothes hanging off his bones, smoking a clove cigarette. He explained to Aziz in rapid-fire Indonesian what had happened. Sara, fresh off the plane, understood none of it. They walked the green corridors. It was like travelling back to the Jurassic era, in a time before man. Yet man had created this, reshaping the earth to his own ends. Logging and deforestation are the biggest threat to orangutans, here in Sumatra and in Borneo, Aziz explained. Palm plantations often take the place of primary rainforest. Once the primary rainforest is gone, there's no way to get it back. The air hummed with insects; moths zigzagged among the ferns. There was no sign of any other kinds of life. Palm plantations are a monoculture and do not support the biodiversity of the rainforest, Aziz said. The animals have nowhere to go. When they come out of the forest, they are usually shot. The plantation worker stopped, pointing to a large spiky cluster of fruit on the ground with his machete. Aziz translated: Palm fruit. He picked a hard orange seed from the cluster and placed it in her hand. It doesn't seem like much, he said, but it's the key to Indonesia's economy. Our country's largest export. When sold to western countries, it is made into ice cream and lipstick, converted to biodiesel for the new hybrid cars. Palm oil is everywhere. But it comes from here. The fruit was hard and waxy in her palm. It doesn't make sense, she said, that we're replacing one fuel with another that destroys the rainforest and contributes to global warming. If we're trying so hard to save the environment, why don't we know about this?

It's just business, Aziz said. Many of the biggest companies are European or North American. This plantation is owned by a company in London, England. People want to do right, so they buy hybrid cars that use biodiesel. They use products advertised as good for the environment, but if palm oil is on the label, it is not clear if it comes from rainforest destruction. The more Sara learned, the more complicated the issue became. None of the players in the palm oil industry took direct responsibility for rainforest destruction, including the governments of the countries involved. The trail of communication was shadowy and convoluted. As long as palm fruit remained a cheap and convenient source of oil, the destruction continued unchecked. The plantation worker stood smoking and looking off into the trees. With a slow, easy amble he led them to a thatched-roof hut and opened the door. On the floor in the corner lay a furry orange heap. We had orders to shoot, the worker explained.

Abdul's hunger and curiosity took him in another direction. He had caught a whiff of something very pleasing. Like a siren, it brought him out of the jungle, bringing his always-hungry belly with him, still full of bananas but wanting more. Posing for adoring fans was hungry work. He headed in the direction of the aroma. Hand over hand he moved through the trees. The jungle whistled and clicked with life around him. He reached a clearing and looked across. Far below, the orang squatted on the ground. The farmer's wife washed clothes in the river, bending and scrubbing as her three small ones splashed and played in the water. Motorcycles whizzed past rumbling convoys of trucks filled with palm fruit. Abdul breathed in the delicious smell from the grove of tall trees. He thought about visiting the farmer's house for dinner again, but that other smell was just too good. He had to descend and cross the clearing first because the forest stopped suddenly and there was no other way. The prickling feeling on the back of his neck warned him of the danger, but he ignored it. He had spent most of his life on the ground, and the orang were almost the same as him, even if they had peculiar habits. Today was Abdul's lucky day. A sweet-smelling fruit had fallen from the tree and lay yellow and spiky on the ground. He picked it up and split it open with his strong hands. Inside lay fragrant yellow seeds nestled in rows. His nostrils widened and his mouth watered with pleasure. He put a seed in his mouth and was transported. Better than bananas. He sucked the soft flesh and spit out the pit. Then he plucked another seed and popped it in his mouth.

Bouncing back over the potholed road in the old truck, Aziz remarked calmly, At least they phoned after they shot it. Sara gripped the window frame because the door handle was missing. Her sentimentality, which she now recognized as a particularly western trait, had not prepared her for the sheer complexity of the problem. In this country people did not share the view that orangutans are cute. They are agricultural pests that pose a threat to their lives and livelihoods. Most people are focused simply on survival. On the back seat, the orangutan lay sprawled, long-limbed, chest wounds bound by clean rags. His eyes were half closed, flickering. Sara kept hoping, praying, it wasn't too late. He had awoken in her motherly instincts she didn't know she had. She wanted to protect him, bring him back from the edge of death, make sure it never happened again.

As he bit into the delicious fleshy seed, Abdul looked up and saw an orang, hand raised and cocked on the trigger. Abdul knew what to do. Still, he was mildly surprised as his body went through the familiar motions without his direction. His arms flew back and the spiky fruit thudded on the ground. Then both his legs failed him; Abdul crumpled to the ground as he had done so many times before. He had practiced for this moment most of his captive life, in the service of entertaining others. The orang stood over him. Abdul looked into his eyes. What he saw was dark and unfathomable. The orang lifted a silver box to his ear and spoke.

The orangutan died on the floor of the veterinary clinic at the research station. Sara's stomach turned to stone as she watched his eyes slowly glaze over and his breathing grow slow and laboured. Then his eyes turned to glass and he was gone. Only then was she allowed to take his hand and hold it, feel the warmth draining from his fingers. The German vet, the only one in the area, had come to the Orangutan Protection headquarters immediately to operate. But it was too late. The pellet tore his aorta, he said. The damage was too great. There was nothing he could do. Anger flared in Sara's heart. They could have shot into the air to scare him away instead. Or played a xylophone out of key like the owner of the local inn who shooed away orangutans who came to pilfer toast and eggs from the restaurant. Music badly played is a strong deterrent to orangutans. They didn't have to shoot him, she said. But Aziz was focused on more practical matters. He went to the truck for a shovel and dug a hole under a nearby palm oil tree. He placed the orangutan in the hole and covered it. The soil was the same colour as the orangutan. Sara saw his wizened, wrinkled face, his closed eyes, the thin line of his mouth, the whiskers on his chin, disappear under the orange earth.

NIGHT DIVERS
LYNN HUTCHINSON LEE

An Allegory, Possibly
    She comes in the dark to take me again to the quarry, step off the ledge out into the starry black air. She's there behind the trees, hands at her sides, peaceful, palms open, inviting.
    If I hadn't let you stay this wouldn't have happened.
    But it would, she says, *I keep telling you.*
    Elva Belyea. Mrs. Borutski.
    Yes.
    They were the first.
    There'll be others, she says. *There'll always be others until we don't need to do this any more.*

⁂

I remember the way it was. There aren't many of us left who've seen or tasted those waters. Springs and wells, puddles, creeks. Lakes, rivers, rain. I hold in my body the touch, the feel, the memory of water and the days when it was everywhere. I smelled the snow on January mornings, drank from streams, leaped into the quarry from a great height. I can think of any part of my body and remember how it touched and was touched by water.
    For about ten years now, since we stopped travelling, Daddus and I have lived in a farmhouse between the Bronte

shores and the old quarry, up the road from my mother's grave. At first Daddus still did business with the fishermen in the shanties down at the lake. He'd set out his collection – ropes, hooks, boots, hardware – at one side of the wharf, and the fishermen laid their baskets of lake trout and whitefish at the other. While they haggled I looked out across the lake where the sky and water met and I couldn't tell which was which. I listened to the waves and seagulls, to Elva Belyea laughing with Daddus and the fishermen.

It happened slowly: little cracks in the clay north of Bronte, dried-up wells, dunes herded by the wind, the Lake Ontario shoreline pulling back and away into mud flats frilled with garbage and weeds. Out past the wharf Charlie Belyea's fishing boat *Elva*, named for his wife, lay on its side in the dirt. Charlie and Charlie Junior and the other fishermen up and left for the city, the farmers too; they vanished like a single flock of birds into the horizon. Some of us stayed on, tending our exhausted gardens. The lines of my hands were etched with dirt. No amount of washing could get it out.

Later the engineers came, the water hunters, the trench diggers, the pumps and drills, the Brothers of the Water of Life and their PrayGuards; and the arms of the Waterlords closed in around us. They marched out over the lands, hunting for buried seas, trapping the lakes and ponds inside chain-link fences. They got everything except the quarry.

The first time diving into the quarry I was with Billy Borutski. Billy knew the land all the way from the Bronte shores up to the Limehouse caves. "Here's Twelve Mile Creek," he said, pressing my finger to the blue vein running from his knuckles to the back of his wrist, "over here's Bronte Creek," sliding my finger across the ridge of his tendon, "and here's the spring that feeds the quarry. And down here somewhere, that'd be Lake Ontario." We knew Lake Ontario wasn't really Lake Ontario any more. It was a cavity, an interval, an opening to something that had once been real. Billy's hand was the only map we had. We spoke the old place names aloud. *Bronte, Limehouse, Palermo.* We were left with highways, parking lots, craters, underground lakes that were grabbed up and whooshed through pipelines and into reservoirs.

Billy lay behind rocks with his slingshot and waited. He could see out to the road where the water hunters drove by, not far from the old Borutski homestead. That Billy. He'd do anything on a dare, you just had to ask him. *Billy. Take out that water hunter there, with one shot. Billy. Put on that blindfold and dive into the quarry.* He had nerve, the whole family did, that's what Daddus said. He said later that's why things caught up to them in the end, with what happened to his family. "Those poor Belyeas and Borutskis," everybody said, and they wondered aloud who'd be next.

◦◦◦

Mrs. Borutski took away Billy's slingshot. Like all the young guys he got sent up north to work on the new waterways. They'd take a river and twist it from north to south, stuff it inside a tunnel. "First, the river's going along minding its business," Billy said, "and then you dig it a new bed, jerk it round, and you got it going off in a whole different direction." He said it was like breaking someone's arm or leg, and that arm or leg never going back to the way it was.

I stood out at the end of the wharf and watched the dirt shift and gather as the lake was pulled back toward the horizon. I dug my fingernails, hard, into the back of my hand. It didn't feel like my hand, it didn't feel like anything. A little whirlwind sprouted up. It nibbled a trail across the dirt, shooting out plumes of twigs and dust, then folded up at the foot of the wharf. Nothing was rooted any more, as if the lands and waters could lift and blow away, leaving us standing on air.

Billy returned from the waterways to find his mother had moved into town, living above the post office with her sister, Elva Belyea. Then one day I came down from the hills to find Elva's post office turned into a Watermart, where we had to line up and buy our water in plastic bottles. Elva protested. "You got no right," she said to one of the Brothers, "no right," waving her arm out to the disappearing lake. "This here's our water." But they were sly, those Waterlords. They repurposed her, made her the Bronte water agent: she got to keep the apartment, but with their cameras watching through her windows.

Each person got exactly ten bottles of water a week. That was for everything, not just drinking. Mrs. Borutski was fed up. "Ten lousy bottles?" she complained to the crowd inside the Watermart. "That's what they give us?" She turned to the PrayGuard at the door. "To hell with you people," she snarled, slamming her money down on the counter and emptying her bottles, one by one, over his feet. The PrayGuard was nearly twice her size. His hands flexed around his gun, his neck swivelled back and forth between her and Elva Belyea. The water splashed off his feet and Mrs. Borutski went on pouring. She said a few things to him that I wouldn't repeat, but she was lucky, his hearing functions must have been switched off. The next day Billy got her out of there and brought her with him up to an empty farmhouse north of ours, on what we still called Twelve Mile Creek. I liked him being nearby, with the quarry between us.

It has three ledges, the quarry does. The bottom one's the low rocky lip where I wash my clothes. The top ledge is the place where we lay and daydreamed, looking into the water, or across the hills down to the mud flats of the lake. Billy would dive from the middle ledge, about the height of our summer kitchen roof. He'd fly out over the water, aiming for the lip at the quarry's mouth, and I never knew whether to look away or watch. I always held my breath, making desperate silent bets on whether he'd break his neck or surface back up into the spray, pumping his fist and yelling.

I was in the shadow of the porch, shelling peas, and Daddus was nodding off in front of the TV. Then he started to yell. "Get over here! Quick!" He was right up at the screen. A reporter opened and shut his mouth, shaking his head at the camera. There must have been nine or so trucks scattered behind him across the highway and along the ditches, though it was hard to see where one truck finished and the next began. Around the edge blinked the lights from ambulances, police cars, a PrayGuard helicopter. The reporter found his voice and gave a little tour: sheets mounded on the ground, blood seeping, here and there an arm or a leg. A jackknifed tractor-trailer. Flattened pickups. A convoy of water hunters' trucks. "The carnage," the reporter was saying as if stuck in a groove, "the carnage."

Then he was over at a water hunter on a stretcher. "It was an angel come for me," the water hunter whispered out of the charred crust of his mouth, "up there." He tried to lift his arm to point at the highway overpass, "right up there on them railings." He kept pushing the words out of his mouth and reached up to the reporter. "She was the colour of heaven," he said. The reporter drew back. "Not kidding you here, man," the water hunter whispered, "heaven."

He died right there on the screen. The last we saw of him the Brothers had gathered round, praying and singing him out of this world of woe. "A martyr for the water hunters, lured to his death," the reporter said, "by some kind of sky-demon."

Late afternoon, hotter and stiller than other winter days, then a breeze came up through the hills from the brackish bits of lake. The flies were hurling themselves at the window frames, hens ruffling in the dust, a dog barking down the road, a faint chorus of voices. Not many people came up here any more except for the odd tramp looking for food, or neighbours from across the fields. This time it was two Water of Life Brothers and their company of stragglers. "Brother George, that's me," said the bigger one, coming at Daddus with his hand out, "and this here's Brother Ed." They told us the usual story: the water-fever was going around, they were looking for the sick. But not since my mother died had a new wave of fever struck the land.

We were supposed to wash their feet, give them food and water, even a bed for the night if they wanted. But they only asked if we'd seen the sky-demon, or if anybody was sick. What about water thieves? Or unreported streams, springs and suchlike? Being all friendly then snooping around, counting the number of water bottles in the kitchen, the number of hens and rabbits in the yard, trying to get the goods on us for the Waterlords. Brother Ed looked around, saw the sheets billowing on the clothesline and said, "Where'd you wash them sheets, then?"

"Wash?" said Daddus. "The sun, Brother, that's all the washing they need." Then he said under his breath, "Next thing you'll be sticking a meter on the sunlight." Brother Ed didn't move. I couldn't tell if he'd heard. He looked at the empty pails by the henhouse door.

"Nobody sick here, then?" he said. "We've come to heal the sick."

Daddus took his Christmas shirt off the line and danced it round the yard. He made a swoop and dive and called out, "Drink like a madman, work like a beaver, pray the Lord keep you from the water-fever," making Brother Ed laugh and the wives turn red.

"Swing your wives under the sun," he went on, "down the river and here they come." The wives scattered and ran to the road, followed, finally, by Brother George and Brother Ed. "Water thieves? Really?" said Daddus, watching them go. "It's the Waterlords and all their gavverbengs that's chorring the panni." The Water Lords, their thugs, stealing the water, *as if such a thing could be stolen*, we used to say before we knew better.

We saw the Brothers later passing by on their way back, and Brother Ed gave us a thumbs-up. "Not sure what that was about," Daddus said, and gave him a flashy grin and a thumbs-up back. There seemed to be extra stragglers this time, more wives than usual, with their bare feet and black teeth, worn grey dresses and dirty hair flapping at their sorry backs. A few of the wives approached. I made them sandwiches and brought a bowl of radishes. They bolted the sandwiches right down, like dogs. "Bless you," they kept saying, hanging on to me like children.

I loosened their grubby fingers from my arms and waist, trying not to seem unkind. They wandered off behind the Brothers, dust curling around their bare feet in the road. Later two or three more wives went past, slowly, in silence. The hens settled into their throaty night sounds, Daddus started snoring, and the moon came up over the trees. I sat at my window to watch the silvery fields.

A shadow came together, a little heap out in the road. Someone was lying at the end of the driveway. I put on my sweater and ran out. She tried to get up but her knees gave way and I half-dragged, half-carried her to the house. I recognized her from the extra wives. Crackling little bones, brittle spine, like a bird she was. I gave her some water, lifted her onto the couch in the kitchen and she stayed there, not moving, for two days.

The third morning she opened her eyes. Her skin was so thin you could almost see a layer of something else underneath. Bluish. She could have been filled with ink. "I'm not sick, you know," she said. "There's nothing wrong, I haven't got the fever." Her eyes closed. At the kitchen table I sat in the rising heat, watching her sleep. Brother Ed could have sent her back here to snoop. *Find the water thieves, the quarry, all the streams and springs.* They could take us away in a pig truck. Or make it a public hanging, Daddus and me on the scaffold down at the wharf. I looked at the frown flickering at her eyebrows, as if there might be an opening for me to pull out a thread of plans or instructions. *Go get the water thieves.* I wouldn't put it past them.

❦

Her name was Grace. By the end of the week her skin was plumper and not as watery, her legs held her up, and every day she walked a little farther. "Thank you," she told us, and sometimes, "Sorry." Sorry for what? But she never said. She hardly spoke. I found things for her to do: sweep the floor, feed the hens, meet me at the top of the hill and help me push my bike, with its load of water, back to the house.

"Won't they be wondering where you are?"

"No, I wasn't a real wife."

"Nobody gets to just wander off. They'll come looking."

"I don't matter."

In the morning, I awoke to the sound of rain. All the pails had been placed under the roof to catch the run-off. Grace was around the side of the house, setting the tin tub under the downspout.

"We're not supposed to do that," I said.

"How will they know?" said Grace.

"We could get hanged for this. Or disappeared."

Grace was turning everything upside down. She was like a needle in my hand, shoved in hard, to make me feel something. Anything.

❦

Billy Borutski was waiting in the quarry. I made sure Grace didn't see me leave. My dresses and nightgowns caught the wind straight off the ledge and settled over the water. Billy had already done his dive. I climbed down, washed my clothes, and we lay floating, looking up at the sky.

"Let's have a snowball fight." That's what I would have said, before. The snow skittering over the quarry, Billy and I on our skates, tearing across to the other side. The air rising from the ice, tasting of the frozen night sky clinking with stars.

"Imagine that feeling again, the snow landing on your face." I leaned my head back as in the old days, opened my mouth to the distant taste of snow. Never would I feel that jewel-like cold again.

We climbed back up to the top of the quarry, stood looking down as we always did. Was the water getting lower? We'd need to go across soon and follow the stream to the springs that fed it. Had the Waterlords already reached the groundwaters from the other side? Were they draining the springs? Sucking them dry?

Then, beside us, here was Grace. "You've got water," she said, looking into the quarry as if she couldn't believe her eyes. My first thought was, *How did she find us, will she tell the Brothers?* Then, *Throw her over the ledge, nobody'll know.* Did I really think that? Billy looked between Grace and me. I remember my arm pulling back for the shove. *Do it. Save Daddus, save yourself, save Billy and Mrs. Borutski, the quarry.* Then I felt her breath, light as a child's, on my shoulder. And was she crying, or what?

⚬⚬⚬

"There's something we need to do." She pulled me out of bed, rushed ahead of me to the quarry. The water was a mirror, throwing up stars from its dark surface. A stone slid out from under my foot, went crashing down to the water, and I barely heard it land. Grace slipped out of her nightgown.

"You need to get undressed."

I protested. "I don't take my clothes off."

"You have to," she said. "The water needs to feel our skin." What kind of drivel was that? But my hands lifted off my nightgown and it dropped to the ground. I stood before her, shivering in the night heat.

I could still throw her over the edge. Or she could throw me.

"Put your arms round my neck," she said. She actually lifted me up. "Your legs, wrap them round me, tight." Her feet shifted on the ledge for balance, her body sticky and damp. I shut my eyes and hid my face in her neck. *She's going to smash me to smithereens on the rocks.* I smelled her sharp sour smell.

If Daddus knew, there'd be hell to pay. Naked like this, our code snapped and broken, just like that, but then all the laws and codes were gone now: the law of rivers, tides, of marshes and bogs, the lap and ebb of the waves on the shore, all thrown up into the air and landing in pieces.

"Don't let go," Grace said in my ear.

The only thing moving was her breath. Then she started to inch her feet out to the edge and stopped.

"Now," she said, and we were in the air. The rock was a blur, the other side of the quarry was a blur, and then the water heaved up at us. We hit it with a crack, everything black and roaring with bubbles. We were deep in the throat of the quarry, the slippery dark wall all around, my lungs on fire, then back up in the cocoon of bubbles, and the water shot us out into the air. I felt my hands, my palms, nerves, fingertips, really felt them. Something had been moved around. Everything out there, inside me. My lungs, voice, bones, skin, all made of water and stars.

The next night Grace brought Billy, then his mother. The night dive, naked, into the dark. I could hear them whooping and hollering after they surfaced, and then the silence of the long climb as we hauled Mrs. Borutski back up the side. I listened to their laboured breathing when we landed, finally, on the ledge. "This is us," said Mrs. Borutski, leaning out over the water, looking into the quarry, out to the streams and springs, "You hear me, son? This is not just you or me, but all of us. All of us here and out there. Everybody."

Elva Belyea came with her daughter Ida. She trembled at the edge while Ida said, "Mother, you're crazy."

"I gotta be crazy. I'm gonna split my head open on them rocks," and Grace lifted Elva as if she were a child.

"Hold tight," said Grace, and they leaped out over the dark.

When they surfaced Elva Belyea was sobbing. "Mother, daughter," she said, trying to wrap her arms around the water, kissing the little waves that were still circling out after her dive.

Elva and Ida came back to the quarry the next night and the night after. Back up on the ledge, after the dive, they didn't speak for a long time. Later they told about the new wall down at the lake, concrete, high as a tidal wave, with gun towers and ramparts, manned by PrayGuards and dogs. As they spoke in quiet voices we looked out over the quarry, our little cradle of water at the bottom of the cliff.

Grace took Ida over to the ledge. "I'm diving into stars," called Ida, as Grace lifted her into the leap. They went twice. The next night Grace said to Ida, "You have to learn to do this now," and showed her how to lift, how to find the throat of the quarry even though it couldn't be seen. "It'll show you where to dive," said Grace. And so, Ida Belyea brought her friends and neighbours from the old shore, climbing up into the hills in the dark of night, holding them as they shook and clung to her, dropping down to the water.

Then out of the blue Grace said she had to go. I watched her walk down the driveway and out to the road. She turned back once to wave. I wanted to run after and make her stay. I went to her room, smoothed her sheets, folded her blanket, lay down on her bed. Outside, the empty road simmered in the air.

Some days after she left, Daddus was at the TV. The reporter called it a terror attack. He was standing by the new wall down at the lake. What happened was Mrs. Borutski was yelling at the PrayGuards, "Take down your damn wall," or something like that. A PrayGuard and his Lieutenant threatened her, and she brought out Billy's slingshot. "I'll show you," she hollered, scooping up a stone, taking aim, and they shot her dead. Right there. Brother Ed was on the TV. He gave a thumbs-up. "We been watching her for some time now."

Elva Belyea and Billy collapsed in our kitchen. I can still hear us all crying, "No, no!"

I must have walked for hours. In just two days the leftover puddles were drying up, and the winds had stopped. The air's holding its breath, the sun glaring off the fragments of lake. Where did the oxygen go? I draw in sips of air, shards in my throat. The depressions are blooming with green murky puddings, heavy and still. A smell of decay. Tiger lilies left to rot in the jar come to mind.

I'm in a giant emergency ward. It's empty. Where's the triage? I was always comforted by the idea of triage even though it leaves you hanging till they tell you what you're dealing with. But at least you know that care is being taken; in triage there's always some kind of hope. Mild or desperate. A place between life and death. You're floating in between.

Here there are no nurses with their brisk friendly arms, no machinery to chirp at you, reassure you that you're still alive. Nobody to draw blood, hand you a blanket. Not even a bandage. But what good is a bandage here anyhow?

Fever. You've got the fever. Call the ambulance, start the siren, lie down in this cool lake to make the fever go away. But there's no cool lake. The lake, too, has the fever. Dry mouth. Can't get enough to drink. Throwing off sheets of sweat, then clammy. Convulsions near the end. A few gasps for effect. Just to let you know it's over.

I'm back on the shore. The old shore, the one from my childhood. The gun tower's quiet. No lights, no sound. The PrayGuards must be out patrolling somewhere. Or they're asleep, bored with nothing to watch or shoot. Here's Billy Borutski, laying asters and goldenrod at the foot of the wall where his mother fell. He joins me on the sand.

The emergency room's still. The floor cooling under my feet. Is this a sign of hope? Or of shutting down? If so, who will sound the bell?

Billy and I fall asleep on the sand. I wake up when he puts his hand in mine. Then we bring our arms, legs, bodies together, if for no other reason than to remind ourselves that we can console without words, for what use are words any more?

We sleep. I don't remember dreaming. Or maybe I did dream. That Grace laid her hand on my brow, her cooling hand, blue as water, and for the first time in weeks the fever lifted and dissolved into thin air. It's the darkest part of the night, just before dawn. I can feel this heavy darkness the length of my bones. Then a shift, the stillness more still, the night more quiet. The fever, is it letting up? Or not? This new disturbance, lightning without the flash. Something out of place.

At the top of the wall a figure floats. The colour of cloud, of sky. But that's impossible. It's her, the sky-demon, the angel, here in our midst. Clouds cover the moon, then disperse, and I see her clearly, naked, hands held up in warning, arms raised above her head, as if signalling to someone or something in the distance, something nobody can see. Her body calling out the end of the water, of all water, or is it the beginning?

I've found my voice. "Billy," and he's awake beside me.

"Who's there?" he calls softly. The figure doesn't move. On the other side of the wall a dog barks, then all the dogs start up, baying and howling. The figure doesn't move.

"What's going on?" People are coming out of the shanties, stopping at the wall, looking up. Some of them start crying, some pray. "What's that up there?" says Elva Belyea. The voices stop. A giant silence broken only by the barking of dogs. The girl's arms stay up, trembling slightly, hovering wings. The light's on in the tower now, moving across the ramparts. It climbs up the girl's body, shines on her face. "Get down," Elva's yelling, "get down!" It's Grace, her eyes looking out over the breach that was once the lake.

A PrayGuard bursts out of the gun tower. Grace hasn't moved. She seems to be waiting for him. His head starts swivelling around and he aims at the crowd. "Grace, run," Elva calls, "get off the wall!" The PrayGuard looks for the person belonging to the voice. He stops. His gun points straight down at Elva. There's a crack as her body lifts off the sand and slams down at Ida's feet. Everybody's screaming. Elva's stomach is spouting blood. The PrayGuard swivels again and shoots. Grace flies up and backwards off the wall. She lands in the dirt on the other side. A muffled thump. The dogs go crazy.

◦○○◦

They don't stop us from burying Elva Belyea and Mrs. Borutski. We carry their coffins, piled with asters and goldenrod, above our heads. The jittery PrayGuards look down, and for a minute, at the foot of the wall, the funeral procession stops.

Mrs. Borutski at the quarry, looking over the water, *This is us.*

Mother, daughter, Elva's words as she surfaced.

We remember Mrs. Borutski whooping and hollering fresh from her dive, Elva embracing the water, kissing the waves, then we carry on up the hill to the old Bronte cemetery.

◦○○◦

Grace appears from behind the pines in the darkest part of the night. She's dragging one foot, but otherwise seems unhurt. She's wearing an odd assortment of clothes – an old sweater of Mrs. Borutski's and a skirt that's too big. She comes forward out of the clearing. The sweater's unravelling here and there, and the sleeves hang down to the ends of her fingers. I can see her skin's bluer than ever, but maybe it's the moonlight spiking down through the branches. This is crazy. "Aren't you supposed to be dead?"

"No," she says, bending down to pull some burrs from the hem of her skirt, "I'm not theirs to kill."

Slingshots, sixty, carved from twigs and branches, waiting under the straw in the old Borutski barn. The quarry, shimmering in the heat. Streams, count them, but there aren't enough. They're drying like puddles under the sun, and then suddenly here are new streams and springs, sprouting and gushing across the lands. Waves appear at the shoreline, the lake announcing itself. I wake up. Billy's out at the henhouse, our boy riding on his shoulders. The day's steaming already, and Daddus is in his wheelchair at the TV.

CAPTURED CARBON

GEOFFREY W. COLE

The shape on the ice floe looked like a woman but Jeje Dhillon knew that was impossible. He floated half a kilometre off the coast of Tuktoyaktuk and as far as he knew he was the only person dumb enough to be stuck out here. He lifted his diving mask for a better look anyway. Maybe it was a walrus or a seal or oil in the shape of a woman. Jeje hyperventilated to prep for the dive. Oil, that made the most sense. The news sites said the slick was still twenty kilometres from Tuk, but the news sites were the lying mouths of the oil companies, and if the woman-looking shape really was oil, that meant the coral was in trouble.

Jeje used the buoy line to pull himself down the seven metres to where the reef grew above the bubbler pipe. Thousands of tiny tentacles extruded from the calcified carcasses of their ancestors and greeted Jeje with their usual enthusiasm.

Hey fellas, he thought at them. *What a lousy day to say goodbye, huh?*

He used hand-holds the coral had grown for him to move across the reef to its easternmost edge, and he took water samples as he went. His boss wanted to make sure the phage they had injected into the bubbler feed line was dispersing all the way across the reef. The phage would splice in some genes that should make the coral a little more resilient if and when the slick made it to Tuk.

Gotta make sure you all get a taste, he thought. *Don't want the crude making you sick.*

The coral usually loved the wild currents he stirred up with his gesticulations, but today they were straining to taste the current coming from the North. They were worried for their little ones.

His lungs were starting to burn: He moved back along the reef and ducked into a grotto the coral had grown at his suggestion. Three little pods grew at the centre of the grotto, each pod filled with thousands of coral planulae. He couldn't remember whose idea it had been to grow the pods – his or the coral's – but it had been his idea to sell them. At fifty thousand dollars a pod, how could he refuse? That was enough to get him back to balmy Halifax.

I'll find a safe home for your babies, he thought as he snipped the base of each pod and placed them in his Otter box.

You take care of yourselves, alright? I'll miss ya. He climbed up the anchor line to the surface.

The ice floe had drifted closer, and when Jeje lifted his diving mask, there was no longer any ambiguity: the woman-shaped smudge on the ice wasn't a walrus or a seal or an oil slick. He swore. Tony was supposed meet him after shift, and she promised she'd have the cash for the planulae in hand. One hundred thousand NAU dollars. He could be on a plane tomorrow.

The woman lay on her side, as if she'd fallen asleep on the ice. Five degrees below freezing, and she was out here wearing nothing but overalls. Jeje swore again and started to swim.

When he pulled himself up onto the ice, her face was the same deep blue as the ocean below. It took him a second to realize he'd seen a much less blue version of that face plastered across all the news sites reporting on the spill. *You're supposed to be dead.* He pushed his fingertips into the frozen skin of her wrist like he'd seen cops do in the movies. *Oh. Maybe you ain't.*

"...is committed to preventing any oil from reaching the coast line. Arctic Energy crews are seeding the affected areas with Petronome, an organism custom-designed by Atrifor to deal with Arctic oil spills. Petronome is a smart-bug that will seek out and metabolize any crude oil in its environment. Petronome will—"

The advertisement had been running on Elvis' music feed all morning, and he was thankful when his phone interrupted it with an incoming alert.

—*Message from Jeje: Need pick-up now. OMG.*

Elvis Jacobson turned his boat around and opened up the throttle. Last time Jeje had sent a text like that, it was because he'd thought the coral were depressed. Turned out one of the calcium and CO_2 bubblers had been blocked, so he hadn't been totally off the mark. This time, though, Elvis feared the kid had found something worse. Smoke darkened the northern sky where the fire boats were still trying to put out the flames on the *Beaufort Endeavour*.

I did the best I could, Anaak, Elvis thought as he steered his boat toward the other end of the reef where he'd left Jeje to collect samples.

He had a good view of the entire nine kilometre expanse of his leasehold as he weaved his way through patches of sea ice. Though there was nothing but neon orange-painted growlers to mark the reef, he could see the shape of the reef below in his mind. Twenty years now he'd been watching it grow, and all it would take was a few days for the oil to kill his livelihood.

Several ships prowled the waters on the northern horizon. Clean-up crews, no doubt, that were dumping the Petronome that Arctic Energy kept blathering about in their advertisements. Elvis worried about that too. From what he'd read, the Petronome was an unknown; neither Arctic Energy nor Atrifor had released anything about the smart-bug they were dumping by the tonne into the ocean. As far as he was concerned, both the oil and the Petronome were a threat to his reef.

I'm leaving everything to you. His Anaak's words came back to him as he reached the mid-point of the reef. *Do something smart with it or I'll haunt you until the day you die.*

He'd thought about going South, like his parents had done, but Anaak had raised him here. Going South didn't seem right. His cousin Randy had purchased a leasehold near Katovik and loved to brag about all the money he got for growing carbon-fixing coral, so Elvis had done the same. The first few years had been good. They were always growing new methane collection systems out in the permasludge back then, and the generating stations where they burned the methane for power were paying good money to capture their waste carbon. But Klomad's licensing fees for their custom coral kept going up, faster than Elvis could bid on more capture contracts. Then the winter ice started coming back a few years ago and he had to buy an upgrade from Klomad to further modify the coral so they could withstand months under the ice. Now he could barely afford to pay the kid.

He hated to admit it, but a small part of him hoped the oil would ravage his reef. The lawsuit would take years, sure, but they'd give him a big payout and he could retire. Go South. Anaak would understand, wouldn't she? He'd stayed long enough.

He could see Jeje on a big slab of pack ice now. The kid was kneeling over the prone shape of a woman lying on the ice. That was odd, but it meant the kid wasn't worried about oil. His reef was safe, just in time for another licensing payment. With a mixture of relief and disappointment, he pulled up along the ice.

"She alive?" he shouted. He tossed the kid a tow line.

"Think so," Jeje said. The kid pulled the boat and the ice floe together.

The woman's skin was blue, her hair looked like seaweed, and her coveralls were frosted with ice. If she was alive, it was a miracle.

"Tie the line under her arms," Elvis said. "And we'll haul her into the boat."

Jeje tied her off. He was good with knots and with the coral. Really, the kid was good with anything that didn't involve talking to other people. Elvis liked that about him. They worked in silence as they tugged and pushed the woman to get her into the boat.

Elvis found an irregular pulse at her neck.

"She's breathing too," Jeje said as he climbed over the gunnel.

"We gotta get her out of those clothes," Elvis said. The kid swallowed hard, the brown skin at his cheeks darkening. "Don't be modest, kid. She'll die if we don't warm her up."

They dragged her into the boat's small cabin. He dug out an old survival suit, blankets and some chemical heating pads, then the two of them peeled the woman out of her coveralls. It was like peeling the clothes off a corpse. The coveralls were burned and torn along her left side, as were the long underwear she wore beneath the coveralls. When they stripped her out of the long underwear, Elvis found the kid staring at her, his eyes wide.

"Never seen a pair of tits before?"

Jeje shook his head and pointed to the skin on the left side of her body. "It healed."

While the rest of her was shades of blue, the skin along her left arm and most of her left side was pinkish and raised, like road rash that had three weeks to heal. Jeje pushed back the damp hair from the left side of her face and there was more of the weird healing skin there too.

"Three days," the kid said.

"Three days what?" Elvis said as he pulled the survival suit over her legs.

"She's been in the water for three days," the kid said. He slid the woman's arms into the suit. "Don't you recognize her?"

Elvis looked at the woman's face as he zipped her up, and sure, she looked kind of familiar, but he couldn't place her.

"The engineer that ran the *Beaufort Endeavour*," the kid said. Jeje packed the heating pads under her armpits. "Marion Lombardo, that's her name."

"Didn't the news say she died in the explosion?"

"If she did, she got better."

Elvis wasn't sure if the kid was joking. He never could tell with anyone under twenty-five, it was like they were a different species. They propped Marion's head up with a life jacket. She still looked dead, despite the slight flare of her nostrils and the bumpy skin along the left side of her face.

"We better call the coast guard," Elvis said.

Elvis reached for the radio. The woman moved faster. Her fingers were ice claws on his wrist, and her eyes were clouded, like Anaak's in the last few years before the cancer took her.

Marion spoke with the voice of a drowned man: "No."

Thirsty, so damn thirsty. Marion downed the bottle of water the older of the two men offered her but it did nothing to slake her thirst. The water sat heavy in her gut and after a moment she spat it all up. That worried the men. The older one looked ready to go for the radio again.

"No coast guard," she said. "No cops."

"You're sick," he said. "We need to call someone."

She shook her head. "I'm alright. I just need to warm up. Please."

The two men looked at each other, confusion plain on their faces. She could understand that. She was confused about so many things, but she knew that the authorities could not get involved. If they did, they would try to stop her.

"Give me a minute, okay?" she said as she leaned back against the life jackets. The older of the two led the younger man back out onto the deck.

She waited until the two men were deep in conversation before she started to move. The boat smelled so good. There had to be something she could drink in here. As she looked for anything to quench her thirst, she disconnected the radio the older man had been trying to use to contact the coast guard, and when she was sure he wasn't watching, she grabbed the phone in the glove box and the back-up battery for the radio and dropped them both out a porthole. The younger one probably had a phone on him; she'd have to get rid of that as well. She'd seen him tapping on something when he'd found her on the ice.

The ice. Marion looked down at her hands, and when she did, memory overwhelmed her. She tumbled into the seat behind the steering wheel.

The sea ice had been thicker than anyone expected. All those years capturing carbon and reducing emissions had finally brought ice back to the Beaufort Sea, and the ice had laid siege to her rig. Alarms rang in her memory – high pressure in the suction line, temperature alarms across the rig – and anything they did only seemed to make it worse. The sound was so awful. She was supposed to be at her daughter's birthday party back in Kitchener, but she'd put off going home to deal with the ice. She'd always hated the sound of children's parties, but the alarms were worse. Then the explosion. She was flying through the air. No, not flying. *I'm falling. And I'm on fire.* Flames consumed her left arm from fingertips to elbow. *Minnie's birthday party. Blow me out, Minnie. Blow me out.*

Then she'd awoken on the ice with this terrible thirst. The fall should have killed her, let alone the burns or the ice-cold sea, yet here she was. She remembered the years of crystalline ambition and hard work that had led to the engineer's position on the *Beaufort Endeavour*, but those memories were like watching a film of someone else's life. She had other memories too, disjointed sensations: the taste of blue, the urge to split, the relief of death. But that too belonged to someone else. The sound of alarms, the hot shame of missing her daughter's birthday, even questions surrounding what should have been her death, all of it paled compared to her thirst.

Her nose found it for her. The bottle sat in a milk crate with several other plastic containers. She unscrewed the lid and drank. The taste made her gag but she forced herself to keep drinking. As she swallowed the final drops, for a brief second her thirst was satiated. With a new clarity of mind, she looked back over at the men on deck. The older of the two was still gesturing at her, then at the line of orange buoys out on the water, while the younger one seemed preoccupied with a yellow Otter box that hung from the belt of his dry suit. He kept touching it, like he had to reassure himself it was still there.

Killing them wouldn't be hard. The old her, the one who remembered Minnie, recoiled in horror at the thought. *You wouldn't dare.* The new her ignored the revulsion. She needed their boat to get to the next rig. The older man wouldn't let her take it without a fight. One quick shove and the ocean would take care of him. The younger man didn't care about the boat, but she couldn't get a good read on him. This kind of analysis was new to her. Before the explosion, she'd bent her mind to the task of how to most efficiently pump oil from its hiding places deep in the Earth. The new her had to master a different calculus, and the young man was an unknown variable. Best to bludgeon him to death with the gaff hook to take him out of the equation.

Her thirst came back with a vengeance. She found another bottle, this one had a different taste but provided the same sense of satiation. She was chugging it when the older man came back into the cabin.

"Jesus Christ," he said. "You're drinking gasoline."

Jeje wished the coral could talk to him up here. They would know what to do.

Gasoline ran out the corners of Marion Lombardo's mouth. She lowered the jerry can, a look of total amazement on her face that Jeje didn't buy for one second. He felt like he could almost understand the woman, like he'd felt with the coral before he finally started to understand their gestures, but she still eluded him.

"Gasoline?" she said. She wiped her mouth and looked at the container as if for the first time. "Oh my God."

She fainted to the floor. Elvis ran over to her. "Coast guard," he said to Jeje. "Now."

Jeje tried the radio but the power line was cut and the back-up batteries were missing. Elvis' phone wasn't in the glove box either. That meant using his phone. Shit. He didn't have a voice plan – too expensive – and a call to the coast guard would put him back several dollars.

"What's the hold up?" Elvis said.

"Your radio is busted," Jeje said. "And I can't find your phone."

The woman moaned and tried to sit.

"Lady," Elvis said. "I think we need to make you throw up." He turned back to Jeje. "I used the phone two minutes ago when you messaged me. It's in the glove box."

Jeje looked over at the woman. Marion stared up at him with her cloudy eyes. *That's how you know a person,* Jeje's father had said when the deputies came to deport him. *The eyes let you look deep into a person. Not to their soul – there's no such damn thing – but past all the bullshit we wear to hide our true selves.* A thin film sat between Marion's true self and the outside world, but those eyes were staring at the phone in its dry bag strapped to Jeje's wrist.

"She chucked your phone," Jeje said. He held up the cut power cable on the radio. "And she cut the radio."

Elvis blinked in confusion. Jeje liked his boss, Elvis was kind and generous as he could afford to be, but the man could be slow at times. Too slow. The woman lunged for the gaff hook hanging on the wall. Jeje grabbed his boss and hauled the big man away from the woman as she spun around, the gaff held like a baseball bat.

"What the hell?" Elvis managed as Jeje threw him to the deck. The woman lunged at them.

Jeje slammed the cabin door shut and locked it from the outside. She screamed at them from within, then hammered the door with the butt end of the gaff.

"What's wrong with her?" Elvis said. He got to one knee as the woman smashed out one of the tiny windows in the door. She tried to crawl through the too-small opening. "Call the cops, Jeje. Now."

Jeje looked down at the phone strapped to his wrist.

"I'll pay for the call," Elvis screamed.

Jeje took the phone out of its case and flicked it on. Tony's message waited for him: *Got the goods?*

"Hold on," Marion said. She'd cut her forearm trying to get through the window and viscous pink liquid seeped from the wound. "Please, I'm not myself." She looked ready to weep. "Something happened to me after the rig exploded. I don't want to hurt anyone."

Elvis didn't look convinced. "That may be the case, but we're still gonna call the cops." He looked over at Jeje and gave him the nod.

Jeje brought up his dial pad.

"What's in the Otter box?" Marion said.

Jeje felt his mouth go dry. The coral would know, he was certain. They would feel that their planulae were in danger. "She's crazy."

"He's been protecting that thing ever since he found me," Marion said. "Why's it so important?"

Elvis looked skeptical. "What's she talking about, Jeje?"

Jeje wanted to retract into the calcified carcass of an ancestor. Elvis wasn't supposed to know about the planulae pods. "Nothing, Elvis. She's crazy."

"Elvis," Marion said. "If there's nothing in the box, why won't he show it to you?"

The big man shook his head. "I don't know what the hell is going on here, but I think I oughtta know what is in the box."

Jeje fought back tears. He put his hand to his mouth to try to stop himself from talking, but it was no use. The coral below must be shuddering in disappointment. "The coral wanted me to do it," he said in a whisper. "They wanted their babies to be free."

"Oh Christ no," Elvis said. "You're stealing from Klomad?"

"Coral want to colonize," he said. He edged closer to the side of the boat. He wouldn't be able to get the life raft out before Elvis could stop him, but he could swim. It wasn't that far to land. "How could I deny them their most basic urge?"

"Fuck that," Elvis said. "You're not stealing them out of the goodness of your heart. How much you getting?"

His buttocks bumped against the edge of the boat. Thirty minutes of swimming, forty max. There was no way Elvis would leave his boat in the hands of this crazy woman. He could swim back to shore, get Tony the planulae and be on a plane back to Halifax tomorrow morning. But Elvis had been good to him all these years. Jeje could make him understand, if only he could explain it right.

"Fifty thousand per pod," he said. "But I'm only gonna sell two. The third I'm gonna raise back home."

"Know what Klomad will do if they catch you?" Elvis was moving closer, like he knew what Jeje was planning. "Selling their proprietary organisms will land you in one of their private prisons. Jesus, Jeje. You've been living under my roof for three years. You know better than this."

The water below the boat was dark. He didn't have his hood up, the first dunk into the Arctic Ocean would be awful.

"Give me the box," Elvis said. The big man put out his hand. "I'll get rid of them, pretend this never happened."

Jeje cradled the Otter box. "I've got a buyer. I don't know what she'll do if I don't have the product."

Elvis went for the Otter box. Jeje tried to fight him off, but Elvis was twice his size, all muscle and instinct honed over a lifetime on the permasludge. "Give it to me, boy. Now." He tore the box off Jeje's belt.

The boat pitched beneath them. Jeje was already off-balance, and his feet slid out from under him, the grey-blue sky inverted, and he fell toward the Arctic waters.

Elvis caught the kid by the ankle as he was tumbling over the gunnel. The kid's head dunked in the water and the drag nearly pulled them both in, but Elvis wedged his knees under the rail and hauled with all his strength.

"Ungrateful little puke," Elvis shouted as he tossed the kid onto the deck. Jeje lay sputtering, seawater pouring out of his nose.

Elvis would deal with the kid later. First he had to deal with the woman sitting in his seat, piloting his boat. She'd tried to toss them both into the ocean with that little manoeuvre. The anger that took him then had been buried for decades. He was thirteen again and his parents were explaining how they were gonna move South to make money that they promised they would send home, but never did. *Anaak will take care of you now.* His blood was liquid fire, his fists granite. His inheritance had bought him the boat; he'd be damned if this woman would take it away from him.

He flicked open the latch and shoved the cabin door, but it didn't budge. She'd wedged the gaff into the jam. Elvis reached through the shattered window to tug the gaff free but she moved faster. She cut at him with his filleting knife. He felt a sting at his right wrist and the knife flicked away, a smear of crimson along its honed edge.

"Stick your hand in here again and I'll chop it off," Marion said. She went back to the wheel.

"You're gonna pay for this, lady," Elvis said, but his voice sounded hollow. The old anger was already seeping out of him. She kept jerking the boat from side to side to keep them off balance. That had to be what was making him lightheaded.

"Oh no," Jeje yelled. "No, no, no."

The kid was scrambling around the deck, looking for his Otter box no doubt. "It went overboard when you did," Elvis said. He sat on the deck to try to get his sea legs back. "Keep pissing me off and I might chuck you in after it."

Jeje shook his head. "Not the box. My phone. I was holding it when I went over." Terror twisted his mouth into a trembling rictus. "We're all alone out here."

The last of the fury drained out of Elvis. He had lived off rage for years, it had kept him up at night and woke him up in the morning, but it had hollowed him out. The past twenty years without it had almost been enough to fill him up again.

"We're not alone," Elvis said. He forced himself to breathe. Three years he'd housed and employed the kid. Sure the kid had made a mistake, but hadn't he made his fair share of dumb moves at that age? "We got each other."

"She's taking us out into the open ocean," Jeje said.

Elvis' vision was a little spotty and cold sweat poured down his neck, but he still knew where they were headed. Tuk crouched on the coastline between the deflated bulk of the pingos that Anaak claimed used to guard the bay. They were heading toward the dark smear of smoke from the still-burning *Beaufort Endeavour*.

Elvis' guts roiled. He hadn't been sea-sick since his first year growing coral. What the hell was wrong with him?

"You're bleeding pretty bad," Jeje said. The kid was looking at Elvis' arm where the woman had sliced him. It had only been a little cut, he thought. Elvis pressed his fingers to it and was surprised when they came away dripping.

"Holy shit."

Jeje shook his head, and pointed into the cabin. "There's a first-aid kit in there. We just gotta get in."

"She'll slice you to ribbons, kid," Elvis said. "No way you can get in there."

"Maybe I can get her to come out."

Elvis pressed his hand to the wound. He had to stop the bleeding or he really might pass out. Then it would just be the kid alone with that woman, and the kid didn't stand a chance. He tried to get his belt off to tie off his wrist but his hands were too slick with blood.

The roar of the motor cut out. Jeje stood over the outboard motor with the disconnected fuel line in one hand. "Now she's gotta talk."

The cabin door burst open. Marion walked onto the deck, gaff hook in one hand and a bottle of lubricant oil in the other.

"Take it easy," Jeje said, his voice trembling.

"Reconnect that line," she said. She took a long pull of the oil, then gestured at Elvis with the gaff. "Or I'll put this hook through his skull."

"Listen to the lady, Jeje," Elvis said. An awful taste filled his mouth, like that medicine Anaak had given him when he came down with scarlet fever in the eleventh grade.

Jeje hesitated beside the motor. He was fiddling with it, but Elvis' vision was swimming too much for him to see what the kid was doing. "Put the gaff down," Jeje said. "Or the motor's going to the bottom of the sea."

The clamp on the motor's mounting bracket: the kid has loosened it right off.

"Not bad, kid," Elvis said. His words were slurring. Blood welled up between the fingers clamped to his wrist, and no matter how tight he squeezed, it wouldn't stop. "Not bad."

Elvis wanted to say more, but his mouth was too dry. He was losing it. Shit, he was going to leave the kid alone with this cloudy-eyed wacko. *I'm sorry, kid*, he tried to say. *So sorry*.

◦◦◦

The older one's head hit the deck with a wet thump. Marion stepped over him and moved closer to the younger man who trembled beside the disabled motor.

"I ain't kidding," the younger one said. "Take another step, and I'll strand us here."

"Do that and your friend will die. He's already lost too much blood."

The younger one's hands shook. "Listen," he said, his voice shaking as much as his hands. "We gotta talk this out or we're all gonna regret it. Why do you want this boat so bad?"

Listen, said the her who should be dead. *You don't need to hurt anyone else.* But the thirst was still strong. *Talk to him,* the dead her implored. Why not? she thought. It would buy her some time. She lowered the gaff.

"I need to get to the next rig."

"The next oil rig? Which one? The *Beifang Dipinxian*? *Hercules 22*?"

"*Beifang*. Then *Hercules*."

"Are you going to blow them up too?"

"Blow them up?" Marion said. And she started to laugh. The sensation was a novel delight. "No. I didn't blow up the *Beaufort*: I was born from its ashes. You wouldn't understand what I plan to do with the *Beifang*."

The younger one held her gaze. His eyes were a dark brown set deep in his thin face and they didn't blink. Like he was looking into her. Understanding changed his expression from fear to wonder. "You want to feed."

Her thirst was still there and the smell from the fuel line the young one held in his hands was enough to make her salivate. "Not the way you think."

His excitement grew. "The most basic urge. Just like the coral, but you aren't coral. You're something else."

"I remember being less than I am now," she said. He wanted to come closer to her, she could see it in his expression. *Keep talking to him,* the old her insisted. *He just wants to know you.*

"The Petronome," he said. "Artificial protists created to metabolize crude oil. They are what healed you, right? They are what changed you. You're a hybrid."

The older her was drowning again beneath the ocean of her thirst, but Marion needed her now. Can we trust him? *We can try.*

"I'm thirsty," she said. She tossed the gaff hook into the water. "Now will you let me slake my thirst?"

He shook his thin head and gestured past Marion. She had forgotten about the old one: why bother thinking about something that was almost a corpse? "You can heal him," the young one said. "The same way you healed, well, yourself."

Her hand had been on fire and now it was almost whole. The parts of her that were many recalled the metabolic pathways they had hijacked to seal up her wounds: the old one's injuries were trivial by comparison. "Healing him will change him."

"He'll die if you don't," Jeje said. "We'll take the life raft and you can have the boat."

She could still kill him. *Why risk losing the motor?* The old her whispered from her tomb. *Give him this and no one else need die.* No, she thought to herself. Give him this and we will live in the old one too.

She sliced open her left arm at the wrist. Pink fluid dripped onto the wound the older one still clutched with his unthinking fingers. While a thin strand of fluid connected the man's wound to her arm, she knew the man's pain. She heard a name – Anaak – and she felt an old, ashen fury. When that viscous line of liquid severed, she lost contact with him, but she knew a part of her lived on within him.

"It will take some time for him to come around," she said. She pointed the knife at the motor's mounting bracket. "Will you re-attach my motor?"

The young one went to work, though he never took his eyes off her. The dead her was quiet in her grave. Once she had the motor idling again, she helped him lower the unconscious older one into the self-inflating raft that the young one ejected into the water beside the boat, then she helped him down into it.

He held onto her wrist after he'd stepped into the raft. His eyes were full of wonder. "You really are new."

She shrugged him off. "He's going to be thirsty when he wakes up."

She went back into the cabin. In seconds, the life raft was a tiny spot on the water behind her. She emptied a spray can of WD-40 into her mouth, and in the calm after drinking, the roar of the motor and the splash of icy water against the hull seemed incredibly quiet. For a moment, she wished for the mechanical quiet to be replaced by the sounds of a children's birthday party. It wasn't the dead her wishing it: this was the new her. The real her. More than anything, she wanted to hear children laughing.

It didn't last long. Soon, there was only the thirst.

REPORT ON THE OUTBREAKS

EXCERPTS FROM THE DRAFT SHORT REPORT TO THE UNITED NATIONS FRAMEWORK CONVENTION ON CLIMATE CHANGE (CONTINUING EMERGENCY AD HOC PLANETARY GOVERNING COUNCIL CONCERNING THE EVENTS OF JANUARY 2060 AND AFTER)

PETER TIMMERMAN

· This Report is in part intended to determine whether the events of January 2060 and after as so widely reported were the result of a long-considered conspiracy – planned and carried out across the Earth in synchronicity – or simply the manifestation of a primal sense of outrage. There is historical precedent (see Subsection 3.B) for some of these actions. As will be suggested at various points, the initial events appear to have been spontaneous; but at some point in the unfolding of the response (see 4.C for Events Reconstruction) at least one form of organization developed to fund and support ongoing activities (see in particular Appendix 1). It is further suggested that this organization or others in some form of emerging global network could potentially pose a significant threat to the Council as the recognized governing body during the current Ruination. In the final Conclusion (Section 6) recommendations to the UNFCCCCEAHPGC will be set out.

* * *

3.B. Historical Precedent

Among previous examples in the Anglo-Saxon tradition, reference is usually made to the heretic British preacher, John Wyclif. Wyclif died in 1384, and was declared a heretic in 1415 at the Council of Constance. After this declaration was confirmed by Pope Martin V, Wyclif's remains were removed in 1428 from consecrated ground, burned, and his ashes subsequently thrown into the River Swift. In September 1658, Oliver Cromwell, the Lord Protector of England during the short-lived Commonwealth died, and upon the return of King Charles II from exile, the new Parliament in 1661 ordered that, on the 12th anniversary of the execution of King Charles I, Cromwell's body and the bodies of others of his party were to be exhumed and posthumously executed. Cromwell's corpse was dug up, hung in chains on Tyburn tree "from morning to four o'clock in the afternoon," and then his head was severed with eight blows. The dismembered body was mutilated further, and thrown into a pit. His head was put on a 20-foot pole and raised above Westminster Hall outside of Parliament, to be pecked at by the birds of the sky. It remained there until at least 1685 when it was pulled down and eventually disappeared. A somewhat related example involves William Burke, the notorious body snatcher of the 19th century, who with his colleague William Hare stole at least 15 corpses and delivered them for dissection to a Dr. Knox of Edinburgh. After his capture and conviction, Burke was executed. Public pressure, including a riot by 2,000 medical students and citizens of Edinburgh, led to him being himself dissected, and his dissected corpse was placed on public show. At least 40,000 citizens of Edinburgh came to view the corpse. Subsequently, his skin was tanned, and made into wallets and tobacco pouches (at a shilling an inch). Other nations and cultures have had similar examples of...

* * *

4.C. Events Reconstruction

The initial precipitating event appears to have occurred in Canada. According to at least two eyewitnesses (one of whom was a participant), late in the evening of New Year's Day, 2060, a substantial crowd (referred to alternatively as a "gleeful, drunken mob" or "a resolute body of citizens") marched en masse to a cemetery on the outskirts of what was until recently the city of Edmonton, and proceeded to dig up the body of Stephen Harper, who was the Prime Minister of Canada in the early years of the Lost Time (his tenure lasted from the early 2000s to 2015). His body was then subject to various forms of mutilation, and then hung from a nearby tree (this part of the event appears to have been unplanned, as a rope had to be obtained, which caused a brief delay in the proceedings), and various other outrages were then perpetrated on his body, including the dangling of a sign from his neck stating (and here reports vary again) either "F_____ OIL SLAVE" or "THE REVENGE OF THE F___ED FUTURE." There is no information on the final disposition of his remains. It is known that in subsequent weeks similar outrages were perpetrated on deceased members of the following groups: oil and gas executives; members of the Canadian

Parliament from the same period of the early 2000s; paid scientists of various lobby groups of the period; and several journalists and editors for certain newspapers and magazines of the period. These desecrations were often accompanied by related slogans such as "JE ME SOUVIENS," "CURSING YOUR MEMORY" and "YOUR OWN CHILDREN AND GRANDCHILDREN CURSE YOUR MEMORY." These actions seem to have generated immediate copycat equivalents in the United States of America, beginning with the gravesites of figures who played important roles as climate deniers and obstructionists during the late-lamented Lost Time, including previously esteemed members of Congress, the Senate, Justices of the Supreme Court, and a loose President or two. It can be confirmed that many of the desecrations took place in sites in parts of what used to be the southwestern United States, though reports from the area are scattered, given the regional consequences of the Ruination. It is known that a seemingly spontaneous movement called "the Trek of Tears" gathered in what is now New Texas and walked south for weeks through the empty desert of Old Texas, and then, upon reaching the ruins of Dallas, proceeded to burn the now abandoned George W. Bush Presidential Center and Library to the ground. The parties to the events then proceeded en masse to the derelict Bush farm in what used to be Crawford, Old Texas, and after sacking and burning everything remaining on that site, sowed the ground with salt.

A month later, a related group embarked on a second "Trek of Tears" from New Oklahoma into Old Oklahoma, and similar damage was done to the gravesite and former family dwellings of the late Senator James Inhofe, once the ranking member of the United States Senate on Environment and Public Works, famous for his obstructionist tactics and promoter of the concept of the "climate hoax." The remains of other figures from the Lost Time across America were also targeted and various sacrileges perpetrated on their memories, particularly the resting places of previously well-known lobbyists and fellow-travellers such as the Global Climate Coalition, Randy Randol, Scott Pruitt and the Dobriansky sisters. Companies and organizations such as the American Petroleum Institute, the Western Fuels Association, the Center for the Defense of Free Enterprise, the Committee for a Constructive Tomorrow and the Competitive Enterprise Institute were also attacked, whether still functioning or defunct. Finally, the bodies of so-called scientists, such as Fred Singer who had denied climate change, were dug up and dragged through the streets of their university towns in a suddenly popular ritual immediately dubbed "Climate Hazing." Throughout all of these cited incidents a mixture of mourning and celebration was evident.

In certain other countries, similar rituals were carried out. To mention just one, in what is left of Australia, a previous prime minister, Tony Abbott, was exhumed and, according to one local report, was boiled and subsequently burned to a crisp in what was referred to as an "oversized billy" labelled "WHAT HE DID TO AUSTRALIA," and finally thrown into the ocean so that he resembled "a Bondi cigar" (reference obscure). Other members of other nations, particularly those with extensive histories of continuing fossil fuel mining, refining, and export, especially during the brief so-called Adaptation Era prior to the onset of the Ruination, have also been targets. The various global and regional Corporations involved in these processes have already been the detailed subject of the most recent Climate Crimes Tribunal Reports available to the Emergency Council, and to keep this Report within reasonable bounds only a list of the related so-called "retroactive retribution" incidents since January 2060 is to be found in Appendix VI.

* * *

5.B. Ongoing Investigation
It is clear that at some point in the outrages significant organizational expertise began to be deployed in the service of these outrages, including the provision of lists of what are colloquially referred to as FCDFFs ("F_____ Climate Denying Earth-F_____ing F_____ers").

These began to be assembled and distributed both clandestinely and openly in various jurisdictions. The lists included maps and locations of cemeteries, gravesites, statues, and archives; quotations from offensive statements in Parliament, Congress, and the popular presses of the period; and thousands of copies of the well-known Lost Time Charts that map the relationship between delay times (as connected to each FCDFF wherever possible) and significant current data sets, including the 2060 level of greenhouse gas emissions in the atmosphere, current global temperature readings, and current mean sea-level (MSL) trends as measured by tidal gauges (see Figure 1 in Appendix 7). Much of the general information was certainly publicly available, but extensive and intensive research was carried out by persons and/or groups unknown on individual targets. Here and in subsection 4.C reference is made to "targets."

Significant effort was made for this Report to determine if there was a databank of targets being generated or already existent, but no such databank has been located. Again, it is not clear if the lists of persons to be exhumed and subjected to "retroactive retribution" were internally generated by individuals who took matters into their own hands in the face of the ongoing Ruination; or were assisted by guiding networks and organizations. At some point in the evolution of the desire to "not let the past off the hook" (in the words of one informant), it does seem plausible that an emergent structure built on the original forms of angry determination has appeared. In this regard, it has been definitely established that at least one organization openly claims a significant role in the more recent events discussed in this Report, especially as concerns funding. In Appendix I, an excerpt from a special clandestine interview with the leader of this organization known as "Sins of the Father" is presented to the Governing Council. It is the considered opinion of the author of this Report that the Council should be urgently apprised of its contents.

* * *

Section 6. Conclusions (to follow).

APPENDIX I:

Recorded Interview: "Sins of the Father" (excerpt)

As a supplement to this report a clandestine interview, following a certain amount of effort, was conducted with the leader of the terrorist group known as "Sins of the Father." Cordelia Koch is a well-known spokesperson for SOTF, the organisation believed to be funding many of the more recent activities outlined in this Report on a grand scale. The place and time of the interview have been withheld.

INTERVIEWER: "Could you explain the aims and goals of your organization?"

CORDELIA KOCH: "Easy. During the Submergencies, we, the children and now the grandchildren of the obscenely rich, initiated SOTF. A group of us were sitting around well inland in some stupid mansion clipping coupons and the usual waste of shit, and I forget who it was but someone said, 'Isn't it interesting that our parents were so insanely obsessed with all those trust funds and estate tax avoidance – I mean there were thousands and thousands of people devoted to this – designed to provide their children and grandchildren with pots of money in their futures, but they were unprepared to spend any of that money to give any of us a planet to spend it on? How f____ insane were they?' And that was the catalyst. We looked out at the Ruination and at ourselves and someone brought us the reports from what was happening in Canada, and we got excited and decided, 'Wow, f____ yes, us too!!!' So, we started. That's how we started. We gathered piles of our rotten ill-gotten gains together and we got organized and now we support all these activities involving serious pissing on the tombs of our beloved ancestors. It's the least we can do, we think. Also, it's a f____ blast."

INTERVIEWER: "You have been accused of terrorism. How do you react?"

CORDELIA KOCH: "At least we aren't meta-terrorists. Governments and others who invoke terrorism in order to achieve a greater terrorism. The Ruination of Earth is ontological terrorism. They were the ones that created the Maldivian Panic and the Methanogenetic Episodes at the outbreak of the Ruination. Everyone else is a bunch of sad f____ers. I mean, look at all those Martians and Muskovites* and the rest of those insanely stupid Cargo Cults. Anyway. Our parents are gone, but their money lingers on, and we are doing our best to repair, reparate their monumental idiocy through vengeance. Did these dead f_____ers think they were going to get off scot-free? And you're in our sights, let me be clear. Not you, you're just a whatever it is you are. What are you anyway?"

INTERVIEWER: "As I said to your guards, I'm writing a report to the Emergency Council about what happened. Piecing it together."

CORDELIA KOCH: "You want to know if we started it."

INTERVIEWER: "That's part—"

CORDELIA KOCH: "Well, we didn't. Those dead F_____ Climate Denying Earth-F_____ing F_____ers started it. That's why I'm allowing this interview, so you can tell your masters. We didn't start it, and we don't control it, but we are happily along for the vengeance ride, you can tell them that."

INTERVIEWER: "Do you have demands?"

CORDELIA KOCH: "Our two demands have been ignored."

INTERVIEWER: "Which were?"

CORDELIA KOCH: "Oh, I thought you knew. Simple. One, a global 'Truth and Vengeance' Commission. And two, we demand of the International Geological Community that this era be referred to in the future as 'The Obscene.'"

INTERVIEWER: "Are you making a joke?"

CORDELIA KOCH: "Yes, haven't you heard? That's what spoiled rich kids do. F____ people around. Your time is up. Out."

INTERVIEWER: "Okay, okay. Thank you for this interview."

CORDELIA KOCH: "Hey, wait, wait, I have one more thing for you to deliver to your masters. Poetry. Ever read any Shakespeare? You've heard of Shakespeare. Wait, give me a second. [At this point she retrieved an old book from a wall library.] Here you go. Henry 6, part 3: 'Had I thy brethren here, their lives and thine were not revenge sufficient for me; No, if I digg'd up thy forefathers' graves and hung their rotten coffins up in chains, It could not slake mine ire, nor ease my heart. The sight of any of the house of York is as a fury to torment my soul; And till I root out their accursed line And leave not one alive, I live in hell.' Now get the f___ out of here."

*Note: these are colloquial and derogatory terms for the new religious believers who have been clustered around abandoned missile sites since the 2030s in the now vain hope of escaping the Earth. They expect a "technorapture" which will enable them to magically levitate to distant worlds and begin the process of seeding the cosmos with humans.

AFTER

JOHN OUGHTON

Voices in the ether… a child crying, a man shouting in some Central European language I don't understand. A woman with a throaty voice and out-of-tune acoustic guitar performing the Doors' "This Is the End" over and over. A man ranting in what sounds like Zulu, with tongue-clicks. A Pentecostal alternating speaking in tongues with imploring any of his sect still alive to contact him. A harsh-voiced woman, a Christer, warning everyone to stay away from their compound, whose location she doesn't specify. "We have lots of guns and ammo. We are the Chosen of the Lord. If you mess with us, we will give you mercy, right through the head. What's ours is not yours…"

Christers, Coasties, Woodmen. Caesar once wrote that all Gaul was divided into three parts, and what's left of North America, galling as it is, follows the same pattern. Before you, unknown and putative reader, demand to know which particular bias has shaped my patchwork history, I will reveal all.

I am a Woodman. Of course, women are just as important in our scattered society as the males, but somehow "Woodpeople" never survived the slang test the way Woodmen did.

I digress. But digression no longer matters, because there often seems no way forward, no clear channel to the future. You can't waste time when time is all we have left. There is only making do, hanging in there, coping. And, now that my allegiance is laid out on the floor like an unrolled tongue, I can say it: Woodmen are good at coping.

All right. Where are we then, humans as a whole? Ironic to say that, because if humans had considered their activities and populations as part of the planetary whole, we wouldn't be in our current position(s). I can't say "fix" because most of civilization is not fixed, but badly broken. Busted, kaput, washed away.

Perhaps... I find it hard to position my prose, to know where to start, a problem endemic in a decaying world, where so much seems to be finishing... I should begin with where I and my Woodmen family of thirty are. We are on a hillside in a boreal forest somewhere in what used to be Canada. I won't get more precise than that, because, I am going to share this, when and if I figure out how to write it, and I don't want my current or future associates to be bothered by those seeking refuge. We get enough of that without fans of the written word – if any remain – adding to the problem.

Pausing, I hear the buzz and shriek of electric chainsaws severing trees into burnable chunks. Despite all the warming, winter nights are still cool here. But cool is one of our treasures up here... Most survivors south of us know only heat, drought, forest and prairie fires, from what I hear. We keep our chainsaws charged with a mix of solar panels, small wind turbines, and a cranky old Honda generator, when we can beg or trade fuel for it.

And now, troublesome audience, I hear you ask, "If things are so deteriorated, how do you hear anything about other places?" Well, I told you Woodmen were adaptable. We have sought out and kept running the only long-distance communication infrastructure that works when most of the copper wires and fibre optics that once threaded the Internet together have long been scavenged or torn apart by encroaching tides and hurricane-force winds.

Yes, short-wave radio. Reception is iffy, often disturbed by storms, solar outbursts, or Lord knows what. But it works enough that we can talk to other parts of the world. Ham radio operators were the precursor to the Net, transmitting music, opinions, news, and sometimes drunken raving over the air. And now that the Net is dead, shortwave rules again.

Right on cue, into the disordered flow of this account breaks the scratchy, static-flavoured voice of Jeremiah over our radio. He's one of the few Christers I can talk to. Oh, he spends a fair amount of bandwidth reading Biblical passages purported to show that these are the End Times, and Jesus will get around to wrapping up our problems in a nice package any day now. He favours the prophets, especially Ezekiel, and the whole Book of Revelations. But in between rants, he sometimes descends from his flaming ladder to talk like a normal person.

"Then I saw 'a new heaven and a new earth,' for the first heaven and the first earth had passed away, and there was no longer any sea…" and he paused, while I could hear him flipping pages looking for another good one. "But the cowardly, the unbelieving, the vile, the murderers, the sexually immoral, those who practise magic arts, the idolaters and all liars – they will be consigned to the fiery lake of burning sulphur. This is the second death."

I interrupted him. "Jeremiah, it's Woodman Mark." He paused and sighed. I was a trial he was willing to put up with, perhaps in the belief that someday he'd convert me to his creed. "The Lord be with you, and all that… Aren't you a bit concerned that Revelations says 'there was no longer any sea' and the sea has eaten every coastal city in the world, and many of the islands too?"

"The ways of the Lord are mysterious, and not always evident to our limited minds," he responded. "But I am assured—"

"Forget it, Jeremiah, I've heard it all before. I can't help but feel that a lot of the Christers have read only the Old Testament. They're big on wrath and vengeance, not so much on loving thy enemy, turning the other cheek, and not judging."

Jeremiah started to sputter, but I cut him off. "Instead of playing the disciple game, let's just be people for a minute. How are you and your family?"

"We endure, Woodman Mark. Our canned supplies are running low, but one of our flock has a good touch with hydroponics. So long as we can still extract water from the ground, we will have food. And I am now a grandfather. My daughter, Faith, has born a son, and they are both well."

"We'll, I'm glad," I said, and meant it. "We may not agree on a lot of things, but so many were lost in the troubles. New life must be welcomed."

"Thank you," he replied. "And we still have enough ammunition to keep the jackals – human and animal – from our door."

My turn to sigh. Christers were remnants of the Bible-belting, proudly gun-owning militia troglodytes that flourished in the US "heartland" and a few parts of Canada. To them, anyone who did not share their beliefs, or had a priority other than bringing the End Times to fruition, were spawn of Satan. "Non-human jackals" refers to one of the sad realities of our time: so many people and animals had died with the warming climate, fast-spreading epidemics that antibiotics couldn't stop, and encroaching oceans. Scavenging species flourished like no others – vultures, sharks, rats, coyotes, foxes.

And the Coasties? They were hardest hit of all. Those who lived in big seaports and along the once-coveted oceanfronts of Florida and California had been decimated, homes and possessions swept away. Only the hardiest and luckiest had survived, trying to eke out a living while nomading around the continent, seeking food and unoccupied homes.

A knock on the door. It was my daughter, Jackie. "Dad, you have to come to council right away! There's strangers at the gate, asking sanctuary." It's been a while since this happened. Our location is relatively inaccessible, and when we venture out to trade or forage, we're careful about not being tracked back to where we live.

"Signing out, Jeremiah," I said, and went to meet the other elders in the tower room of our palisaded enclave. Camouflaged with pine branches, this is where our council meets. The long views its narrow windows afford help our deliberations go further.

I nodded to Prim, our facilitator. We don't use the term "leader" since we govern by consensus and consultation. Leaders, as humanity found to its sorrow, too often are bought out by those with the most money and power.

Prim signalled to Manjeet, our resident electronics geek. She had cobbled together a video surveillance system, complete with remote speaker and microphone, that let us see who was at our gates. She flipped a switch, swatted a recalcitrant component, and an image flickered onto the council room's screen. It was a young couple, he bearded and bulky, she slim. They were stretching after their bumpy ride on a beat-up ATV painted in green and brown camo, its rack and tank loaded down with bags and the carcass of a deer.

"State your name and allegiance," Prim ordered.

"I am Don," a deep voice answered over the scratchy audio, "and this is my partner, Chris. We are Coasties from what was Washington State. We ask sanctuary."

"What skills or gifts do you bring?" Prim continued. "Our resources and space are limited. We cannot afford to admit anyone who does not contribute."

"How do you think we made it all the way from Seattle on this piece-of-shit ATV?" Don asked, adding a grin so we could see he wasn't angry. "I'm a mechanic. I can keep most engines and machines going, and I've traded my skills for gasoline and ammunition to get us here."

"Ammunition?" Prim's voice went up a tone. "Sentries, show yourselves." At the squared-off corners of our front wall, our best shooters stood up, pointing their rifles at the couple. "Now take out your weapons, and lay them down in front of you."

"Relax," Don said. He slowly pulled a rifle from its scabbard on the side of the ATV, and laid it on the ground. "Tell him, Chris."

"We have only the rifle for hunting and self-defence," she said in a clear contralto. "We have not shot anyone in our journey, although we had to threaten a couple of bandits."

"Very commendable," Prim said. "What skills do you bring, young woman?"

"Health and birthing," she said. She rummaged in a bag and slowly drew out a thick medical book and a stethoscope, holding them up. "I can deal with most first-aid situations, and I apprenticed with a midwife for a year before we decided to try our luck inland."

The other elders were nodding. We could use a mechanic and a nurse. Who couldn't?

"Last question," Prim said. "How did you find us?"

Chris looked at Don, then answered. "We kept asking people who trade with others if they knew of any settlement that we might fit into. We heard about your group. No one told us exactly where you are, so we kept exploring. We figured you'd be on high ground, where you could watch out for troublers. Finally last night, with binoculars, we spotted a few lights in your enclave."

Prim nodded, and we elders looked at each other. We were going to have to tighten up our nighttime blackout procedures. Prim surveyed the group, and got enough thumbs-up to take it to the next stage.

"All right," she said into the mike. "Wait there, and the elders will confer. Do you agree to let us hold your weapon while we talk?"

Don and Chris assented, and waited beside their ATV. Our sentries pointed their rifles and ordered Don to back away from his weapon. He did so, and Vince, one of our food growers, collected the rifle.

"I like them," Elder Shayna said. "They seem sane, and we can certainly use the skills they bring… and their vehicle."

The rest agreed, except for one woman, who had a long-standing and well-justified suspicion of large men. "How do we know they won't cut our throats while we sleep?" she asked, scowling. "You can't just take strangers on their word."

"Susan has a point," I said. "How about one month's probation, while they spend their nights in the isolation cabin?"

Prim took a vote, and all but Susan went along with my proposal. "Fine, but I'm sleeping with a knife beside me," she added.

Prim picked up the microphone and offered the new couple the deal. They had a month to prove their skills and ability to cooperate. During that time, they would stay in the cabin built for those who developed infectious diseases or had psychotic outbreaks. Its door locked from the outside. There was a honey bucket for overnight needs. And, of course, they must follow the rules of our group. Everyone works as hard as he or she is capable. No one can hoard food or other supplies. Any disputes – between themselves, or with others – must be taken to the council for mediation. Finally, they let no one outside the group know our location.

Relieved, they agreed. We unbarred the gate and let them in, then introduced them to all members who were not out foraging. Our children stared at them open-mouthed. They don't get to meet many new people, as it's too risky for them to venture far outside the palisade, and not the right era for casual visitors. One shy little girl reached a hand towards Chris's long red hair, fascinated by the first ginger she'd met. "It's all right," Chris said, kneeling to greet her. "You can touch it." Several men gathered around the tired ATV, prodding its tires and debating its usefulness.

I stepped outside, and looked at the dispassionate stars, sending us their illumination from light-years ago, instant replays on the galactic level. Would Don and Chris fit? Could we trust them? I only knew that there's no way forward without risks. I took a big breath, stretched my creaking frame up towards the constellations and went inside. I lay down beside my partner, Anya, and hoped for the best.

It was a good month for Chris, Don, and the group. He got our generator running more smoothly, and found and fixed some short circuits that had been reducing our solar panels' output. He got our old 4X4 truck back on the road... Well, there's hardly a road worthy of the name nearby, but the vehicle was starting and stopping again at the whim of the driver.

Meanwhile, Chris had efficiently repaired some cuts and a broken bone, and helped deliver a healthy girl, the newest member of our group. It was good to hear a baby's cries and happy gurgles again. She also proved to be a good listener and an emotional support to those whose problems were more moral or spiritual than physical. Don didn't say much, but he pulled more than his share of the workload, and his fixer-upper skills were well beyond mine.

The council decided to end the couple's probation. We helped them build their own cabin and they moved their few things in. Life fell into its usual patterns, work parties and projects during the day, family time at night except when we had music or storytelling. Chris and Don mostly kept to themselves in the evening, although Chris had a good clear singing voice, and sometimes joined our impromptu kitchen music efforts. It was summer, and our gardens were producing a bumper crop. We had potatoes, corn and cabbages to store for the winter.

Don and I did have some contact, as the one problem with our location was finding a good supply of fresh water. We had a stream coming down the hillside, but it dried up by midsummer. We recycled and purified water from laundry, dishes and bathing, but we always needed more. One of our tribe, Lynn, decided to try her hand at dowsing; her Y-shaped stick jerked sharply downwards about fifty metres outside the palisade wall.

We had a pump, a stock of seasoned bamboo we had traded some food for a while back, some garden hose and a few boxes of assorted clamps, couplings, taps and spouts. Could we somehow drill a hole to the water, then pump it into our compound? Did we have enough electrical wire – a hot commodity since commercial mines had gone out of business, so copper was scarce – to connect the pump to our generator inside the walls?

With a problem like this, I'd alternate between sketching possible solutions and trying to connect various bits, alternating the two activities until something works. Don's approach was different. He laid all the useful pieces out on open ground, walked around them and thought for a long time, saying nothing, tugging at his beard.

He came up with a scheme I thought brilliant. "The big issue is not getting the water into the compound," he stated. "We've got a pump and enough pipe and couplings to solve that one. It's drilling a hole down to the water, and then keeping it open so it doesn't clog that worries me."

I nodded. Don selected the thickest bamboo sections, and showed me what he had in mind. First, we'd dig down with shovels to get any rocks out of the way. Then we'd carve a point onto the end of the biggest bamboo piece and run garden hose through it, with a connector at the top of the bamboo. We'd use a plumber's wrench to turn the bamboo, and a sledge to lightly tap it into the ground. He thought we'd feel a lessening of resistance when we hit water, and we then could run the pump to see if it sucked up any fluid.

It worked. We had to add a second piece of bamboo on top and use it to drive the first piece deeper, but we found a spring of clear, sweet water. Once we got rid of the worst leaks in our mismatched joints, the worn pump drew enough water to fill the reservoir we'd made of cedar, lined with plastic sheeting. We even filled our standby plastic jugs. Don gravely shook my hand when he finished the project.

I sleep a couple of rooms away from the radio, just in case. We have a few Woodmen friends who alert us to incoming bad weather, or worse, groups of marauders in the area. One night I woke up with a start, as Anya snored lightly beside me. Had I heard quiet voices from the radio room, or had I imagined it? I got up carefully, pulled on my pants and a sweatshirt, put my ear to the door and tiptoed to the radio room. No one was there. The radio was warm to the touch, but it's nearly always left on, that didn't mean anything. I thought I caught a whiff of sweat that wasn't my own. I still wasn't sure whether the voices were dream or reality.

A week later, when I was helping to repair some rotten logs in a friend's cabin, I messed up my thumb. It got caught between two logs that shifted, and some small splinters were driven into it. I could see the result would be a nasty bruise and blood blister, but those I could survive. Infection, however, was a concern. Cradling my wounded digit, I called Chris from the kitchen – it was chili and preserves-making season – and showed her my wound.

She clucked her tongue in concern, and applied a cold pack to lessen the swelling and numb the pain a bit. Then she extracted splinters, bathed my thumb in antiseptic, applied an antibiotic lotion, and bandaged the now-throbbing appendage.

I thanked her, surveying her handiwork, and said, "I'm so glad you and Don have joined us. You add a lot to our little clan."

To my surprise, I saw she was quietly weeping. "How did we come to this?" she asked in a hopeless tone.

"You mean the end of civilization as we knew it? The Internet, art galleries and museums, schools, hospitals, peacekeeping troops, international cooperation? My opinion is the problem was that an economy premised on profit and eternal growth of consumption was bound to crash eventually. The earth just didn't have enough space and resources to support seven-some billion people intent on having a luxury car and a large-screen TV set. And we gave away too much power – or money, the same thing – to big corporations who wanted to make the last possible buck from petrochemical resources, and the hell with consequences. In fact, some of that money went to buy bad science and publics relations flacks to deny global warming was happening, or was important. As a species, humans are pretty good at creating technology with short-term advantages, not so good at predicting future problems from it. Many people were just too misled by religion or ideology to listen to scientists, no matter how many warnings they were given." I stopped, seeing my analysis was not calming her.

"Or is that not what you meant by 'this'?" I asked.

She shook her head, the tears still flowing. I lifted her chin so I could see her eyes, and took her hands as gently as I could, given my oversized, white-plastered thumb. "Tell me."

"I can't keep doing this," she murmured. I wondered if she meant her nurse duties, but this was not the time to interrupt.

She withdrew a hand to wipe her tears, then confessed in a rush, "Don and I lied to you. He's not even my partner. We're just playing a role. We're not Coasties either. We're Christers from Alberta. Our site there is too small and hard to defend from others. We found you by homing in on your shortwave signals, not by asking locals. We're supposed to gain your trust and then help the rest of our group take your place over. Don's already been on the shortwave telling them where you are. They are coming. They've got lots of weapons, and don't like taking prisoners. After all, we're the Lord's Chosen Ones."

Dumbfounded, I stared at her. "So why tell me now?"

"Because our leaders lied to me," she said. "They told us you were degenerate pagans and Satanists, maybe even cannibals. You don't follow the Bible, so you must be evil."

"And we're not?" I asked.

"No, I only see good people helping each other, working hard, loving their children. I see people with different skin colours and religions getting along. You share what you have with each other, and don't abuse anyone."

"How long do we have?" I asked.

"A couple of days, I think," she responded. "Their vehicles are old, and keep breaking down without Don to fix them."

Action time. I thanked Chris for her honesty, and called the sentries to get their guns. We pulled Don away from the water pump he had been oiling, and marched him to the isolation cabin, where we locked him in. He seemed resigned to his fate, no doubt figuring he'd be rescued soon enough. Chris was left free, but someone accompanied her all the time in case she had another change of heart and tried to release Don or use the radio herself.

After a long and intense council meeting, we came to a decision. We couldn't defend our site long with so few rifles and limited ammunition. The attackers could just burn down our wooden walls and get in that way. Fortunately, we had a fallback. Years ago, we had found a large cave above our location. Its opening was small and easy to camouflage. We set up a human chain to move food, water, sleeping stuff, the radio and our smaller generator and storage batteries up there. We disabled the water pump and main generator by removing a couple of key parts that couldn't easily be replaced.

Don was a problem. As much as we could have used his skills, he gave no indication of changing his allegiance. When I tried to persuade him to follow Chris and really join us, he stared defiantly and muttered Bible verses at me. We couldn't leave him alive. He knew too much about our resources and strategies. Nor could we confine him in the cave. Given his strength and mechanical abilities, he'd not stay a prisoner long. I explained all this to him, and passed in his rifle, then one bullet.

"We don't want to kill you," I said, "even though you've lied to us and betrayed us. I'm sure you believe you'll go straight to paradise, but you'll have to open that door yourself." He nodded.

In a few minutes, I heard the shot, then the slump of a heavy body.

And now I'm safe in the cave, with all the others. We wired up our remaining sticks of dynamite around the enclave, and ran buried wires to our cave. The Christers arrived, with threats and cajoling over a bullhorn, then broke down the main gate. I heard shouts of despair and outrage when they found Don's corpse. One fired a quick burst of automatic fire into the air. It wouldn't be long before someone found our cave's opening.

My finger is hovering over the detonation button. Our council was evenly split. Do we blow the invaders up and rebuild our site? It would be a violation of the peaceful way we've managed to live up to now. But if we don't protect the peaceful ones, who will be left to rebuild a new and possibly better civilization? Or do we undertake a difficult and dangerous trek to find another site before winter comes, and let them have our home?

They left the decision to me, since I alone abstained from voting, in doubt about which way was best.

My finger hovers.

WEIGHT OF THE WORLD

HOLLY SCHOFIELD

The edge of the stainless-steel laboratory sink pressed into Gurpreet's distended belly as she forced herself to eat her lunch slowly. Even the nauseating lab smells didn't quell her urge to gulp it down. A wave of dizziness hit her and she sank sideways, rapping one elbow against the counter. Her oatcake flew out of her hand.

After her head cleared, the under-counter cabinet handles gave her enough leverage to ease herself back onto her feet. The oatcake had landed dead centre in a nearby gel tray, splattering gel into the tray next to it. It was already soaking up moisture and turning a dingy grey. She couldn't let food go to waste, not since the Super Winters had started, and certainly not since her pregnancy.

She was holding the sodden lump in her hand when Dr. Mohammad strode in from the clean room. "Eat over the sink. I told you before." He readjusted the elastic band on his grey ponytail and added something rude in Arabic.

She popped the slimy mess in her mouth and licked her lips. "Understood. I'll clean up these two trays in just a moment. And I've prepped all the others. Oh, and we're out of buffering solution."

He grunted as he made a notation on a nearby screen.

No matter how hard she worked, he seemed to think she was still completely unsuitable for the job. She sank into her rickety swivel chair, needing to rest for just a minute. She *was* unsuitable. Her genetics background *did* make her a poor mining lab technician. And a baby the size of a large Thanksgiving turkey in her stomach, and the accompanying constant hunger, were just adding to her poor job performance.

She squeezed her eyes shut and scolded herself. It didn't matter that she was doing work far removed from her genetics post-doc. Dr. Mohammad's trial to extract heavy metals from remote northern marshes was still valuable. If researchers kept chipping away at the world's many problems, they'd solve them. There wasn't any question. Research would be humanity's savior; she *knew* that deep in her bones. The stupid mindlessness that the eighth month of pregnancy had brought had just made her temporarily forget that.

Dr. Mohammad's angry muttering faded away as he headed back into the clean room.

Snow battered against the windows. She opened her eyes and shoved the empty lunch container into her purse, and then spent a moment futilely digging to the bottom for a stray mint or a leftover crumb of oatcake. Her stomach gnawed like a trapped animal. Last night, with Damian tossing restlessly beside her, she'd dreamt of her mother's chicken biryani. Cardamom, garlic, and the almost-forgotten succulent smell of real chicken.

She was suddenly sweating. Cursing her hormone imbalances, she levered herself out of the chair and, careful to avoid the computer cables taped haphazardly across the cracked tile floor, walked to the lab window. Cold glass against her forehead helped a bit. Last night's huge dump of snow still clogged the unplowed streets. Someone, probably homeless, wrapped in a parka and several scarves forged against the January wind through a thigh-high drift, then stopped to rest a mittened hand against the half-buried Western Alberta Research Centre sign.

Seven winters of this hell. Arctic warming had started it all, altering the jet stream, slamming lengthy cold fronts across Canadian prairies, a cascading effect of heavy snowfalls, disastrous spring flooding, and drastically shortened growing seasons.

The person below continued trudging by, one step at a time, until they were out of sight. Their dogged effort made Gurpreet feel guilty; she turned back to the worktable just as the hallway door opened.

Joseph Liew, the Centre's finance director, strode in, tablet in hand. He couldn't be bringing good news. There was never any good news, not anymore. Gurpreet tugged at her frayed lab coat but it wouldn't close over her belly.

"Where's Mohammad?" Joseph avoided her eyes, just as he had last month when he'd told her that her genetic engineering project had been put on permanent hold. He'd blamed the Supreme Court's ruling against any type of genetic modification research. Her research budget had been frozen and her lab door padlocked. 'Allocated but not Assigned,' Joseph had called the fiscal process.

Before she could reply, plastic sheeting swished and Mohammad strode in from the clean room's antechamber. "Liew! What do *you* want?"

Joseph flicked fingers at his tablet, clearly stalling. It must be very bad news. She tried not to dislike the man. At least he'd reassigned her to Dr. Mohammad's lab and accepted her decision to waive maternity leave. With Damian laid off from his construction work until at least June, her Centre minimum-wage pay cheque was the only thing keeping the two of them from joining other Albertans starving in the streets – with the current economy, there were no other research jobs to be had in Canada, the U.S., or even overseas. Unless, of course, she transferred to the Centre's Heavenly Soy project, but that was out of the question.

"Don't shoot the messenger, Ahmed." Joseph put up a hand. "The numbers are telling me—"

"Numbers don't speak." Dr. Mohammad tore off his clean suit and threw it in the lab's trash bin.

Gurpreet started to rise. Maybe the suit could be sterilized and reused if it was retrieved right away. They were down to one last carton of twenty.

"I'll make it quick, then." Joseph rasped a hand over his brush cut. "Your project has been slated for early shut-down."

Gurpreet sat back down with a thump that sent the old chair rocking.

Dr. Mohammad threw his arms up. "I need the full year I'm budgeted for. The year you *committed* to."

"I'm sorry, Ahmed. I don't have to tell you that the board's focus is on reducing the effects of climate change. Retrieving heavy metals using microbes is a low priority compared to inadequate global food security, induced seismicity, and extreme weather events."

Gurpreet put both hands flat on the worktable and pushed herself to her feet. Enough was enough. She'd held herself back too many times. "If you want to fix the food problems, then the government – *all* governments – should lift their GMO bans. *And* the mammalian-piscine stem cell ban. Think how many people we could feed with vat-grown meats. With chicken, beef, even… even pork." She forced herself to stop and take deep breaths. Her little speech had probably been no use, and her Sikh father would be horrified if he was still alive, but she'd had to try even though it made her heart pound. She rubbed her belly to soothe the little person within.

Sure enough, Joseph's only reaction was to suck on a tooth. "I could tell you about fiscal considerations and the risk evaluations the board has—"

"Risk! What do they know of *risk*!" Dr. Mohammad towered over both of them. His face was as red as her own must be. "Science is *about* taking risks! Especially with money!"

Joseph's thin lips tightened further. "I went along with you, Ahmed. When you hired a plane to take you up north, when you incurred extra flight charges for the buckets of mine tailings you brought back, when you demanded the only remaining lab with a clean room—"

Dr. Mohammad snorted. "Risks that *will* pay off, given enough research dollars." He assumed the dry sardonic voice Gurpreet knew he used for his Mining Economics 101 lectures: "If Canada's economy is to recover, it won't be via the energy sector, it'll be manufacturing. And that requires rare earth elements. It's not as if China can supply us given all their own recent climate change problems."

"I'm sure you're right, Ahmed. Nonetheless, we'll be closing you down." Joseph adjusted his tie.

Gurpreet twisted her loose wedding ring around and around. What did "early shut-down" actually mean? This was January. Damian would find work by June at least, when the snowpack would finally melt. All she needed was five months. Dr. Mohammad's budget was supposed to run right to December. And Joseph had to give them *some* notice.

Arms crossed, Dr. Mohammad remained silent. Too proud to ask the timing, probably. And too angry – it was rumored he'd punched Joseph in the face last spring over Heavenly Soy.

"How long do we have?" Gurpreet broke the silence.

"Three weeks. Four at most."

The room swayed and Gurpreet managed to plop down on the swivel chair before everything went dark.

By the second-to-last day, the project, in a drastically reduced format, was nearly wound down. Gurpreet had managed to keep up with Dr. Mohammad's frenetic pace, endlessly smearing bacteria-filled mine tailings onto gel trays and inserting electrodes, following Centre protocol of photo-documenting every step.

The bacteria, from a slough in the northern Alberta foothills, began to fascinate her. Their minute response to an electric current run through the inoculated electrophoresis gel was especially fascinating. It was far too soon to tell if the extraction process would be viable but at least they'd been able to do several replications at different amperages and pH levels. This was valuable work even though the growth rates had all been disappointingly slow.

The results wouldn't be definitive enough to be publishable, but it was exciting to do real science again – for the first time since her study to increase drought resistance in burrowing owls had been halted. She blinked away tears at the memory of sending some of the last burrowing owls in existence away on silent wings into a greying forest ravaged by pine beetles.

Mostly, she worked alone. Dr. Mohammad had been spending less and less time in the lab, always out on mysterious errands yet coming back emptyhanded. Once, she spotted him standing in the parking lot with the Centre's receptionist, waving his hands in furious discussion. The stout young man had kept shaking his head, almost in tears.

Tomorrow, she'd be unemployed. After a sleepless night last week, she'd finally sent Joseph a lengthy email, turning down his offer of a position working on the Heavenly Soy trials. She couldn't force herself to help with the study, she just couldn't, despite the quadrupled salary and permanent contract. She'd read all the reports. Preliminary studies had shown strong indications that the weevil-resistant soybeans devastated honeybee populations through a complex ecological chain of disaster. Despite that, the Centre had moved ahead with human trials regardless of the terrible long-term environmental risk. The soy had been the only food crop developed and approved prior to the GMO ban.

Gurpreet massaged her stomach. Had it really only been seven years since GMO – under strict governance, of course – had shown such promise? And a broader definition of "endangered species" had temporarily been somewhat effective in helping slow the destruction of the world's biodiversity? And her marriage had been happy and carefree?

Until humanity, in all its short-sightedness, had taken far too many unnecessary risks. Risks with the environment that had caused the spread of many bird flus, mad cow disease, and pesticide-resistant bugs that now plagued the world's wheat, corn, and barley crops. Risks with carbon emissions that had accelerated climate change. Risks that were tearing apart civilization.

To be fair, she and Damian had also taken a huge risk, conceiving a child even as the country's infrastructure collapsed around them. But that was a hope-filled risk, a small light in a snowstorm. Wasn't it?

Outside the window, the darkening sky leered. Trees had given up the struggle to break free of their icy shrouds, broken twigs dangling. Over the past few years, all her hopes had swirled away like scraps of garbage in the frigid wind.

Her stomach growled again. She tapped her screen and called up her dietary intake spreadsheet. With the baby due any day now, it was getting enough Vitamin D, folic acid, and calcium. But no meat and few vegetables meant a shortage of some amino acids and less than optimal weight gain. Homemade yogurt, nutritional yeast, and whey-based goat cheese didn't quite bridge the gap – she needed protein of all kinds.

One more day in the project. She'd do what she could. She entered the clean room and pulled a gel tray from the portable rack, careful not to disturb the balled-up clean suit bootie that braced the rack's broken wheel. Only a few more trays left to document. She'd need to fetch a step stool to be able to reach the top row.

On this lower tray, her analyses indicated that the *Acidithiobacillus* bacteria were indeed a previously unknown species. And a robust one. It was recovering astonishing amounts of tungsten and molybdenum. She ignored her heartburn and sore back and concentrated on taking detailed notes.

"Gurpreet, what the hell have you done?"

She rose awkwardly in the small space. She hadn't even heard Dr. Mohammad come in. He slid a tray from the top tier of the rack just above her eye level.

He thrust it down at her and she squinted at the label. It was one of the final two trays she'd prepped a month ago on the day Joseph had axed their study. "Did you spit on these?" His clean suit rustled with his annoyance as he pulled down a second, identical tray. "These are both contaminated. *Mokhak gazma!*"

Telling her she was as stupid as a shoe didn't clarify the problem. Gurpreet set down her tablet and peered over. The two trays held shiny brown globs of something: much, much larger growths than the other streaked trays. Then she remembered dropping her oatcake that day. Had she resterilized the tray before Dr. Mohammad whisked them away to the clean room? She couldn't remember. Damn pregnancy brain.

She bit her lip and the baby kicked her hard. If the experiment was ruined, it was her fault. There was no more gel, no more trays, no more time.

"I'm sorry, I must have—" She broke off. The huge blobs looked strangely familiar. And the fluid leaking off them had a particular golden sheen and a sharp odor she knew from her genetics work. "Dr. Mohammad, is it possible that—?"

"Nothing is possible, not here, not anymore!" Dr. Mohammad clattered the trays back onto the rack and rubbed the stubble on his face. He looked like he hadn't slept in weeks.

"Bear with me for a moment, please. I probably did contaminate the two trays with my lunch." She ignored his tightening mouth. "My oatcake that day – every day – was spread with nutritional yeast. I culture *Saccharomyces*, the active stuff, using beetroot juice at home. You know, for the baby's health. I can't afford multi-vitamins and..." She gripped her stomach as the baby kicked again.

Dr. Mohammad picked up a beaker rimmed with mud and shook it at her. "This was the *last* of the slough sample. This was the *last* of the bacteria. When the ice buildup broke the dam, the marsh silt was swept downstream for *miles*. There is no more, *do you understand!*" He slammed down the beaker, cracking the base in a jagged line. Plastic strips of curtain fluttered behind his ponytail as he stalked into the clean room's antechamber.

With wild hope, Gurpreet remembered an eight-year-old science journal she'd read a few days ago, curled on the sofa while Damian watched a movie. "Hang on! Please! The rapid growth with hardly any sugars to feed off of, that's unusual for yeast, right? And this yellow liquid leaching out. Possibly amino acids. Do you remember that study in *European Journal of Microbiological Methods*? About similar bacteria-yeast interactions?"

Dr. Mohammad called through the curtain. "Bah! I skimmed it. So what? This growth not likely similar now, is it!" The wrenching sound of a clean suit zipper being torn open then, "Silly girl. Even if it was, how could we study it for the *years* that would be necessary?" The lid of the suit disposal bin banged against the wall.

Gurpreet pressed a hand against her aching lower back. How indeed?

And even if they could, that wouldn't feed a hungry nation. Canada's food security problems were complex and intertwined – the Super Winters with their massive snowmelt leading to crops rotting across the prairies were only one horrific contributor among many. She tried to keep up on the world's developing climate crises but there were just too many to follow and there was no point in stressing the baby.

On her endless cold walk to work today, a gaunt woman had peeled off a long food bank line-up and poked at Gurpreet's lab ID card dangling over her parka. "I used to be a university professor," she'd whispered in a husky voice, leaning too close. "I used to *believe*."

Gurpreet had had nothing to give her. She'd whispered, "Sorry," and hurried off as icy pellets of snow stung her face with a thousand pinpricks. She'd looked back once from the edge of the courtyard. The queue of huddled forms had turned almost invisible by the fine curtain of snow. But her dogged trail of footprints was clearly etched across the snow-covered cobblestones. She'd made it this far. That had to mean something. It had to!

The only solution was determination and teamwork. She would let others figure out distribution systems and all the many other issues surrounding Canada's starvation – and she would continue to do her small part in moving scientific knowledge forward the best she could.

She picked up the contaminated tray and sniffed it. The vinegary smell made her empty stomach gurgle.

That evening, she texted Damian she was working late. She told Dr. Mohammad she needed to stay behind to wash out some equipment and, as proof, prepared a large beaker of a bleach-bromine solution, leaving it prominently by the sink.

After Dr. Mohammad left, she spent forty minutes pushing a fridge-sized mass spectrometer from the genetics wing to the geology lab, past Joseph's darkened office door.

Bit by bit, piece by piece. That's how science was done.

One machine down, one to go.

Dripping with sweat, she parked the machine in a corner of the geology lab by the window.

Outside, snow continued to fall. Her footprints from this morning had been totally obliterated.

She wiped her forehead on her lab coat sleeve and trudged back to fetch the equally large laminar flow hood.

The next day, the final day of the project, Gurpreet arrived a few minutes early. The hallway lights had already been dimmed as maintenance personnel began to shut down the wing. She hurried through her chores, taking the rack of gel trays out into the main room for disposal after final notetaking. Perhaps a future researcher could follow up on them. Maybe if she put the notes on a public website, if the mine tailing bacteria were not as rare as Dr. Mohammad believed… if, if, if. A storm of "if's" threatened to engulf her like this morning's sleet. Her stomach thrummed, burning from too little food and too much weak tea.

As the clock ticked maddeningly fast, she was almost grateful that Dr. Mohammad hadn't bothered to show up. She wanted to sequence the genes from the two trays with the unusual growth, now centered on a sterile lab mat under the laminar hood. No time like the present. She broke off the routine documentation of the racked trays and started pipetting from the yeast-infected samples under the hood.

Joseph stuck his head in the door. "Gurpreet." He looked left then right before stepping into the lab, clearly relieved not to see Dr. Mohammad. "How's the baby?"

"Ready to make an entrance any day now." She tried to mirror his tight smile. The man was only doing his job. She sniffed. Was that fried fish wafting off his suit? Her mouth watered.

They chatted for a few minutes about nothing, Gurpreet's eyes more on the clock than his face.

As she was about to politely tell him to leave, Dr. Mohammad barged in, slamming the door against the wall. "Liew!

Why do you continue to harangue me? Get out!" His fists clenched and he circled around in front of Joseph as if to manhandle him out. He bumped against the rack of gel trays Gurpreet had been cataloguing, sending it rocking.

Joseph took a step backwards. "Ahmed, relax. I've only come to see if I can facilitate your final day."

With one foot, Dr. Mohammad nudged the rack a few centimetres forward. "See these trays? We're about to dump them without really knowing what's on them. That's what rushing an experiment leads to!"

Gurpreet clutched her rounded stomach. She didn't dare interfere for the baby's sake. As she watched in horror, Dr. Mohammad shoved the rack again, harder. The faulty wheel caught on a cable and the neatly-labeled trays clattered off onto Joseph's shoes – a slimy heap of smashed gel slabs, cracked plastic, and broken dreams.

A moan escaped Gurpreet's lips. Now there was no way to finish taking notes. The experiment had been ruined. And all that remained of the unique bacteria lay in the two trays under the flow hood. The two contaminated trays.

She bit her lip and waddled over to the roll of paper towels that stood near the sink. The assay results beeped and she tossed Joseph the roll as she automatically glanced back at the screen.

Then she took a longer look, tuning out Dr. Mohammad's rant, Joseph's fussing about his shoes, and the incessant beeping.

"Dr. Mohammad?" She repeated his name three times before he wound down his tirade. "Come look. Please. I'm not sure I believe it but sequencing indicates the yeast is a new variant of *Saccharomyces*."

Dr. Mohammad furrowed his brow. "Impossible."

"The assay indicates it's an epigenetic change with a full range of proteinogenic amino acids—" Gurpreet glanced at Joseph's face and simplified it for him: "The bacteria may have changed my homegrown yeast to a super-yeast, a really nutritious food source that doesn't need many sugars to grow fast…"

She shut off the beeping noise with a shaking finger. If further trials gave the same results, it meant cheap, easy protein for her baby, for the city, perhaps for the world. Humanity had a chance.

"This project is ended, remember?" Joseph threw the dirty paper towel in the garbage can. "No more funding."

"Probably just microchimerism anyway," Dr. Mohammad said. He was still glaring at Joseph and his chest continued to heave.

Gurpreet looked at the data. "The assay says not. Since it's a well-known strain of *Saccharomyces cerevisiae*, no need for substantial equivalence. No issue with allergenicity." She clarified again for Joseph: "This yeast variant might be completely edible and breed true."

Dr. Mohammad came closer, eyeing the screen. "Years of lab studies, of clinical trials ahead. And how would we ever grow huge quantities? Not on gel, certainly."

"Maybe on a sawdust slurry? Sawdust from BC is cheap and plentiful." The pine beetles, aided by climate change, had seen to that.

However, it was all an academic exercise without funding. She turned to Joseph. "Could you authorize a study? It *is* food. Non-GMO food."

"Heavenly Soy is taking all the budget available. I'm sorry."

"Right. Heavenly Soy." Gurpreet rudely waggled her thumb. Sikhs didn't believe in heaven.

She sank into the swivel chair. Damian's comment that morning came back to her. He'd pushed his portion of oatmeal toward her and spat out, "I don't know how you bear it. The weight of it all, I mean." Then he'd thrown himself down on the couch, no longer even making a pretense of looking for snow shoveling work.

Damian had given up.

Joseph had given up.

Even Dr. Mohammad had given up.

But she wasn't going to. Not yet. The sky always held a glimmer of light even in the worst of snowstorms.

She cupped her hands over her stomach, not sure if this morning's angular bumps were feet or knees or elbows. She wouldn't let her baby down. She wouldn't let herself down. She just had to buy some time. And that was true of the yeast as well. The bacteria consortium was completely irreplaceable, as unique and as precious as her baby or burrowing owls. The bacteria might be going extinct, like the burrowing owls, but *science* wasn't extinct. Not yet, it wasn't.

Science was just endangered.

With that thought, she sat up straighter.

"Joseph." She cleared her throat. "Correct me if I'm wrong. The burrowing owl budget has been 'spent' this year, correct? 'Allocated but not Assigned'?"

Joseph gave a slow nod, probably feeling he was humoring the deranged pregnant woman in the chair.

Gurpreet's voice cracked again. "So it's available for something endangered but not extinct?"

"Holy shit." Dr. Mohammad said, his voice loud in Gurpreet's ear. "That's all the bacteria left." He pointed at the two innocuous brown lumps.

"The endangerment definitions don't include bacteria," Joseph said. "You know that."

Gurpreet rubbed her belly in slow circles.

Dr. Mohammad sneered. "So, simply because of a definition, the world's greatest potential foodstuff will be trashed. Is that what you're saying, Liew?"

"I didn't write the—"

Gurpreet interrupted. "Hey, that's right. Foodstuff. It's not the *bacteria* that need to be endangered to fit the definition, it's these particular few cells of yeast." She looked at the assay size estimates. "There's only about two hundred million of them." It really wasn't much.

Behind her, Dr. Mohammad sputtered, "By definition, yeast can't be 'endangered.' It's a microorganism, for pity's sake, not a—"

Gurpreet cut him off too. "Doesn't the Centre's own definition simply read 'organism,' thereby not excluding microorganisms? Check, please, Joseph."

"I don't think—"

"Please, Joseph."

He ran a finger down his tablet, stopped, and pursed his lips. "Hmm, yes, there's the phrase: 'organism.' One of those older open-ended definitions that they never tightened. I can try for a few dollars, I suppose." He paused and his dark eyes met hers. "But for Ahmed's salary only, though. There is no way any sort of budget going forward allows for an assistant. I'm sorry, Gurpreet, but you are laid off in any case."

She swallowed the lump in her throat. "Joseph, I'll work without pay if this project can go ahead." She and Damian would manage, somehow, even if they both had to set out begging bowls on the sidewalk.

Dr. Mohammad snorted. "No need, Gurpreet." He poked his finger into Joseph's chest. "I've found you out. I know you altered the Heavenly Soy budget and redirected funding to it for a hefty bribe from a certain food conglomerate."

"That's a lie!"

"I have my sources."

Joseph flushed dark red. "You wouldn't dare!"

"Wouldn't I?"

A long moment and then, "All right, all right. Let me see what I can do." He tapped his tablet then said, "Hold on. Here's another roadblock." He read aloud: "'An at-risk wildlife population becomes endangered when it suffers a population reduction of fifty percent or more within a short time.'" He pointed at the two brown masses. "Half has to have died. That's not the case here."

"Well, we can certainly facilitate that." Gurpreet shoved her chair back, checked that the camera had recorded the full contents of both trays, and then fetched the beaker of cleaning solution from the sink.

With one hand still on her belly, she splashed a good dollop of fluid over the nearest of the two trays.

One side of the brown glob darkened and bubbled.

Joseph's intake of breath was audible across the room.

Dr. Mohammad squeezed her shoulder, hard. "Do you know what you've just done, stupid girl?"

Of course she did. She'd just killed half of humankind's best chance at survival.

She blinked several times, the sharp odor of bleach stinging her eyes. "If you're going to punch me, Dr. Mohammad, please hit my face, not my stomach."

He grunted and strode over to Joseph. "I'd say this organism is definitely endangered now, right, Liew?" He shoved his face into Joseph's. "Better go allocate our funding. And damn quickly."

As the door banged shut, Gurpreet looked up at Dr. Mohammad. "You were bluffing about being able to prove the bribery, right?"

He shrugged, calm again. "The guy is a good accountant. Very tidy." he said. "Not like you. Now, clean up this mess. We've got work to do." He stumped away to the clean room, mumbling under his breath.

Gurpreet half-smiled. Teamwork between the two of them, finally. They'd need that in the long days to come.

Then she soaked the partially-blackened blob on the first tray – thoroughly killing it this time. She carefully documented the process and took her time – the way science is done.

LYING IN BED TOGETHER

RICHARD VAN CAMP

Warlike and just what the doctor ordered. Holy, cow. What a night! Valentina!

Valentina…

Valentina!

The way she crouched and then sank into me as she squeezed the back of my neck and whispered, "I got you. I got you."

Her tattoos: a figure-eight between her breasts, encircling her shoulders and her muscles. She's marked in the old ways: her legs, arms, feet and hands. And she's scarred: scorch scars on her hip and bruises all over her. Fresh stitches under her left rib. My God! A warrior! The sweep of her hair over my hands as I held on and the low guttural growl of me trying to hold back but losing every time myself to her completely and the hunger as we buried each other to the hilt. Holy, man, the hunger for each other. We became the night!

And who knew suffering could be so glorious? What a goddess. Sweet mercy. I am in awe. I had no idea… I just… no words… I am a brand new man and I am hers now. Completely.

And on today of all days: my last day as a Handi Bus driver. I'm free. We could hit the city, help get her car fixed, rock out. What can I cook her? Porridge, heavy cream, blueberries. Toast. Jam. Oh I'm going to spoil her.

Last night while she was in the shower, I fried up some caribou meat with lots of butter and salt, fresh veggies with tonnes of butter and a swab of minced garlic. I used my couscous from Kaeser's, the garlic blend. All of this took 20 minutes. As I cooked and got all three of my pans and pot going, I boiled up some mint tea, all of which I picked myself out at Tsu Lake. Oh she was hungry. She was glowing from the shower.

And now she's back.

"Shhhhh," she says, walking back into the bedroom. She's dressed. Hair wet. Ready to go. Her clothes, in this light, are different. She's used sinew to mend tears and there's a logo now that I see on her right arm – the skull of a caribou. Did she have that on last night? And why does she smell like smoke?

"Shhh?" I say and reach out my hand. "Can I make you coffee? Are you hungry?"

She shakes her head. "We have to go."

"Where?" I ask. "The Pelican? I can cook for you—"

"No," she says. "We have to leave."

I frown. "And go where?"

She points to the sky.

I wrinkle my nose. "What?"

"Goddam you," she says, suddenly serious. "Why didn't you listen to me?"

"Listen?" I ask. "I did everything you wanted me to last night."

"No," she says and hands me my pills. "What are these?"

My pills. I've had the worst splitting headaches the last year. It feels like a 747 is taking off in my head. I almost go into seizure if I don't get to them in time. "Those?" I ask. Oh no – those were in my bathroom, behind the mirror. *Don't tell me she's psycho.* "They're for my migraines."

She shakes her head. "Those weren't migraines. That was us trying to reach you."

"Us?" I say. "Who's 'us'?"

She points up. "Us."

"Okay," I say and pull the blankets close. I'm still naked. "What are you talking about?"

"Remember what I said last night?" She asks. "Remember, I said you were needed."

At the dance. Roaring Rapids Hall aka Moccasin Square Gardens. I nodded. "Yes."

"And remember how I said you called me?"

I don't want to blow this with her, but I don't know what she's talking about. "Yes."

"The men who were after you have all agreed to stand down. This is because of me. I showed them something."

Seriously, Gunner and his bros aren't going to beat me up? "Okay," I say. "What did you show them?"

She sits on the bed beside me. "Close your eyes and focus."

I close my eyes and nod.

She places her hand on my head and I see a series of brutal flashes and I hear hissing.

Footage. How? I'm whipped into another time: footage. Grainy footage. Something huge – not human – walking through smoke. Screaming. Praying. The *pop pop pop* of guns firing. Screaming. Something behind it crawling through smoke. To the left, bodies are rolling in water of froth. Children. People. Upside down. Parts of them. Rolling with the tide. People running. Praying. All languages. Running. The something-human walking the earth is hit by a huge gun and falls, kneels, gets back up. Throws its head back and screams. Gets up. Keeps walking. Three beings following. One without arms. Another flying low to the earth, human face, spinning its body around its neck. Then a scream that hurts my head and breaks the feed and a cut to a forest that isn't moving and hundreds of things are standing still. Arms up and towards the sky. Their backs. Skin is hanging off their backs and one is ramming a tusk through another one's head. One is raking more skin off of the back of another and rolling it and passing it to another. Valentina's voice going, "Go go go go" as she grips a long spear, and people with us are moving, slowing to crouch behind this field of beings praying under a full moon.

I take a big breath and come back. "What the fuck was that?"

"I warned you," she says. "You were supposed to stop the Tar Sands."

"Me?" I say. "How?"

She lets her breath out. "Not just you. Everyone. We sent dreams back and I know you received them."

I look at her hands. What is she holding? Nothing. "Those were nightmares. How did you do that?"

She looks at me. "Our daughter taught me."

I get the shivers. "Our daughter?"

"You and I have a girl. They're scared of her."

"Us? How? Prove it," I say again. "You can't do this… shit to my head… and not have me asking questions. Just talk to me."

She looks at me, studies me. She then points to my jeans on the floor. "You still don't believe me? Okay, in your left pocket two days ago was a shell casing. We put it there ten years from now. Your mark in the future will be your right hand bathed in yellow pollen. You will leave it on the trees to signal that the area is safe for what's left of us."

"Safe?" Shit! I did find a shell casing from a huge gun in my pocket when I was getting dressed. "From who?"

"It's *what*," she shakes her head. "*What's* coming is already here."

"Wait. What are you talking about? You sound like something out of *The Terminator*. Don't lie about anything and just tell me."

She looks so tired. "You already know what I'm talking about."

"I don't," I say. "Just start at the beginning and tell me."

"The ammunition of the world lasts three days. That's it. We hold them off for three days and then they rule the earth."

"Who?"

"The Wheetago."

"The Wheetago," I say. "Okay... when?"

"When is the year the caribou do not come down from the coast?

I look around the room. "It's now. They didn't come down. The Elders just met and are worried."

She nods twice. "Then it's now. This is the year they return."

"Wait a minute. Come on. That's a story."

"Do you know what I saw three days ago?"

"Three days... in the future?"

It was supposed to be a joke but she nodded and continued. "I saw Hell. There were thousands of dancers. All Native. Fancy dancers. Shawl dancers. Button blanket dancers. They save them for the end."

I swallow hard. "Go on."

"There were fields of bodies around them and they were dancing. Some had been dancing for days, but it was the older women who lasted because they had discipline. The younger ones were bleeding through their moccasins. The drummers had their left feet pulled off so their right feet could balance and keep time. They'd had their eyes sucked out. They were singing blind and some had their tongues missing."

"My God," I say.

She starts to cry. "What's worse is if you couldn't dance anymore, the Wheetago – and there are thousands of them – they can't wait to rip you apart in front of your family."

"Oh, shit. But what are they dancing for?"

"It's not what. It's who."

"Okay, so who are they dancing for?"

"The mother. There is a queen. She is eating and giving birth. She vomits Wheetago out of her mouth."

I cover mine.

"Hell is coming and you're a part of it. You're a prayer warrior and you're also my husband."

I swallow dry as my heart blooms. "What?"

She nods. "There's a future war but not in the way you think." She wipes her eyes. "Site C Dam, Muskrat Falls, Standing Rock…"

"What… now? That's happening now."

"It all goes wrong. It's a setup for meat."

I close my eyes. "Meat?"

She ties her hair back. "Our meat."

I reach for her arm. "How? Why?"

She pulls away. "For the Wheetago and their mother."

I swallow dry. "What?

She looks directly at me. "You will name her 'The Mother of all Tusks.' She is born because when they expand the Tar

Sands they uncover a Wheetago who bites her. It's all destined."

I close my eyes. *Why did this feel real? Why did I already know this?*

As I tried to process all of this, my neck started to burn from hickeys; my back was shredded from her claws and she bit my shoulder through. It started to ache. I shook my head. No headaches. Holy sweet mercy! It's 7:48 am. Usually by now I'd be gripping my head, rocking back and forth praying to be thrown into a sea of ice to stop the pain. "What if you're wrong? What if you're, like, in a coma and dreaming this or I am?" I thought of that Facebook meme: *What if the adventures of Indiana Jones are the dreams of Han Solo while he's locked up in carbonite?*

"Don't believe me? What is coming back has been waiting for global warming for many of their lifetimes. They are patient. Starving."

"So, they've been doing what all these years under the ice?"

"Praying."

I felt a throom of energy blow through me. What did I really know about her? There were rumors that Valentina was a deity, that she was a being of forever, that she'd come back through my grandfather's life time to witness the signing of the treaties. When was that? 1899 for Treaty 8 in Fort Fitzgerald and Treaty 11 in 1921. She downed Gunner and his buddies last night to save me from – what did she say, a broken spine? Last night in the dark we made ferocious love. Holey moley, but is she sane? "Valentina," I say. "You can't just drop this on someone. I need more proof."

"Okay," she said. "Tell me the story your grandfather told you. The one you never wanted to believe."

I sat up. "My grandpa?"

"Tell me," she said, "about what Pierre saw in Fort Fitzgerald when he was a boy."

I remembered. "My ehtse," I started, "wanted to work with the men in Fort Fitz when he was a young man. He wanted to help unload the barges. He even lied about his age. Holy, man, he said, they worked you hard but they fed you good."

She nodded. "Go on. This was when?"

"The 30s, I think."

She glanced out the window before looking at me. "Go on. Hurry."

I swallowed and thought about this. The terror of Grandpa's story started trickling back.

"As he was making his way with the men to receive their work orders, he saw someone chained to a hill. I have seen this hill. It's low and solid." I'll never walk on it. "This person was tied to the hill face down. There was an old woman guarding this person with a long willow. Thick. Like a staff. As they got closer, there were people saying, 'Don't look at it. It's a Wheetago.'

"Of course, as he got closer, he snuck a peek.

"This person chained to the hill was shivering, shaking, trembling. He or she had rubbed their own feces into his or her hair. They'd eaten their own lips, their own fingers and one whole side of their face.

"This person looked up at my grandpa and their eyes met.

"He froze.

"This thing raised its arms off of the ground and, as this happened, my ehtse felt the strength leave his body.

"He collapsed.

"The old woman turned and started whipping the Wheetago and yelled in Cree, 'Let him go.' It did."

She nodded. "That is only a glimpse into their power. They can stop shells from firing. They eat their own lips, and most of their fingers. They are always suffering. The more they eat, the hungrier they become; the more they drink, the thirstier.

"But in the future – our future – they have started to decorate themselves for something. They have Oracles that can kill from a distance. Some have sewn and pushed sticks and antlers into their bodies. These are older than Christ and they have been counting on our greed as humans to warm the earth so they can return. That thing on the hill, it was a scout. You're going to call them 'Hair Eaters' in your life.

"We just saw them – you and me and our girl – praying in the thousands, looking at the moon. They shiver like bats. Their corridors are growing."

"Corridors?" I ask.

She nodded. "Their range now is expanding globally to 144 miles per day."

"Stop," I said. I realized that my jaws hurt. I'd been grinding my teeth as I listened and dug into her truth. "Okay. Okay. If I believe you, what am I in the future?"

"Besides being my husband?" She sits beside me and runs her hand up my arm. "Because of you, I give birth to one of the greatest Wheetago hunters of all time: our girl." She nods and levels her eyes in the direction of somewhere I didn't know. "You've honoured me. You've called me. Now it's time for us to leave this place and train. Got it?" She held her hand out to me.

"Okay," I say. "If this is really true… I need you to do that thing again. Show me something. No tricks. Bring me your worst memory from the future."

She nods and holds out her hands. She offers them to me to show me she's holding nothing.

I nod.

"I'm not sorry you see this," she says, as she places her palms against my ears and I hear a roaring and I see people picking blackberries along burning hills. Some are walking back to their camp. I realize as I zoom in closer that they are all women and men who are dragging themselves somehow and still walking. They have finished picking berries and are carrying buckets. Ahead of them are people kneeling and rolling berries with their fingers to create a jam. They then dig into people's open skulls that are tied to trees to mix the brains with the berries. These people have no hair, no hands, no feet yet they're still alive. Screaming, drooling, twisting. There are seven creatures on a hill watching, like priests. There is a flame flickering above each of their heads. They are decorated for war: huge antlers rise through their skulls and throats. On top of a hill watching them is a bull Wheetago. It is hunched, huge and trembling in its ferocity. It has the mouth of a hammerhead shark because of a thigh bone rammed through its cheeks. It stands on a hill of human and animal bodies torn in half and drained. This Wheetago sniffs and reads the wind. A *Patroller*. I somehow know this. Behind it are more hills with more bodies with more bull Wheetago all perched like pawns. A *Shovel Head*, we call them. Patrolling. Guarding. Behind them is the biggest hill of all. We see the Queen. She is a human giant, giving birth to more Wheetago through her mouth. Hundreds of Wheetago approach holding human heads like chalices served up as offerings. Brains are mixed with blackberries. The Queen licks blood from her mouth and drinks from the skull. Then another. Then another. She looks directly in my direction. Her eyes say it all: she hates the world and she hates us. She makes a grabbing motion towards me. She wants her children to kill and eat the world. She holds up a skull. It's upside down. It is the face of Valentina: eyes open. Looking up. Mouth torn apart. An ear hanging from a braid. Beside her they have a girl. Two Hair Eaters – *Splitters* – we call them, hold a little girl down. One steps on her arms as another rips her legs apart and I realize this is our girl. "NO!!" I scream. The Mother of All Tusks throws her head back and howls.

The seven priests raise their hands to the sky.

The bulls join her.

Then the females.

And I see a flash.

I come back. Ears ringing.

I'm shivering, cold, terrified.

It is the end of the world and we have caused this by doing nothing.

"See?" She says.

"Wait," I say and hold my hands out. "You died? That was you? The girl beside you…"

She nods. "This is how we die if you don't come with me right now."

I start to panic. I saw my daughter. She was screaming, scared, praying. "Valentina, wait…"

"We have to go." She kneels down and kisses me.

"Wait," I say. "Wait, wait, wait… You and I…"

"We have a few years," she says and smiles. She's crying.

"What is our daughter's name?" I hear myself asking.

"Ehdze," she says.

"For the moon," I say.

She nods and smiles with tears in her eyes. "For moonlight."

"Whoa," I say and get the tingles. That was always my favourite word in Tlicho: my language.

"Hurry," she says. "Everything starts now. I Double Dogrib Dare you to take my hand and we'll leave. But you can never come back because there'll be nothing you want to come back to."

I look around. This house. My life. The world I know or knew. I take her hand just to see what will happen. Valentina. The one who calls the snow. The woman in all of the pictures of the treaty signings if you look close enough. Now. Still the same. Ageless and war-torn. "Ehdze," I say and get the tinglies again. *Moonlight.* I take my wife's hand

she squeezes

we vanish

and are reborn into the war ground of Earth and the return of the Wheetago…

REEF

GEORGE McWHIRTER

I come down with Darren Downey out of tall conifers through salal and other shrubs to the shore. Coves scallop the coast here. Long-ago eruptions on the volcanic mountains behind them cooled into the hard, Late Cretaceous granite which splay spits of rock like fingers, webbed with grey sand, into the water.

As Darren Downey counts, the bodies laid out along the tideline extend like a regimented extension of his index finger. Once summed, then summed again, he moves that same index finger to his lower lip and rests it there. Darren Downey is the President and Prime Undertaker of Ocean Interments, Reef Restoration and Exoskeletal Services: OIRRES.

Crabs, huge ones – not Dungeness, but not unlike – move like dark bruises, or the disease that takes their name, cancers, across the corpses, but have metastasized post mortem, visibly eating into those newly laid-out after the OIRRES finely enacted ceremony of dedicating their remains to the reef.

"One cove was all it took for the cadavers when we started," Darren informs me. He draws my attention to the slipway, to the mobile barges, mounted on multiple small wheels with chubby tyres, where ranks of skeletons, already stripped for the battle of beating back excess acid in salt sea, have been lined up and loaded – a corps of alkaline Canutes.

"Amphibious, adapted from the military's small landing craft," Darren tells me. "As you can see, once our donors are cleaned to the bone, we ship them on our amphibians to where we are rebuilding this side of the spit with human coral."

"Reef replacement routine?"

"Not routine – rite!"

I can see Darren thinks my question too cold and quickly conclusive. I ask another. "Excuse me, Darren. Might I ask – did you have this many crabs when you started?"

"As few crabs as bodies. But the demand meets the supply. They multiplied along with donors, such as yourself, committed to the reef." Darren has deliberately chosen to use a word from the classic sea-burial service. "The accelerated growth and deposits from their shells augment the calcium from the cadavers."

"The shells and nippers look gargantuan, but what do you mean by demand meets supply?"

"In several short crab generations they have multiplied to fit the food source. In nature, the size of the task dictates the size of the tool to carry it out."

As diligently as a tailor's scissors, I imagine the crabs' nippers cutting through me, gliding along, as if following the chalked white outline on the cloth for a new bespoke coat. But I know their work will be choppy and in no way as smoothly ceremonial and sweetly prolonged as I would wish. Still, what will I feel, what will I care?

Darren Downey wears a black tunic and pants in a material as solid and close-woven as serge, formal and practical wear for services and heavy-duty supervision, and if its high circular collar were white, he'd look the clergyman he also happens to be. But what am I? Voyeur, scientific observer or prospective interee – something of all three, and something more, someone born into and soon to die in trade. I've grown up with graveyards and their evolution from burial places to sites where there's no interment at all. My great-grandfather, then grandfather, my great-uncles and uncles were gravediggers at Mountainview Cemetery in Vancouver from when it was new and lightly populated. Unobstructed views of the mountains then from its headstone-heavy slopes. Tall men, my forefathers and uncles, six foot three to six foot six in their socks. They dug until they were down to their noses, which meant the grave stood six feet deep and finished. They sighted the hills from the grave's end, always pointing north to the mountains, as if looking through a periscope. "Up," they would shout and climb up the wood-ladder into broad daylight; they said the world always grew darker, down there where they earned their living, and climbing out of a finished grave was like coming back to life.

 I was on my father's knee when I first heard this and they were already old men, complaining of aches inherited from their labours. My father complained along with them about the mechanical diggers that made him feel like he was working on a building site. He was old enough to have apprenticed with spades. The rattle and roar of engines and the cranking up and down of the digger on the tractor was a desecration to him. Nothing like the solemn scrape, scrape of cleaning the long-handled spade that bit through into the hard pan and tossed both earth and grit above-ground with a long upward sweep of the arm and twist of the wrist.

 Crabs, instead of spades or mechanical diggers, do the job of excavating here, but directly on the bodies. When Darren Downey sees me looking and cocking an ear to the clatter of crab nippers and clash of carapaces on the beach, he tells me,

"You should hear the noise sometimes when open warfare breaks out. They battle all across a cove, and it's like Agincourt, shields and swords clashing."

I raise my eyebrows and he asks me to forget what he has just said.

"Agincourt *is* a bit over the top. I'm sorry if I inflate a repetitious scene with an outrageous comparison, but I confess, I *am* trying to impress and give you some idea of the dimensions and historical importance of the campaign we are waging here. So much reef dissolving, and too few deceased and praiseworthy people, like yourself, to do what needs to be done. In that respect it is a constant battle for donors. But then, you did ask for a preparatory tour. To see what you are getting into."

I put my finger in my mouth, take it out, hold it up in the air, and he looks at me as if this is my gesture for him to stop, absolutely stop. I grimace and hasten to assure him. "I'm sorry. I was just wondering why the smell isn't that strong. Because the wind is strong, am I right?"

"And off the ocean, yes."

"And away out there over the Pacific Ocean. Where it's really the East and Asia, they'd understand what you are doing is a tradition. That cult in India, which leaves its dead for the vultures to eat and carry off into the sky in their beaks."

Darren Downey nods, "Tibetan sky burials, where birds of prey carry out the excarnation. A wise man . . . a priest told me we who eat should prepare to be eaten as a repayment, a penance. The priest I quote is one of our consultants."

"Excellent," I say and look up into the sky and then out at the spit. "I'm ready." Darryl Downey follows my line of sight to the spit's long finger and end knuckle digging into its origin in the bedrock.

For a long time before things went from bad to worse for me, medically, I have been gathering data on similar funeral services and their business model, which Darren Downey hasn't got to describing yet. I have only seen the facility and the machinery at work – crabs scavenging over the grey hulks of flesh as efficaciously as the ragged and exhausted wreckers in the ships' graveyards of Bangladesh.

Yet, in your regular graveyard, how long does it take to worm through a fine wooden coffin and convert the lately dead flesh into earth? The longstanding craze for cardboard coffins to accelerate the process is laudable. I have a cousin, Martin, who keeps up our family tradition of grave digging, spade in hand, on Vancouver Island, near Port Renfrew. There is a graveyard patronized by geriatric hippies and cultists, who eschew cardboard, wood or any covering, who want the dirt tossed directly onto their faces. Others pay extra to be eviscerated and interred in burlap bundles around the roots of trees. No mechanical diggers for that specialized packing and spadework. The process makes me think of September and October rituals with potted hyacinth bulbs, forced to bloom indoors in the middle of winter.

I didn't find all this out until I drove my father there, at his request, to be buried by one of the family still labouring at the family's traditional trade. I had dropped the back seat of his old station wagon to fit him in, threw a rug over his coffin. He had not specified a casket of any kind, but had insisted on the rug going with him, one my mother said would suit my father down to the ground (every irony intended). Not a rug really, an old Mexican blanket they had bought on holiday. The never-take-no-for-an-answer seller raced after them through the market, reducing the price with every step they took away from him. It bore Mexico's national emblem, an eagle with a serpent plucked from a thorn tree, writhing between its talons. They bit into his back, metaphorically, every time he sat down on his favourite chair, where my father draped their purchase for the duration.

My father also loved that chair, a wing-back, and gladly died in it. He would have been buried in it, too, if it hadn't been anathema to my cousin, who did, God bless him, joke about the prospect. A sitting-up burial would be a first for the Island, maybe the only one since the time of the Pharaohs, who liked both the sitting-up and the standing-up kind. My cousin Martin calls me Cousin Will, never William, just Will.

"Jesus, Cousin Will, his old stinky, half-rotted blanket will do, not this thing."

He was referring to the coffin in the back of my father's station wagon, pulling the old Mexican blanket off it and rapping his knuckles on it like it was a walnut dining-room table my father was lying under, dead drunk. Which is exactly what he saw it as. "A fine big thick-topped table I'll make you out of that. Didn't you know we don't use these? Too much waste. Turned into a table it will last you a lifetime."

"Make the table and keep it," my mother said. "Now, you two get him out of it and bury him in his blanket." Then, after a pause, "If you like, sell the table or keep it when you've made it. I don't want the thing."

She turned to look at my wife, Carol, who gasped at the "keep it"/"sell it" sentiments. Carol had just got out of our car and come up with our son, Jordan. I had to explain that they weren't going to toss Father out and sell the coffin while it was in perfect shape.

Then, I got to work on one end of my father, gripping him by his woolly ankle socks while my cousin took hold of him by the shoulders. I expected Cousin Martin to tell me that socks, shoes and suit were a waste and should be passed on to the homeless. At the same time, I wondered if the tulip trees in that Island burial ground were actually more lush because of their human fertilizer. Their early blooms shone as anachronistically bright as spring-white hyacinths in January.

My wife, Carol, and son, Jordan, had arrived in our Mini-Cooper runabout. More a racing car than runabout, but Carol was glad it was too small to fit a corpse into. Unless (she thought this was terribly funny) she became one in a road accident during the trip over from the mainland. That was more likely to happen after her post-burial and pre-wake vodkas at Burley's Pub on the short hop to my cousin's.

"I think Jordan and I should go see your cousin's workshop with you," Carol declared her drunken curiosity as soon as Jordan had parked the Mini for her beside me in the station wagon. After showing my mother into the house Cousin Martin came out with an apprentice – or hick friend in coveralls – I assumed, to help him transform the coffin into a dining-room table right then and there, ready to be taken back home by my mother if she wished in the back or roof of the station wagon.

"I bet he makes a fortune out of recycled coffins," Carol whispered in my ear.

"That's a distinct possibility, and a fresh direction I should add to my study of the trade. A secondary industry in recycled coffins."

"Or Cousin Martin just sells them to anybody who wants to buy a coffin when we're not here." Trust my son, Jordan, to think that.

"Don't think so," I told him.

"Okay," Jordan said, "but I'd think better of Cousin Martin if he turned the tables on Granddad's loss by actually making his coffin into a table and getting somebody to buy it for a profit."

His mother grinned at him, for speaking her mind. Jordan's own business is bespoke 3-D printing of specialized parts, like missing legs for antique tables, out of matching wood fibre fed into the printer. He moved ahead to get first-peek at Cousin Martin's shop, where sawdust and wood whorls spilled like a wild Berber carpet over the dirt floor to the door Martin left open when he went in with his coveralled accomplice or apprentice. The moment Jordan moved a step ahead of her, Carol lifted her leg and gave him a kick in the rear end.

"I want the table, if it ever gets made. I won't let my mother-in-law or your father's cousin sell it. After the money we put into that coffin. Paying extra for a composite, recycled walnut. Whatever the hell that is?"

"Shavings of walnut, bits and pieces glued into a solid piece," I explained.

"Okay, but to go into *a hole in the ground*, like it's supposed to. Not a table."

Gallantly, Jordan held out his arm in the workshop door, inviting his mother to huff and come in.

You need hazard no guesses, given my background, that the death industry would be my lifetime study – one, vastly over-exploited. You need only Google it to find 6 Stocks To Die For: Making A Killing In Caskets, Funerals… But then, my books and academic studies have morphed into many analyses of how abundance is made out of absence, a utility out of unbeing. Most companies turn mortality into money; OIRRES includes transubstantiation. This is Darren Downey's main point of principle and design for the company.

"When we first started, the authorities tested for contamination of fish stocks, as if we were a fish farm. They sent investigators posing as donors, who had us walk them through to the point of facilitating their departure, but the only departure they experienced was when we waved to them leaving through the gates."

"Understandable. It was illegal."

"Not now. Desperate situations demand divine remedies is how I put it. The planet's in a pickle, everything is so bad the Spaniards will have bacalao straight from the sea, no boxing and curing in rock salt required. I'm so glad that those who come to us see beyond their demise, that there is another life for them in the continuing life of the ocean. They look like you look now. Your cancer is terminal?"

"As terminal as the inexorable crab it is, but indeterminate as to the day and the hour it finishes its work. If it gets too painful, I will time my own dying with proper assistance."

"And your wife and close family support you in that and your choice of last rites on the reef? Many come with their wives, or their husbands, as the case may be, to see where they have dedicated their bodies, if not to the deep, then to lessening the bitterness of the sea we share."

"Carol, my wife, would need to brace herself. A stiff drink or two, and after that this would not be a place of great ritual, but what word can I use for it, Carol's ribaldry in the face of death? And she would want to know what's in it for you."

"A business, of course, where every part of it has a second use. I'm proud of that. Not one morsel in the matter is lost to future sustenance of the sea or our species. We consume and we are consumed."

I haven't a shred of doubt Carol would gag on what he means, and to Darren Downey's face.

When we boat over behind the chubby landing barges to the reef-rebuild along the deep inside of the granite spit, I look through the glass inspection bottom of the boat.

"We could use a large barge and just dump, but we place the skeletons as best we can."

I can see much has collapsed – ribs have broken, sunk and forked over hip bones, out of the arranged dispositions. Fish thread through the hip cavities and rib-bone arches, appearing from behind the fine sea fur on the deeper bone deposits. They come up, turn suddenly and dive back down to avoid the new gently drifting down remains, femurs coming apart from hips, shin bones and arm bones descended, as if to beat the fishes off into a respectful distance.

"Our charitable work," Darren Downey sighs, "planetary charity, can't survive on donations and payment for the funeral expenses alone."

He looks down into the water and rubs his hands together, obviously, at a job well done.

"The crabs?" I ask.

"Exactly. We sell them directly to restaurants and at various retailers."

"Surplus to those for operations, I would surmise."

"Precisely, but with one extra. Like returnable empty bottles, the shells have a deposit, clearly marked on the bill, and refundable with their return."

"I have checked. You are sole suppliers and retailers."

"Of course, at select outlets. Handling pick-ups and deliveries. We keep within a geographic range to make it feasible. The same trucks that deliver bring back the empties."

He smiled at me. "Each reef replacement is specific and local. It is also very important for visitors, who don't have to travel to the ends of the earth for the funeral services."

I have data on the wholesale and retail of the crab meat trade, and more data on the listings for Crab Convertible Enterprises (CCE) on the TSX and DOW along with the names of the principal stock-holders in OIRRES. All donors are issued a set of shares as investors in both companies, a fine touch. I haven't confined myself to OIRRES and CCE's effect on the local economy. With the weather warming and the proliferation of turkey vultures here on the coast and inland on the Cascadia Range and Rockies, I have been gathering data on the start-ups with East Asian money and age-old cult experience in the process of sky burial. Articles have been written in newspapers, but none have done a thorough analysis of this secondary transfer of wealth from the dead to the living. *The Economics of Expiry and Expiation*, I'm thinking of as a title, but something much more rigorous and academic will have to be found before I finish.

My wife and son say my lifetime study puts my dying at two removes for me; into an abstract intellectual pursuit on the one hand, and a business, subject to statistics and financial analysis, on the other. They say I relish becoming a statistic when I die.

Nonsense, I have told them. This is why I am here talking to Darren Downey, making my arrangements. Carol and Jordan will not only get shares but, as part of my commitment, a receipt for the charitable donation. In these times, it won't be hard to explain to Carol why the previous government wrote it into the tax act as a concession to the terminally ill and their surviving families. Jordan – jokey Jordan – will make a terrible pun, something like how he always thought, but never told me I was very crabby person. I'm sure he will ask me if he can be excused from coming to visit and watch while I am being eaten and made into crab meat. He will sit with his current wife, turn to her and look at her face to see how disgusted she is with him and with me. It is why his relationships never last – he can be as caustic as he is gleeful about being caustic. He loves to turn people upside down, then try to shake laughter out of their pockets. Then, being who he is, he will confess that he can be a very crabby person himself.

Nevertheless, it's a grisly serious subject and situation. I will have to talk up how the old and sick here have always walked off into the wilderness and the snow to do away with themselves when they are no longer of use. Remains have been bundled up and hung in trees in parts of this huge country. Carol, Jordan and his current partner don't have to deal with it right this moment. My timeline could be a year or several. My oncologist tells me that post-op some fight and live longer, some don't and live just as long. I don't know what writing another book on what I have always been writing about is fighting or giving in, but I always have been and am about to be completely consumed by my subject. Turned into crabmeat, and Jordan would be right... a product in the expiational economy. Carol, Jordan and his current partner will be able to say at Thanksgiving, "We eat this crab in remembrance of him."

Lord, what have I been calling Jordan? He's my son. That side of his character doesn't come out of nowhere. The wonder is how Carol has stayed with me till the death-do-us-part time. Then, doesn't Carol tell all and sundry that I might as well be dead, or a zombie when I'm working? For her the till-death-do-us-part has come time and time again because of my occupational obsession. Carol's other complaint, "Boring-as-hell poets are the only people who put more words into the subject than you – minus the demographic maps, charts, ratios and all that analytic shit." After which, she'll switch to a different tone of voice and add, "It's always a relief," and I'll ask, "What is?"

"When you're gone with the dead and out of my hair."

I suppose I could take that as an endorsement for my being here making arrangements, doing research at Ocean Interments, Reef Restoration and Exoskeletal Services.

I look down again from where Darren Downey has shut off the motor to wait for the chubby landing barges to pass back to shore. The fish reappear below, blip in and out of the new architectural accretions on the reef. Then, they stop as if waiting to see if our boat will discharge any more osseous combatants into the sea, then they swim up, looking at us through the glass.

I swear their eyes ask me, "When are you going to drift down out of your skin and join this rampart against the acid sea?"

There I go, being un-academic and anthropomorphic. The fish don't know a thing about what's happening to them and the fish don't care. Could they do anything about it, if they did?

"Tomorrow," I whisper anyway, "but not tomorrow and tomorrow. One tomorrow soon, I will, I promise."

AFTERWORD

DAN BLOOM

What is "Cli-fi?" It is many things: a new literary genre, a meme, a motif, a buzzword, a warning flare, an alarm bell. Take your pick. Basically, Cli-fi was created as a platform for writers to use, upon which they could frame and flesh out their stories.

Cli-fi has also drawn the attention of mainstream literary figures such as Margaret Atwood and Barbara Kingsolver. New novels and short stories embracing Cli-fi are now being published every month. Some are dystopian, some are utopian. They might also turn out to be crime thrillers or detective yarns. They take place in the past, the present and the future.

Since most North Americans now accept man-made global warming as real, writers need to use their creative spark and passion for social responsibility to emotionally move readers about a possible disaster that could claim much of the planet within the next 30 generations of humankind.

That's the time frame I envision: 500 years before the Climapocalypse hits for real. For now, life is good, life is wonderful, we are lucky to be alive and thriving in the first decades of the 21st century. But things could take a turn for the worse, our moment of punctuated equilibrium could end, and that's where the power of Cli-fi comes in, serving as a wake-up call for this generation of Canadians and future generations as well.

And so it is no wonder that Margaret Atwood put out a challenge to Canadian writers, young and old, to respond to the reality of climate change. And with a new government in place in Canada that has appointed a minister responsible for Climate Change, Canada is, in terms of policy, legitimizing an appreciation and acceptance of what we face, something that writers and film directors can distill and define in their creative works.

I am an optimist. I believe in the power of art and literature to transform lives and transform society. What Nevil Shute did with his 1957 novel, *On the Beach*, Cli-fi writers can do with their stories and novels now: shine a spotlight on the most pressing issue ever facing humanity.

This anthology does just that. It looks to change hearts and minds in Canada, and beyond our borders – to answer, in creative terms, a call for a type of writing that has not yet entered the artistic consciousness nationwide, or worldwide. This is an important step in the right direction.

ABOUT THE AUTHORS

Dan Bloom of Taiwan and the United States is a writer, filmmaker, environmental activist, and the editor of *The Cli-fi Report* (www.cli-fi.net). He is the inventor of the term "Cli-fi."

Wendy Bone of Java, Indonesia, is a Canadian writer currently taking her MFA in Creative Writing online at the University of British Columbia while teaching English and freelancing. Her journalism, fiction and poetry have appeared in *Prism International*, *Room*, *Creative Nonfiction* magazine, and numerous other publications throughout Asia and North America. www.wendyboneabroad.com

Geoffrey W. Cole of Toronto has had short fiction appear in *On Spec*, *Clarkesworld*, *New Worlds*, Exile's *The Playground of Lost Toys*, and *Imaginarium 2012: The Year's Best Canadian Speculative Writing*. His work has been translated into Spanish, Romanian, Italian, and Catalan, for which he recently won the Premis Ictineu for best translated story. He has degrees in biology and engineering, and is completing an MFA in Creative Writing at the University of British Columbia. He is a member of SF Canada and SFWA. www.geoffreywcole.com

Phil Dwyer of Toronto is a journalist, essayist, travel writer, and fiction writer whose works have been published in over fifteen international publications, including *The Financial Times*, *The Times* (of London), and the *Globe and Mail*. He is an alumnus of the Humber School for Writers.

Leslie Goodreid of Barrie, Ontario, is currently putting the finishing touches on two new fantasy novels. In 2015 she was winner of the Canadian Authors' Association Poetry Prize.

Lynn Hutchinson Lee of Toronto has had her written/spoken word poems and short fiction appear in *Romani Folio*, *Drunken Boat 22*, International Online Journal of the Arts; *Bridges and Borders*; *Sar o Paj*, *Kafla Intercontinental*; *Diaspora Dialogues*; at events such as *Call*

the Witness, Roma Pavilion, 54th Venice Biennale (Venice, Italy), BAK (Utrecht, Netherlands), National Museum of Contemporary Art (Bucharest, Romania), *Canada Without Shadows* (spoken word sound installation, with chirikli collective). Her recent exhibitions include *metanoia* (Workers Arts and Heritage Centre, Hamilton, Ontario), and *Musaj te Dzav* (*I Have to Leave*), with chirikli collective (Gallery 50, Toronto). www.chiriklicollective.com

George McWhirter of Vancouver was born in Belfast, Northern Ireland. He is the author of ten books of poetry, eight books of short and long fiction (including Exile's *The Gift of Women*), and four books of literary translation. His recognitions include the Commonwealth Prize for Poetry (shared with Chinua Achebe), the Ethel Wilson Fiction Prize, and the F.R. Scott Translation Prize. He served as the inaugural Poet Laureate of Vancouver.

Rati Mehrotra of Toronto has had short stories appear in *AE – The Canadian Science Fiction Review*, *Apex Magazine*, *Abyss & Apex*, *Inscription Magazine*, Exile's *Clockwork Canada*, *ELQ/Exile: The Literary Quarterly* and many more. Her debut novel, *Markswoman*, will be published in early 2018. www.ratiwrites.com
@Rati_Mehrotra

Nina Munteanu of Upper Tantallon, Nova Scotia, is an ecologist author of award-nominated speculative novels, short stories and non-fiction. She edits for Eagle Publishing House and the European zine *Europa SF*, and writes for *Amazing Stories*. She currently teaches writing at George Brown College and the University of Toronto. Her latest book is *Water Is...*, a scientific study and personal journey as limnologist, mother, teacher and environmentalist.
www.NinaMunteanu.ca www.NinaMunteanu.me

John Oughton of Toronto is a recently retired professor of Learning and Teaching at Centennial College. He has published a mystery novel, *Death by Triangulation*, five books of poetry, most recently *Time Slip*, several chapbooks, and over 400 articles, interviews, reviews and blogs. His poetic biography *Mata Hari's Lost Words* has just been published in a new edition. He is a member of the Long Dash writing workshop. He is also a photographer with three solo shows and several book and magazine covers to his credit.

www.joughton.wixsite.com/author

Linda Rogers of Victoria, British Columbia, is poet, fiction writer, a songwriter and arts journalist. She was Canada's year 2000 People's Poet, a former Victoria Poet Laureate, and a former President of the League of Canadian Poets and the Federation of B.C. Writers. Her works include numerous poetry collections, children's books, and adult novels including, *The Empress Trilogy*, *Say My Name*, *Friday Water* and most recently Exile's *Bozuk* ("Broken"in Turkish), the story of a broken woman seeking the "better angel of her nature." Her recognitions are national and international awards, including the Leacock, Monday, Bridport, Cardiff, Montreal, MacEwen, Livesay, Kenney Acorn Rukeyser, Arc, Benjamin Franklin, Voices Israel, Prix d'Anglais and National Poetry Prizes. She is currently co-writing fiction with Ben Murray, a Canadian poet she met at the Kenney Awards in London. Their first renga-style novel, *The Arioso Game*, was shortlisted for the great BC novel search in 2016.

Holly Schofield of rural British Columbia is the author of over 50 short stories. Her works have been published in *Lightspeed*, Exile's *Clockwork Canada*, *Tesseracts*, the Aurora-winning *Second Contacts*, and many other publications throughout the world. New stories will soon appear in *Young Explorer's Adventure Guide*, *Brave New Girls*, and *Analog*. www.hollyschofield.wordpress.com

Kate Story of Peterborough, Ontario, is a writer and performer born and raised in Newfoundland. Her first novel, *Blasted*, received the Sunburst Award's honourable mention. She is the 2015 recipient of the Ontario Arts Foundation's K.M. Hunter Award for her work in theatre. Recent publications include short stories in World Fantasy Award-nominated and Aurora Award-nominated collections, and she is proud to have been included in several Exile collections. This year her third novel, *An Insubstantial Pageant*, comes out with ChiZine Publications. www.katestory.com

Peter Timmerman of Toronto is an associate professor in the Faculty of Environmental Studies at York University. His first monograph on climate change, "Vulnerability, Resilience, and the Collapse of Society," was published in 1981, and was followed by multiple publications on climate change and its impacts for Environment Canada and other organizations. He was the co-chair for the Canadian NGO Earth Charter process for the Rio Earth Summit in 1992, a founder of the Canadian Coalition for Ecology, Ethics, and Religion (CCEER), and is a member of the Canadian Forum on Religion and Ecology (CFORE). He continued through the 1990s and 2000s as a public activist and author on topics such as genetic manipulation, climate change and coastal cities, and nuclear waste management. He now works primarily on environmental philosophy and ethics, with a special research focus on Buddhism and long-term sustainability in South and Southeast Asia. He recently co-edited *Ecological Economics for the Anthropocene*, a volume of papers for Columbia University Press on the ethical foundations and future of alternative economics.

Richard Van Camp from Fort Smith is a member of the Dogrib (Tlicho) Nation, from Fort Smith, Northwest Territories. He is the author of two children's books with the Cree artist George Littlechild: *A Man Called Raven* and *What's the Most Beautiful Thing You Know About Horses?* He has published a novel, *The Lesser Blessed*, which is now a feature film with First Generation Films. His collections of short fiction include *Angel Wing Splash Pattern*, *The Moon of Letting Go and Other Stories*, *Godless but Loyal to Heaven* and *Night Moves*. He has authored four baby books: *Welcome Song for Baby: A Lullaby for Newborns*, *Nighty Night: A Bedtime Song for Babies*, *Little You* (translated into Cree, Dene and South Slavey) and *We Sang You Home*, And graphically he has written two comic books, *Kiss Me Deadly*, and *Path of the Warrior*, and the graphic novels, *Three Feathers*, *A Blanket of Butterflies*, and *Spirit*. His newest works are the novel, *Whistle*, and a graphic novel, *The Blue Raven*. He has also had a variety of cinematic adaptations done of his work.

Halli Villegas of Mount Forest, Ontario, is the author of three collections of poetry: *Red Promises*, *In the Silence Absence Makes*, and *The*

Human Cannonball, and a book of ghost stories, *The Hairwreath and Other Stories*. She received Honourable Mention for two of her stories in the 2010 edition of The Year's Best Horror edited by Ellen Datlow. She was the co-editor of the anthologies *Imaginarium: The Best Canadian Speculative Writing 2012* and *In The Dark: Tales of the Supernatural*. Her genre work has appeared in anthologies that include *Chilling Tales 2*, *The White Collar Anthology*, *Bad Seed*, *Incubus* and *Girls Who Bite Back*. After selling her self-started publishing house, Tightrope Books, she now has an editing and manuscript evaluation business, In the Write Direction. And with Bruce Meyer, she is co-editing for Exile *That Dammed Beaver*, an anthology of new Canadian comedy, due in autumn 2017.

Seán Virgo of Eastend, Saskatchewan, was born in Malta and raised in several countries before becoming a Canadian at the age of 32. His short fiction and poetry have won awards on both sides of the Atlantic. He has published a novel, short story collections, and poetry collections, and has worked in theatre and mixed-media as writer, director and performer. His most recent fiction collection is *Dibidalen, ten stories*.

Frank Westcott of Alliston, Ontario, is a poet, short story writer, lyricist, musician, and a former educator with Special Education certification. In 2011 he won the Carter V. Cooper Short Fiction Award/Best Story by an Emerging Writer for "The Poet" (published in Exile's *CVC1* anthology). In 2014, his poem "And She Lay Herself Down" was a finalist for the Gwendolyn MacEwen Poetry Award (published in *ELQ/Exile: The Literary Quarterly*). In 2016 "It Was A Dark Day ~ Not A Stormy Night ~ In Tuck-Tea-*Tee*-Uck-Tuck" was shortlisted for the Carter V. Cooper Short Fiction Award/Best Story by an Emerging Writer category (published in Exile's *CVC6* anthology). www.FrankWestcottPoet.com
www.facebook.com/frank.westcott.9

Bruce Meyer of Barrie, Ontario, is the award-winning author of over 50 books of poetry, short fiction, non-fiction, literary journalism, photography books, and textbooks. Among his recent titles are *Testing the Elements, The Seasons, The Arrow of Time, The Madness of Planets, To Linares,* and *Portraits of Canadian Writers*. He was winner of the Gwendolyn MacEwen Prize for Poetry in 2015 and 2016. He was the inaugural Poet Laureate of the City of Barrie, and teaches at Georgian College in Barrie and at Victoria College in the University of Toronto.

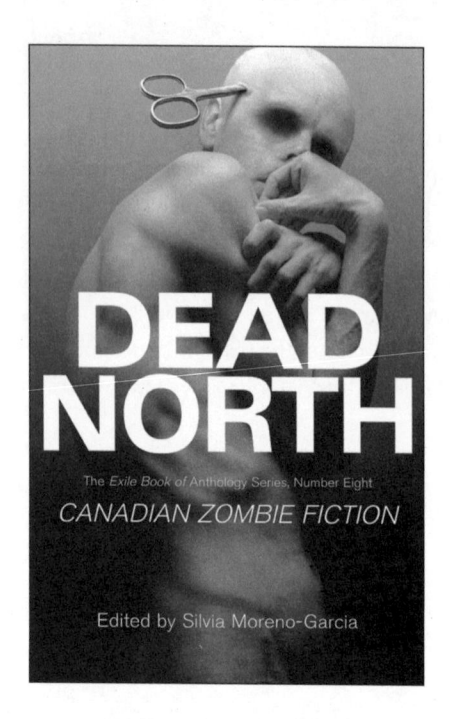

DEAD NORTH: CANADIAN ZOMBIE FICTION
EDITED BY SILVIA MORENO-GARCIA

"*Dead North* suggests zombies may be thought of as native to this country, their presence going back to Aboriginal myths and legends…we see deadheads, shamblers, jiang shi, and Shark Throats invading such home and native settings as the Bay of Fundy's Hopewell Rocks, Alberta's tar sands, Toronto's Mount Pleasant Cemetery, and a Vancouver Island grow-op. Throw in the last poutine truck on Earth driving across Saskatchewan and some "mutant demon zombie cows devouring Montreal" (honest!) and what you've got is a fun and eclectic mix of zombie fiction…" —The Toronto Star

"Every time I listen to the yearly edition of *Canada Reads* on CBC, so much attention seems to be drawn to the fact that the author is Canadian, that being Canadian becomes a gimmick. *Dead North*, a collection of zombie short stories by exclusively Canadian authors, is the first of its kind that I've seen to buck this trend, using the diverse cultural mythology of the Great White North to put a number of unique spins on an otherwise over-saturated genre." —Bookshelf Reviews

Featuring stories by Chantal Boudreau, Tessa J. Brown, Richard Van Camp, Kevin Cockle, Jacques L. Condor, Carrie-Lea Côté, Linda DeMeulemeester, Brian Dolton, Gemma Files, Ada Hoffmann, Tyler Keevil, Claude Lalumière, Jamie Mason, Michael Matheson, Ursula Pflug, Rhea Rose, Simon Strantzas, E. Catherine Tobler, Beth Wodzinski and Melissa Yuan-Ines.

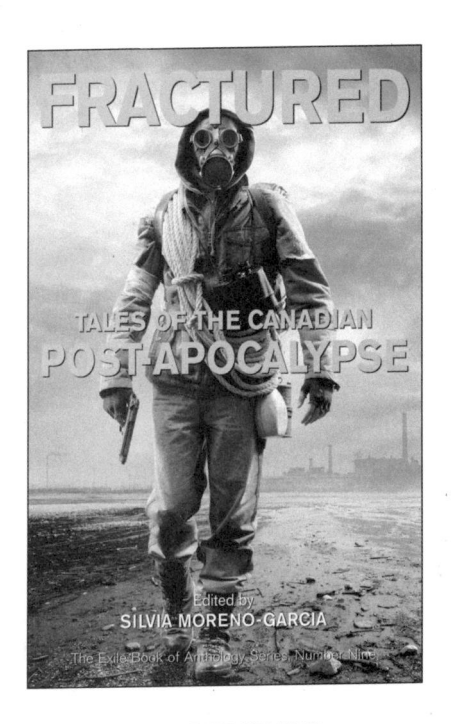

FRACTURED:
TALES OF THE CANADIAN POST-APOCALYPSE
EDITED BY SILVIA MORENO-GARCIA

"The 23 stories in *Fractured* cover incredible breadth, from the last man alive in Haida Gwaii to a dying Matthew waiting for his Anne in PEI. All the usual apocalyptic suspects are here – climate change, disease, alien invasion – alongside less familiar scenarios such as a ghost apocalypse and an invasion of shadows. Stories range from the immediate aftermath of society's collapse to distant futures in which humanity has been significantly reduced, but the same sense of struggle and survival against the odds permeates most of the pieces in the collection… What *Fractured* really drives home is how perfect Canada is as a setting for the post-apocalypse. Vast tracts of wilderness, intense weather, and the potentially sinister consequences of environmental devastation provide ample inspiration for imagining both humanity's destruction and its rugged survival." —*Quill & Quire*

Featuring stories by T.S. Bazelli, GMB Chomichuk, A.M. Dellamonica, dvsduncan, Geoff Gander, Orrin Grey, David Huebert, John Jantunen, H.N. Janzen, Arun Jiwa, Claude Lalumière, Jamie Mason, Michael Matheson, Christine Ottoni, Miriam Oudin, Michael S. Pack, Morgan M. Page, Steve Stanton, Amanda M. Taylor, E. Catherine Tobler, Jean-Louis Trudel, Frank Westcott and A.C. Wise.

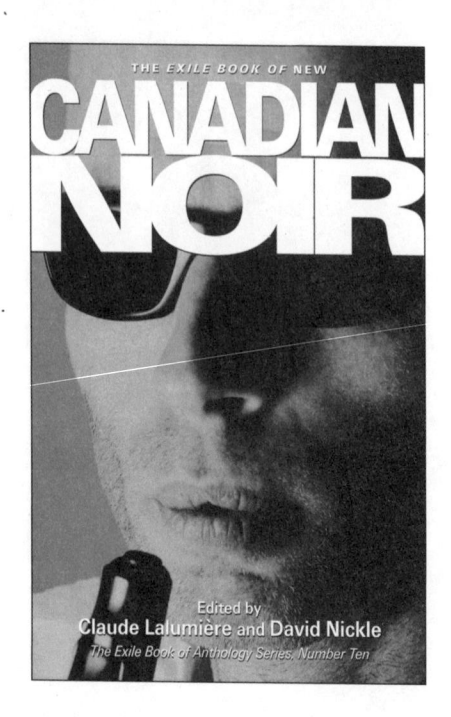

NEW CANADIAN NOIR
EDITED BY CLAUDE LALUMIÈRE AND DAVID NICKLE

"Everything is in the title. These are all new stories – no novel extracts – selected by Claude Lalumière and David Nickle from an open call. They're Canadian-authored, but this is not an invitation for national introspection. Some Canadian locales get the noir treatment, which is fun, since, as Nickle notes in his afterword, noir, with its regard for the underbelly, seems like an un-Canadian thing to write. But the main question *New Canadian Noir* asks isn't "Where is here?" it's "What can noir be?" These stories push past the formulaic to explore noir's far reaches as a mood and aesthetic. In Nickle's words, "Noir is a state of mind – an exploration of corruptibility, ultimately an expression of humanity in all its terrible frailty." The resulting literary alchemy – from horror to fantasy, science fiction to literary realism, romance to, yes, crime – spanning the darkly funny to the stomach-queasy horrific, provides consistently entertaining rewards." —*Globe and Mail*

Featuring stories by Corey Redekop, Joel Thomas Hynes, Silvia Moreno-Garcia, Chadwick Ginther, Michael Mirolla, Simon Strantzas, Steve Vernon, Kevin Cockle, Colleen Anderson, Shane Simmons, Laird Long, Dale L. Sproule, Alex C. Renwick, Ada Hoffmann, Kieth Cadieux, Michael S. Chong, Rich Larson, Kelly Robson, Edward McDermott, Hermine Robinson, David Menear and Patrick Fleming.

PLAYGROUND OF LOST TOYS

EDITED BY COLLEEN ANDERSON AND URSULA PFLUG

A dynamic collection of stories that explore the mystery, awe and dread that we may have felt as children when encountering a special toy. But it goes further, to the edges of space, where games are for keeps and where the mind plays its own games. We enter a world where the magic may not have been lost, where a toy or computers or gods vie for the upper hand. Wooden games of skill, ancient artifacts misinterpreted, dolls, stuffed animals, wand items that seek a life or even revenge – these lost toys and games bring tales of companionship, loss, revenge, hope, murder, cunning, and love, to be unearthed in the sandbox.

Featuring stories by Chris Kuriata, Joe Davies, Catherine MacLeod, Kate Story, Meagan Whan, Candas Jane Dorsey, Rati Mehrotra, Nathan Adler, Rhonda Eikamp, Robert Runté, Linda DeMeulemeester, Kevin Cockle, Claude Lalumière, Dominik Parisien, dvsduncan, Christine Daigle, Melissa Yuan-Innes, Shane Simmons, Lisa Carreiro, Karen Abrahamson, Geoffrey W. Cole and Alexandra Camille Renwick. Afterword by Derek Newman-Stille.

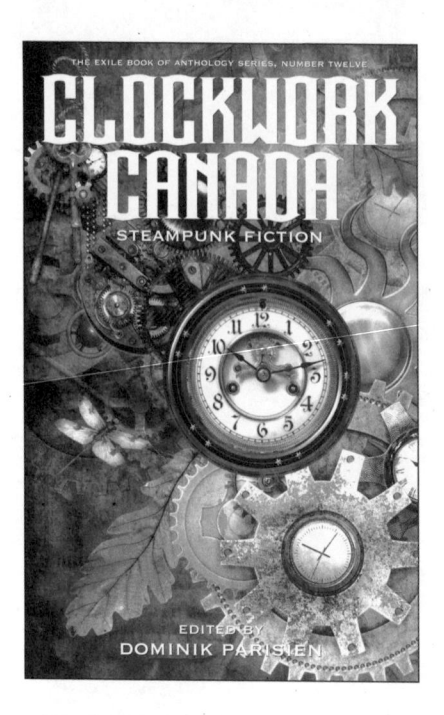

CLOCKWORK CANADA: STEAMPUNK FICTION

EDITED BY DOMINIK PARISIEN

Welcome to an alternate Canada, where steam technology and the wonders and horrors of the mechanical age have reshaped the past into something both wholly familiar yet compellingly different.

"These stories of clockworks, airships, mechanical limbs, automata, and steam are, overall, an unfettered delight to read." —*Quill & Quire*

"[*Clockwork Canada*] is a true delight that hits on my favorite things in fiction — curious worldbuilding, magic, and tough women taking charge. It's a carefully curated adventure in short fiction that stays true to a particular vision while seeking and achieving nuance."
—*Tor.com*

"...inventive and transgressive...these stories rethink even the fundamentals of what we usually mean by steampunk." —*The Toronto Star*

Featuring stories by Colleen Anderson, Karin Lowachee, Brent Nichols, Charlotte Ashley, Chantal Boudreau, Rhea Rose, Kate Story, Terri Favro, Kate Heartfield, Claire Humphrey, Rati Mehrotra, Tony Pi, Holly Schofield, Harold R. Thompson and Michal Wojcik.

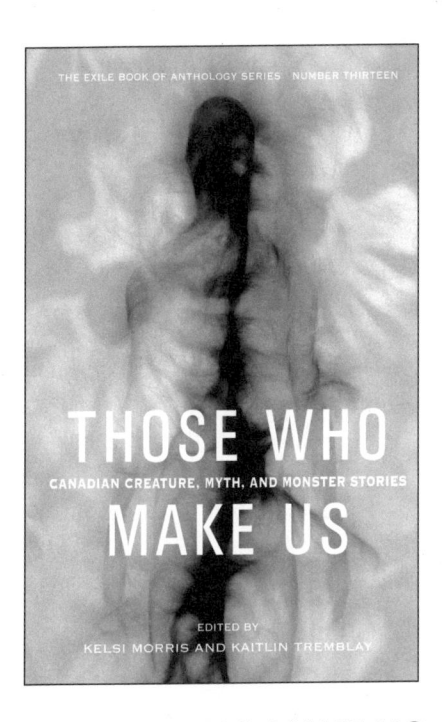

THOSE WHO MAKE US:
CANADIAN CREATURE, MYTH AND MONSTER STORIES

EDITED BY KELSI MORRIS AND KAITLIN TREMBLAY

What resides beneath the blankets of snow, under the ripples of water, within the whispers of the wind, and between the husks of trees all across Canada? Creatures, myths and monsters are everywhere…even if we don't always see them.

Canadians from all backgrounds and cultures look to identify with their surroundings through stories. Herein, speculative and literary fiction provides unique takes on what being Canadian is about.

"Kelsi Morris and Kaitlin Tremblay did not set out to create a traditional anthology of monster stories… This unconventional anthology lives up to the challenge, the stories show tremendous openness and compassion in the face of the world's darkness, unfairness, and indifference." —*Quill & Quire*

Featuring stories by Helen Marshall, Renée Sarojini Saklikar, Nathan Adler, Kate Story, Braydon Beaulieu, Chadwick Ginther, Dominik Parisien, Stephen Michell, Andrew Wilmot, Rati Mehrotra, Rebecca Schaeffer, Delani Valin, Corey Redekop, Angeline Woon, Michal Wojcik, Andrea Bradley, Andrew F. Sullivan and Alexandra Camille Renwick.

FORTHCOMING ANTHOLOGIES

OVER THE RAINBOW: FOLK AND FAIRY TALES FROM THE MARGINS

EDITORS KELSI MORRIS AND DEREK NEWMAN-STILLE

Fairy tales are often about the encounter with the strange, fantastic, and otherworldly. They are frequently used as texts of warning, inspiring conformity by telling people what they shouldn't do. In *Over the Rainbow* we explore the power of fairy tales as texts of resistance, as ways of speaking back to those power structures that try to get us to conform.

Over the Rainbow uses fairy tales to smash tradition and reshape it with (dis)enchantment, to bring readers into the woods where transformations and new beginnings can happen, playing with traditional tropes in unconventional ways, offering a shattered-mirror image of our world and our imagination. This includes an exploration of fairy tales through all genres – horror, humour, slipstream, steampunk, cyberpunk, science fiction, urban fantasy, magical realism, etc., along with non-Western tales – that push boundaries into the strange and otherworldly.

At the time of publication, some of these anthologies are open for submissions. Open call information for any and all forthcoming anthologies: www.exilepublishing.submittable.com

ALICE UNBOUND

EDITED BY COLLEEN ANDERSON

Lewis Carroll (Charles Dodgson) explored childlike wonder and the bewildering realm of adult rules and status, which clashed in bizarre ways. Many characters in his tales are anthropomorphic, whether talking cards, crying mock turtles or saucy Tiger Lilies. Over 150 years later, people still recognize characters from Carroll's works.

Time has passed, and myth became fairy tale, evolving to resonate with each generation, showing the triumphs of the common man, the humble and generous woman who outsmarts tempters, jailers and evil stepmothers, or the trials and tribulations of seeking the unknown. We might not truly want to live in the world of Alice or have to deal with mad queens and bandersnatches, but what if that Wonderland ceased to exist on a separate plain, and melded with our modern world? How would these characters fit in, and what would they bring or change? Are we ready to accept *Alice Unbound* into our hearts and let the Jabberwock in the back door?

THE FOOD OF MY PEOPLE

EDITED BY URSULA PFLUG AND CANDAS JANE DORSEY

Speculative writing, whatever the sub-genre, is full of food scenes. Food can be integral to the magic, the meetings, the processes of narratives from hard Sci-fi to high Fantasy. For all of us, eating is a symbolic and magical act, a transformation, a covenant, a ritual, a comfort, and a necessity, and this awareness has been expressed in story – all the way from myth, legend and fairy tale to modern speculative writing – in many memorable ways. Alice eats and drinks to participate in Wonderland, Ripley's alien has to feed its young, Persephone eats the pomegranate seeds and spends half her life in the Underworld, the witch entices Hansel and Gretel with food to become food, the food in *2001*'s famous white room is spookily nutritious and generic, and *Soylent Green* is people.

We can't live without food, but sometimes we can't live with it, either. In literature and in history, food-themed stories have had a darker side: starvation, poisonings (whether intentional or accidental), struggles with eating disorders, and more. We're all drawn to candy coatings (in this case, literally) but at times the story is about how the missing ingredient ruined the feast.

A recipe is a feature of each story.

THAT DAMMED BEAVER: NEW CANDIAN COMEDY

EDITED BY BRUCE MEYER AND HALLI VILLEGAS

Canadians have a unique, if not odd, way of looking at themselves and at the world. We see the chaotic and the absurd all around us, and it is our resilient sense of humour that allows us to laugh when facing the truth, or at times to avoid crying. What a nation finds funny, and how it embraces humour, is key to what makes a nation great. From SCTV to Kids in the Hall to the Mercer Report, generations of Canadians leave 'em laughing. Eliciting the guffaw, the snicker, the gut-buster, the wry twist of a smile, these are the moments when our humanity is revealed, and embraced.

While one of our greatest exports has been our distinct sense of humour – one of the enduring myths about Canada is that we are a nice people, polite, but not necessarily funny. This collection showcases that Canadian writers have put that idea of the peaceable, quiet, subdued North to rest. These stories share our greatest capacities to be human/humane with readers across the country and around the world – the experience of what makes us laugh. So, what is funny about the Canadian experience? What sets us apart, and what makes us laugh? Canada's diverse communities show others something they might not have realized about themselves, and what they share in spirit with everyone across the country.

Three Native Canadian Anthologies

BAWAJIGAN: VISIONS, NIGHTMARES, AND REVERIES

EDITED BY NATHAN NIIGAN NOODIN ADLER AND CHRISTINE MISKONOODINKWE SMITH

Dreams have always played a powerful role in Indigenous cultures across Turtle Island: they have changed the course of history, and served as warning, insight, guidance, solace, or hope. In *Bawajigan* (Anishinaabemowin for Dream) we gather fictional stories and art about what it means to dream and be Indigenous, how dreams weave their way through our realities, how they impact history, lived experience, and the stories we tell each other and the world. These can be lucid daydreams, waking trances, hallucinations, reveries, reoccurring nightmares, revenge-fantasies, fever-induced delirium, coma, sleep-paralysis visitations, sleep-walking disorders or sleep deprivation, communication with non-human entities, messages from beyond the grave, cybernetic ghosts, vision-quests, ceremony, or ghost-dancing hopes for the future – all while you just try to make it through the week.

A collection of fictional stories and art-based works by Indigenous writers. These are *our* stories about the strength and power of dreams – stories that *all* may share in and grow from.

ONWAACHIGEWIN: PREDICTIONS, POSSIBLE FUTURES, AND SINGULARITIES

EDITED BY NATHAN NIIGAN NOODIN ADLER AND CHRISTINE MISKONOODINKWE SMITH

A collection of fictional stories and art-based works by Indigenous writers about what it means to glimpse the future, how foreknowledge and foretelling can serve as warning and protection, or be a matter of survival. From omens, spirit guides, migration stories and the Seven Fires Prophecy, to predictions encoded in wampum, cowrie shells, beads, birch-bark scrolls, petroforms and petroglyphs. There are many ways of seeing the future: scrying, divination, the study of entrails, astrology, necromancy, numerology, scientific calculations, Ouija boards, ventriloquism, dowsing rods, tea leaves, fortune cookies, cards, and the casting of bones. There are also many visions of the future, from the end of the world, near disasters, fears of global warming, collapse, and lost loves, to close calls, divine interventions, change and transformation, to hypothetical biologic or digital immortality. How does luck, freewill, and fate or destiny fit into the equation? How do animals sometimes know things before humans? Can aching bones predict the weather?

These are stories that reveal and revel in the strength and power of prophecy.

AKI: LAND AND TERRITORY
EDITED BY NATHAN NIIGAN NOODIN ADLER
AND CHRISTINE MISKONOODINKWE SMITH

This is the third of three volumes featuring fictional stories and art-based works by Indigenous writers. What does Mother Earth mean to us, from creation stories of Miikinakominis (literally, the land that used to be a turtle), to one's home or homeland(s), or being on the Rez, or in the urban metropolis. What are the connections one has to the water, metals, stones, plants, animals, and the other beings that share space with us? What are the consequences of the collision between Indigenous and non-Indigenous cultures when it comes to power or justice; isolation or loneliness or empowerment; strategic or military conflict in places of contention; if it's Reserved land or Crown land? And how do places of burial, places that are scarred or bear the marks of trauma, places that are haunted, affect us as individuals or as a people?

These are stories about how the land is a source of inspiration, strength, and power.

Exile's $15,000 Carter V. Cooper Short Fiction Competition

FOR CANADIAN WRITERS ONLY

$10,000 for the Best Story by an Emerging Writer
$5,000 for the Best Story by a Writer at Any Career Point

The 12 shortlisted are published in the annual *CVC Short Fiction Anthology* series and *ELQ/Exile: The Literary Quarterly*

Exile's $3,000 Gwendolyn MacEwen Poetry Competition

FOR CANADIAN WRITERS ONLY

$1,500 for the Best Suite of Poetry
$1,000 for the Best Suite by an Emerging Writer
$500 for the Best Poem

Winners are published in *ELQ/Exile: The Literary Quarterly*

These annual competitions open in November, and close May 15.
details at: www.TheExileWriters.com